CU00661196

STAYING ALIVE

By the same author:

Wherein Lies Justice, Book Guild Publishing, 2013

STAYING ALIVE

Barry Johnson

Book Guild Publishing
Sussex, England

First published in Great Britain in 2014 by
The Book Guild Ltd
The Werks
45 Church Road
Hove, BN3 2BE

Typesetting in Baskerville by
YHT Ltd, London

Printed and bound in Great Britain by
CPI Group (UK) Ltd, Croydon, CR0 4YY

A catalogue record for this book is available from
The British Library.

ISBN 978 1 909716 10 0

Acknowledgements

I extend a sincere thank-you to David Smith, who read an early draft of this novel and lent encouragement with a nice line in honesty. To Her-indoors, who puts up with me spending hours in front of the second love of my life – my Apple Mac computer, which has saved me from the reality of this world so that I can live in the exciting world of Jake Robinson. And to Hayley Sherman, who did another thorough job, picking up my inconsistencies, suggesting amendments and raising pertinent queries.

1

I lay there in bed. The duvet was a crumpled untidy heap halfway off the bed. My cold feet stuck out the bottom. It had been another miserable night. The killing of Jase Phillips in prison just kept nagging at me. Yes, he'd killed Major Michael Carmichael in Iraq but that in itself didn't justify the sentence or any sentence. I knew it wasn't my fault but I blamed myself – stupid really. I watched shadows float across the ceiling as clouds passed in front of the early morning sun. I could hear the distant rumble of London's morning traffic as the rush hour got underway. That day was just another day but I'd decided, today I'd start to do something about the Jase Phillips killing and I knew The Family, with their power and position, would oppose me. I'd said that before, perhaps a hundred times, but now it was keeping me awake at night. What to do was the question. Let's get some breakfast. Perhaps thinking is better after food. So I fried two eggs using olive oil as part of my healthy diet and had them with toast, but it didn't seem to make any difference so I went to work.

My job was interesting, demanding and enjoyable. I just loved working for Sir Nicolas, the best defence barrister in the UK. Time was just flying by and I'd taken over Frances's flat in central London. I still missed her. I don't suppose we could have gone through the Bolivian experience without becoming very close. That we lived to escape the American Mafia and the Bolivian organised crime syndicate and get to

1

La Paz was a minor miracle, but then it all went pear-shaped and I lost her. I suppose I'd thought we would settle down together, though I don't think either of us was a settling-down person. We were independent, self-sufficient but we were also in tune. Now she was dead, killed by the effects of the Mafia attack in Bolivia and I was taking too long to get over it.

It had been a good move from the special section of the security service to working for a top defence barrister, and Sir Nicolas had me dashing about all over the place. In the main, I was interviewing career criminals, dodgy witnesses, psychopaths and crooked policemen. I suppose that sounds negative but it wasn't really. Sir Nicolas's job was to defend them and most of them really needed extensive and intensive defence. They were arrogant and cynical. They were so intent on not admitting anything to anybody just in case they admitted to doing something wrong and most didn't really think they'd done anything wrong; they just dug a big hole and then fell into it. Funny really, most of them were highly intelligent, highly successful, had extensive friendship circles but were morally deficient. In general, Sir Nicolas defended the ones who were unlikely to get caught, too clever or powerful, and if they did get caught they could afford to get Sir Nicolas Ross QC to defend them.

Life was good but the killing of Jase Phillips in prison just kept nagging at me. I just couldn't shake it. An honest, tough, likeable infantry sergeant sent to prison for killing an officer who was on drugs. He killed the officer, Major Michael Carmichael, to save the lives of a whole platoon and now he'd been murdered in prison. Major Michael Carmichael was the son of Rupert Carmichael, Earl of Charnforth, who was the head of The Family, the most powerful political and criminal dynasty in the country. In my view, killing the officer was necessary. But who killed Jase? Who ordered the killing and why? It had to be The Family, but why? Could it just be payback? No, it had to be something more. The Family was too clever, too subtle and too careful to risk murdering somebody. It had to be more than payback; there had to be a reason and a very big reason.

It was a fine spring day and I soon arrived at Holborn Station. I could get to most places I wanted or needed to go in London by using the underground. I suppose I'm one of those strange people that regard the London Underground as one of the Seven Wonders of the World. The sun was shining, the pigeons were pooing and the sparrows seemed to be spritely, hopping about like mad things, collecting crumbs and looking forward to summer. As the sun was out we had the usual mixture of sun-loving nutters in short sleeves or off-the-shoulder summer dresses looking for an early suntan, and the ultra conservatives with overcoats, hats and scarves in case it snowed. London's a wonderfully cosmopolitan place. It was a pleasant day for the walk from Holborn Station down the Kingsway to the Strand, where Sir Nicolas had his chambers just a stone's throw from the Royal Courts of Justice. Not that he appeared much in the Royal Courts of Justice, usually only on the rare case when one of his clients had been found guilty or some other barrister had made a cock-up and Sir Nicolas was going in to sort it. I got a kick out of walking through that wide, black, shiny door of the chambers and entering a different world.

I suppose you could call Sir Nicolas's chambers ostentatious but only after you'd entered. Now that's a daft thing to say, how would you know until you'd entered? You moved from a busy main thoroughfare through a very wide black, shiny door with some discreet brass plaques on the wall to the left-hand side and you entered wonderland: quiet, modern with exquisite paintings hanging on the walls over superb oak and leather furniture and deep, deep pile carpets. There, Samantha the receptionist was freestanding. By that I mean she wasn't hidden behind some barrier isolated from the visitor. I would watch her walk to a client or visitor, hold out her hand, take a firm cool grip and say, 'Good morning, sir. How can we be of help to you?' It was the way she said 'we' and 'help to you' that put them at the centre of the universe. Just watching her walk was a delight and many male clients must have thought they'd died and gone to heaven when this exquisite angel smiled at them and her friendly blue eyes flashed a welcome. I'm not sure what female clients thought but they were very few. Funny that, but Sir Nicolas only dealt with heavyweight criminals and I suppose there are few women in that league. I suppose it's good that in some areas of life equality doesn't reign. The few women clients that he had had usually murdered their husbands or, to quote the modern parlance, partners. Normally, when I read the brief, I thought, 'Good on yer gel,' as our handyman, when I was a boy, might have said. The males in question seemed to me to deserve to be bumped off.

The chambers were luxurious. The staff, like me, that worked in or from the chambers, revelled in the expensive surroundings. We enjoyed the quiet smooth efficiency of the operation of the defence of people who needed defending and the extraordinary record of the successful defence of people who seemed as guilty as sin. The denizens of these offices were the people I'd hated when I was a military policeman. They could take my painstaking and extensive investigation, which proved beyond a shadow of a doubt that a person was guilty, and destroy my evidence as if it were a mere comic book. They wouldn't now. I'd learned so much that I knew what information was required to achieve a conviction. It's so much more than establishing the facts and the links between the facts. I'd watched Sir Nicolas drive a coach and horses through rock solid evidence with just three or four simple questions and watched the jury doubt the evidence and move in favour of the accused. Now that I understood the questions he and his partners and juniors were likely to ask, I'd be able to compile the evidence, not as a policeman aiming for a trial but as an avenger aiming for a conviction. My military police training didn't really equip me for that nor, as far as I could see, did any other police training.

That morning was like any other morning and there was this vision of loveliness that illuminated my day. It was Monday, nine o'clock, when I walked into the chambers. As it turned out, this was a special day, the beginning of a special adventure, well, perhaps more than one special adventure.

'Good morning, Sam.'

'Good morning, Jake. My name is Samantha, and Joseph would like to see you.' I knew that would be about my expenses, late again.

'Thank you, Sam – oh, sorry! What do I have to do to call you Sam?'

'Sleep with me.'

'Is that an invitation?'

'Good Lord, no; it's just the requirement.'

'Ha hum, I see. Is the boss likely to be free this morning?'

'You know that for you, Jake, Sir Nicolas is always free.'

Sam and I had developed a special bond; well, I thought so. We sparred but I could never penetrate her defences, even though I knew that she wanted me to. Well, even a mere mortal can dream.

I took the lift to the top floor, silent apart from the zip-zip as it passed each floor. Vera, the wicked witch of the west, who pretends to be Sir Nicolas's secretary, was, as always, waiting. I knew she was a witch because I never saw her use her expensive Apple Mac, but she produced enough documentation each day to demolish a small forest. Not just a sizable wood but a small forest and, not only that, she was never rushed. She always had time to chat to those she wanted to chat to and the others were too scared to speak to her. One look from her and they turned to stone, dumb, or they became mumbling wrecks. Yes, she was definitely a witch.

She greeted me, smiled at me, reassured me that Sir Nicolas would see me shortly and asked me to wait. For some unaccountable reason, she liked me. I suppose she was about fifty-something, her hair gripped back in a tight grey bun with, as always, her immaculate white blouse under a dark fine wool suit. Apparently, she lived on her own and it was said that she was a member of the Salvation Army, but I couldn't image her with a tambourine or tuba marching down the road or standing outside Marks and Sparks singing carols at Christmas in her blue uniform and a bowler hat with a turned-up brim. Did the Salvation Army have witches? No, I didn't think so. Perhaps it was just a vicious rumour that she was in the Salvation Army.

I sat on one of the expensive chairs and relaxed. The outer office area was quiet with exquisite paintings hanging on the walls. These were different from the ones downstairs. Downstairs, they were expensive, original, eighteenth-century street scenes of London or the criminal courts as they were then. I was told that a couple in the reception were by William Hogarth. They were probably the prison scenes. Up on this floor they were modern impressionist paintings verging on the abstract. I liked these much more. Every time I looked at one I saw something different. I was told that a couple cost over half a million but that was the sort of figure I couldn't get my head around for a painting. The matching furniture was modern and beautifully crafted, standing on a deep, deep-pile carpet. No, that was wrong; the furniture stood *in* the deep, deep luxurious carpet.

Sir Nicolas never spent long with any client when in his chambers. He saw the clients, bemused them with his charm

STAYING ALIVE

and handed them over to one of the barristers to whom they unburdened their souls. He then dissected the findings with the QC. There were some juniors but mainly they were QCs working for Sir Nicolas. I believe that was why irrelevancies didn't divert him or use up his expensive time unnecessarily.

The door opened and Sir Nicolas showed out a well-dressed man in his fifties. They shook hands and said their goodbyes, and Vera took the man to the lift. The door shut and there was silence as Vera went back to her desk. I'd recognised the man. He was an MP who apparently had done a silly thing in the Far East that had resulted in some sort of financial irregularity and he'd been caught.

Five minutes passed and Vera spoke. 'Sir Nicolas will see you now, Jake.' She had precise, cut-glass pronunciation and always used correct grammar and appropriate words. How the hell did she know? There must have been a 'free now' light on her desk because she hadn't appeared to contact him. She was definitely a witch with extra sensory perception.

I walked towards the large oak door and Vera, who was there before me, tapped so gently that I couldn't hear the knock on this side of the door, so how Sir Nicolas was supposed to hear the tap on his side I never understood. She then opened the door. Perhaps the tapping was just for show.

'Jake is here to see you, Sir Nicolas.'

When she introduced clients they got their full handle: Mr Antony Peter Grandstand Top-Notch Gerard to see you, Sir Nicolas, or Superintendent Graham Blackmailer-of-Old-Ladies-and-Seducer-of-Young-Girls Paterson to see you, Sir Nicolas, and if it were one of the partners it would be Mr Fredrick James pain-in-the-arse Peebles QC to see you, Sir Nicolas; but not with me. With me it was just plain Jake, not Captain Jake Robinson George Cross. It made me feel I

7

belonged. I supposed outsiders and mere staff needed full titles irrespective of their power and standing in the world, but people who belonged didn't simply because they belonged.

'Come in, Jake, grab a pew.'

He had this rich, round public school voice. Strange really as he went to a grammar school and was brought up by his single parent mother with his two brothers on a tough council estate in Neasden. But it did show sometimes in the words he used. His father was an army private killed in the Korean War, so I supposed he was in his late fifties perhaps early sixties. Mind you, both his brothers had done well. One was a surgeon and the other, the youngest, was a career criminal. Well, he worked in the City, so that amounts to the same thing and I heard he was considering standing for Parliament.

I sat at the small table. We always sat at the small table. It was a ritual. Coffee would come in in about two minutes, after we'd sat down and dispensed with the general chitchat before business began. There we go. It wasn't Vera, though. Vera didn't demean herself with serving coffee and the like. She sent in one of her acolytes from the coven. One day she was going to see my fantasy about her and then she would cast a spell and I would disappear in a puff of green smoke. Yes, it would have to be green as Vera was into saving the environment.

Coffee that day was served by Grace – Grace by name and grace by nature. She'd turned serving coffee to an art form – the positioning of the cups, the elegance of her movements as she manoeuvred the pot and jug of hot milk or cream, depending on the client's choice – but it was her fingers that fascinated me. She seemed to have more and longer fingers than anybody I'd seen and they seemed to move independently but in total rhythm. And she always asked Sir Nicolas how he wanted his coffee despite the fact that it was always the same. She knew I was a hot, black and sweet, so that's what she gave me. I remember the first and only time she asked and when I said hot, black and sweet she blushed. I must admit I flashed my eyebrows up and down, but women like Grace frighten me. When serving me coffee she smiled, fluttered her eyelashes at me and withdrew. I was terrified to smile back in case my smile was misunderstood, or was she just getting her own back on me as a junior witch might?

The coffee serving ceremony completed and Sir Nicolas and I left alone, I started, 'Sir, something has been bothering me.'

'Yes, Jake, I wondered when you'd get round to talking to me about it.'

'Is it that obvious?'

'No, it's just the lost look in your eyes when you're not focusing on work. Tell me about it.'

'It's about Jase Phillips.'

'Yes, bad business, Jake, but murder in prison happens.'

'But not to someone like Jase Phillips.'

Sir Nicolas had been the judge at the trial and had resigned from the bench after the court martial verdict that freed the two young soldiers was overturned. He subsequently went back into private practice and this was when he employed me as what he called his private police force.

'I know what you think, Jake. You think Mabry ordered the killing to prevent us getting the verdict overturned.'

Now why would I think that? How could I have been so cynical? My covert cynicism was nearly made overt.

Mabry was now in the cabinet as Home Secretary and was a senior member of The Family. He was the half-brother of Michael Carmichael, the major that Jase had been convicted of murdering. Only a handful of people knew about that relationship. Of course there was no confirmation, just straws in the wind when I'd been involved in Barrow Jones's Special Section of MI5.

I thought about the court martial that had acquitted Jase Phillips and his co-accused Mike Munro, and the over-coming of 'double jeopardy' because the 'acquittal was tainted'. Sir Nicolas told me that had been the work of Antony Bray, Major Carmichael's cousin. Bray was the personal private secretary to the then Home Secretary, James Bradshaw, and a rising star in The Family. I wasn't available to testify at the subsequent court case as I'd been shipped off to Bolivia. Jase had been found guilty and sentenced to fourteen years and Mike had been released.

My view, as the investigating officer, was that Jase was justified in killing Carmichael given the reality of the battle situation. Anyway, Bray was now dead, assassinated from a smartly aimed bullet and Mike had been wrongly blamed. I shot the right honourable bastard Bray, but Mike had set it up for me and died immediately after the shooting; his choice, suicide by police officers from SCO19 Specialist Firearms Command. Six bullets from four police officers hit him, he fired only three and none directed at the police, and the enquiry found that justifiable. Me, cynical? Come on! I think I had justification for my cynicism.

'Yes, sir. If Jase had been released or just retried, the whole Carmichael case would have been front page news again and our illustrious Home Secretary's links with him may have been revealed and other information about The Family could have been made public.'

My view was that the only way to break the power of The Family, with its hold on senior government and industrial positions and its Mafia-like criminal infrastructure, was press exposure, but insignificant accusations were useless. It needed something like a major court case.

'You do like to live dangerously, Jake. Why don't you go and talk to Mabry? He knows you.'

'I doubt that I could get past the bureaucracy now. Anyway, I doubt he would talk to me.'

'Oh, I think we might just be able to fix that.'

I seemed to know so many people who could fix things or who knew people who could fix things. I suppose it was all about this thing called networking but in the case of legal people, politicians and the wealthy old families, it was just an old boys' network, the rich and powerful scratching the backs of the rich and powerful. Me, I was neither rich nor powerful but, luckily, I knew a few people that were.

2

It was six in the morning and I was lying in bed trying to build up enough energy to get up and go for a run. Jase Phillips was again on my mind. My phone went; it was Vera. Did the bloody woman never sleep? Perhaps witches don't need sleep.

'Jake, Sir Nicolas spoke to Mr Randolph Mabry last night and he'll see you in Portcullis House at ten. Just ask the receptionist and he'll direct you to the allocated office.'

It was short, to the point and complete. What else could I possibly need? I supposed I'd better wear a smart suit; though, I didn't think I really needed to impress anybody. I'd had my blue Crombie cleaned so that was easy.

I went for a run then dressed appropriately for a meeting with the Home Secretary and even arrived early, so I watched the Thames from Victoria Embankment. I could see the restaurant ship Hispaniola moored alongside and decided I would really have to bring Sam here one evening and as for the necessary qualification to call her Sam, I'd have to work on it. The Thames had stunning views from the Victoria Embankment. I thought perhaps we could have lunch on The Symphony with its all-glass super-structure to enable views of some of London's landmarks as it tootled along the river. Apparently, one of these waterborne restaurants had live jazz music. I wondered if Sam liked jazz.

I wandered along, past The Battle of Britain Monument. It was exactly opposite the Ministry of Defence and close to

Big Ben and Westminster Pier. For some reason I thought that was appropriate. I'd never seen it before. It showed aircrew running to their aircraft, some resting in full flying kit on the grass and fitters and mechanics working on the aircraft. Time was running away from me and I had to hurry to get to Portcullis House. I arrived at three minutes to the hour. It was odd that. I had this horror of being late but I'd been taught to never be too early.

The whole thing went as Vera had said. A pretty young man met me in the entrance area. I wondered where they found them. 'Contacts, Jake, contacts.' I could hear Sir Nicolas's dulcet tones in my ear.

'Captain Robertson?'

My guide had the public school accent, I might have known. His vowel sounds indicated north of the border and he also had the soft effeminate lisping of an extrovert gay and elements of his expensive clothing reinforced it: the soft, loose cut of his expensive suit, the broad tie with more and brighter colours than usual in the regimented civil service bureaucracy and the floppy handkerchief in his breast pocket.

'Um, no, Robi*n*son.'

'Oh, I'm sorry; it's the Home Secretary's handwriting.' As he said 'Oh' he placed his index and middle fingers of his right hand on his right cheek just below his cheekbone. Dislike washed through me. You see; I have this quirk of accepting responsibility. I dislike people who blame others when they can check to get things right and if they can't check they should still accept that they're the one in the wrong. But that was never going to happen in civil service or political circles; they had to be right all the time, even when they knew they were wrong. Oh, cynical me!

'Would you like to walk this way?'

I was very tempted to say, 'No, daahling, I like the way I walk,' but I restrained myself. It was odd how some people

13

irritated me. Howard was a homosexual and Gabriel was an extrovert gay but they didn't irritate me; they were my friends.

We went to the lift, up two or three floors and along a balcony passageway that had pictures of members of Parliament hanging on the inner wall to a bunch of offices. I looked over the balcony rail at the side and down onto a restaurant area with lots of people in small groups talking. Such was the way of real power in Government. The office we went into was huge with a long table and the Home Secretary was at one end with a pile of papers in front of him. A drab-looking woman was sitting near him: one of the minions that toil through mountains of paper, scrutinise millions of words, ensure everything is correct, the bedrock of the civil service, but are largely ignored by the hierarchy. Still, they'd safer pensions and greater job security than toiling productive workers who provided that security.

Mabry was like he always was, with fair, receding hair, long at the sides with twin bald patches on top and a crew cut clump in the middle. He had tanned skin, an aquiline nose and piercing blue eyes. He oozed power and authority and his sharp tongue had made many an MP in the House hate him, but with me he'd always been pleasant.

'Come in, Jake, please come in and sit down here. Charles, please ensure we're not disturbed.' Charles pouted; I'd no idea why. Mabry turned to the woman and said, 'Please give me fifteen minutes, Jacky.' She obediently, silently and neatly gathered up her papers with no indication of emotion and we waited for them to leave. 'Now, Jake, what can I do for you? Sir Nicolas implied it was important.'

'It's about the killing of Jason Phillips.'

'Yes, bad business and you want to talk to me.' There was a thoughtful air in the way he said it. 'I can understand why you think I ordered it.' So he'd reached a conclusion as to why I was here or perhaps Sir Nicolas had told him. 'It was a relief when it happened as it got me out of a hole, but I didn't order his killing or even suggest it.'

'I didn't ask, sir.'

'No, I know you didn't but it must be in your thoughts, Jake.' He looked at me with those intelligent, analytical eyes that gave nothing away. 'We've known each other a fair time; perhaps you could call me Randolph.'

Now that was a real surprise. Most people called him Home Secretary or Sir or introduced him as the Right Honourable Randolph Mabry. Why was he drawing me into his circle? How many people outside of the bounds of power and privilege would call him by his Christian name? Yes, it would definitely be a Christian name as he came from that social group that believes it has a duty to attend a church every Sunday even if they show no evidence of believing what is preached there. My cynicism was growing with every passing month that I had contact with the politically powerful.

'You're right, Randolph.' I was mildly uncomfortable calling him Randolph. It wasn't that he was the Home Secretary; it was more that I didn't want to be on first-name terms with a senior member of The Family, the most powerful criminal group in Europe. 'It seems logical that you'd order his killing. If you didn't, have you any ideas who did?'

'You're assuming it wasn't just a prison killing.'

'It seems that this is the first killing in Peasmarsh.'

'I see you've been doing some homework. Murder in prison is fairly rare. Prisoners are one and a half times more likely to die from suicide, three times more likely to die from an accident and forty-two times more likely to die from natural causes.'

I wondered why politicians go into the 'it's not as bad as you think', assuming the listener thinks the worst and then put in some statistics or a disclaimer. I was impressed he knew the statistics though, but as I didn't he could have been making them up.

'No, I believe you're right; his killing was ordered. By whom or why I've no idea; but it was of great benefit to me. If you and your friends had managed a retrial all sorts of things we wouldn't want aired may have come out.'

There you go: both statistics and a disclaimer. It wasn't me, Officer, honest, and the '*we* wouldn't want' spread the targets for giving the order.

'Such as?'

'Such as what?'

'Such as the things you "wouldn't want to come out".' The *you*, I hoped, planted it back in his domain.

'Come on, Jake, you can't expect me to tell you that.'

'But it may be one of those things that could give me the clue to finding his murderer.'

'True, very true.' He nodded and thought and then reached a decision. 'Well, you know my cousin Antony Bray had the original evidence tampered with and you also know he was behind the overthrow of the dismissal of the first case and the conviction of Phillips in the second case. You also know he couldn't have ordered Phillips's killing because you shot him.

'You seem quite convinced I killed Antony Bray.' Bugger, he'd done the politicians' trick of diverting me.

'Look at the evidence, Jake. It points to Munro but you know and I know that he was in no state to accurately fire that rifle. You were in the vicinity and you were in league with him and you wanted Antony dead. I understand that.'

Now, how did he know I was there? Kitty Halloway the senior investigating officer had 'lost' all the information that connected me to the crime.

'As I said, I owe you too much for rescuing my sister and, and um, Sister Theresa.' It's extraordinary that he still perpetrates the lie about 'his sister' when he knows I know she is his daughter and Sister Theresa is her mother.

16

'What was it that Jase might have known that would cause somebody to have him killed?'

'There are a number of people who would want Michael's name unsullied but enough to take the risk of murder? Not sure about that.' He was using avoidance. Sounding helpful and saying nothing. Another politicians' trick.

'What about somebody wanting to get at you?'

'Could be, but I'm in the dark, Jake.' He was thinking. 'Jake, old bean,' he began again - he occasionally did this old-world, upper-class charm stuff - 'I've some spare cash lying around.' What an understatement; he was a multi-millionaire, probably a multibillionaire. 'About fifty grand. If you find out who killed Phillips that fifty K is yours.'

'You're on, Randolph.' It wasn't the money, although it would come in handy. Running a flat in London wasn't cheap and the death duties on Frances's legacy, my ex-boss in MI5 and girlfriend who left me all she owned, hit my nest egg. It was just that it had to be The Family that had Jase killed. Mabry was the head of the political and non-financial criminal wings of The Family and had no reason to lie to me, but he was actually giving me nothing. So he knew something that he didn't want to tell me. That told me it was ordered and not just a prison killing. If I could get enough straws in the wind I'd be able to build a straw stack but would it help me find the answers I wanted or would a gust of wind blow it away.

'Would anybody else in The Family have Jase killed?'

'If I knew that, Jake, I'd point you at him, but I'd insist you didn't kill him.'

Very interesting. This meant that if I found out and I, by some mischance, killed the killer, my new friend Randolph had clean hands. I liked Jase and I knew, given time, I could nail his killer. I'd lost people I liked in Iraq and in some of my little adventures with the MI5 Special Section, but that wasn't what was nagging at me. Why would Mabry be

17

worried to the extent of fifty grand to find out who killed Jase Phillips? And why would he have wanted me to look into the killing when as Home Secretary he had the whole damn police force to find out, not to mention his own goons and goonesses. Conclusion: he wanted this entirely private. Not just private but carried out by someone he trusted.

'Curiouser and curiouser!' cried Alice.

I agreed with the Right Hon. Randolph Mabry, Home Secretary and one of the top criminals in the country, that I would find out, for the princely sum of fifty grand, who killed Jason Phillips, but more than that I would find out who ordered the killing and why.

I nipped back to the chambers and spent the day going over the court transcripts and my notes. Nothing! That night in bed I went back over the information as I remembered it; perhaps there was some clue along the way. I just lay there painting pictures of what happened on the light, rose-coloured ceiling (I like ceilings that aren't white. Funny that! They're kind of relaxing. I had them painted a very pale shade of the colour of the carpets.) and went back step-by-step: my investigation, the court martial and bits along the way. Nothing new came to mind.

Carmichael's reputation was restored with Jase going to prison. It seemed a hell of a lot of trouble just to restore the reputation of your cousin but I suppose that's what The Family was like, close-knit and supportive. The murder of Jase could be due to the legal team of Sir Nicolas Ross, solicitor Keith Todd and defence barrister Roland Parsley, with me sitting on their coat-tails, deciding to challenge the second trial. Even before we got underway Jase was murdered in prison, stopping our challenge in its tracks. Who else but The Family would want to stop the challenge by killing Jase? Who else but Mabry, Carmichael's half-brother, would order the kill? Perhaps Rupert Carmichael, Earl of

Charnforth, his father and head of The Family, now that was likely. I'd been thinking about this for months. I'd reached the conclusion that I must do something or go right round the bend. There must have been more to this than the reputation of an army major, even if he was destined to be a big wheel in the army and The Family, and that was something I was going to find out. I was becoming evangelical about this and not only that; the Home Secretary was going to pay me for it.

3

The next morning found me in Sir Nicolas's palatial office with coffee served by Faith, another of Vera's acolytes. Funny how all those in Vera's coven had inappropriate names for junior witches: Grace, Faith and I shouldn't be surprised if there was one in the stationery cupboard called Hope or Charity. Jake, stop fantasising. Faith had a very different approach to serving coffee from Grace. Faith was into military precision. It was as if an army drill sergeant was snapping out orders to her: lift spoon, two, three, load with sugar, two, three, dunk sugar, two, three, stir, stir, stir and not one flicker of a smile. She even did everything with a straight back.

Sir Nicolas asked me how the meeting went.

'The Home Secretary – he thinks I should call him Randolph – told me he didn't order the killing of Jase. In fact, he wanted to know who did order the killing and he offered me fifty thousand pounds to find out.'

'Why are you telling me? And why now?'

'Well, you did ask and I work for you and I'd like to find out who killed Jase. It seems it would be a good contract for the practice, although it's likely to lead to a prosecution rather than a defence.'

'Do you think this practice would earn much from this contract?'

'Well no; by the time the cost of my employment has been deducted and I've hired, say Howard and Nicky for any bits

I can't do, and you've had to replace my services for however long, you'd probably break even.'

'At last you're beginning to see what is required in business, Jake. But I'm intrigued. If Mabry didn't order it I wonder who did and why. Somebody is playing a long game here or it's a cock up. The questions are, is it somebody within The Family or is it somebody planning to use it sometime to attack The Family? If it's within The Family, was it done to rehabilitate Carmichael or was it to, at some time, disgrace and replace Mabry?'

'Perhaps it was just to bury information, sir.'

'Now that's much more likely. This will be a tough one, Jake, and if you're right, dangerous.'

I knew with that statement that I had a goer.

'There is, as far as we know, no evidence as to who killed Phillips. The trail is now cold but that has the advantage that nobody would expect an enquiry.' He was thinking. He often just stared at whomever he was speaking to when he was thinking but he didn't really see them. His vision was turned inwards. I had the impression that he was seeing things inside his head like an internal video. His eyes looked upwards and sometimes moved to the right and sometimes to the left as if he was looking at something in his memory files and using that information to construct an action plan or build a way forward.

'It's not clear yet how to proceed on this but my view is you'll have to go back to the very beginning and build the picture from scratch.'

'When you say the beginning, sir, where do you think the beginning is?'

'Good question, Jake; let's see what we can uncover from the police enquiry but you're going to have to gather evidence and bring it from obscurity into the bright light of day. What's your view?'

'I think I'll have to go into the prison and find out who

did the killing. Then find out who in the prison or from outside of the prison gave that order and then work back up the chain. We know, or rather I believe, Mabry didn't order the killing so the more we can eliminate the clearer those in the frame will become.'

'That means you'll need to be undercover in the same prison and same cell block Phillips was in.' He again went into his internal viewing mode. 'I think our friend Barrow can throw some light on what we need to do to get you incarcerated.'

'Incarcerated' – what a lovely word. However, it was the 'getting free again' that was my only concern.

4

Two days later, I was in Thames House waiting outside the office of Barrow Jones, my ex MI5 special section boss. He was now very senior and in common with all very senior people you have to wait to see them. It demonstrated their importance if you had to wait. It wasn't like this in his old section. Barrow never gave a stuff about status, but from what I could observe here, his underlings did. Their status was dependent on his status so they were trying to make Barrow look important; therefore, a mere mortal or member of a sub species, such as me, had to wait. Just as I was running all this through my mind, Barrow came to the door of his office.

'Have you been waiting long, Jake?'

I raised my eyebrows.

'I do apologise. I spend more time waiting to see people who are waiting to see me than actually seeing them. The inefficiency is throttling me. Come in, come in! It's great to see a member of the old team.'

I find that all great leaders have this simple way with words – *the* old team, not *my* old team. And he was a great leader, always able to make things happen so that you could achieve. He had this way of giving you the information you needed while treating you with consideration and supporting your decisions, enabling you to take responsibility for what you achieved. That was the main thing about him. I always felt it was what I wanted to do not what he wanted me to do; although I knew he was the person directing my efforts.

We shook hands and I followed him into his office. We settled into a right-angled corner settee with a round table set within the confines of the seating area. Then a stiff woman came in and asked, 'Would you like coffee, sir?'

'Hot, black and sweet for Jake please and my usual, Ms Sweet, and when Jake comes again can you get him in here as soon as possible. He's a very important person; his time is extremely valuable.'

She looked at me, and clearly didn't think I could possibly be important, then back at Barrow. 'Certainly, Sir Barrow,' she answered and left.

'Sir Barrow? What on earth is this about?'

'The silly buggers knighted me, Jake.'

'When?' I hadn't heard.

'Must be a whole month now. I toyed with the idea of saying no but it was made clear to me that saying no wasn't acceptable.'

'Can I ask why you were knighted?'

'That's an extremely good question but I've absolutely no idea what the answer might be. It says services to the security of the United Kingdom, but in reality they get a certain number each year and somebody decides who to give them to. I think this year they gave them to people with odd forenames.' He smiled and shook his head. 'You've done more for the security of this country than I ever have. I've never risked being killed; you have.'

'No, Barrow, I just don't have an odd first name.'

He started to laugh as Ms Sweet came in with the coffee and from the look on her frosty face, laughing was an infringement of protocol.

'Shall I pour, Sir Barrow?'

'No, I think not, Ms Sweet. Jake here has a range of very technical skills including the ability to pour coffee and to kill people, so I think it would be much safer for all of us to let him pour.'

Her eyes widened and she backed rapidly out of the room as if I was about to strike her dead and as soon as she'd gone, we were both laughing.

'I don't think I can put up with this much longer. I'm going to have to reorganise this lot and staff it with human beings and I want a replacement for the old team.'

I knew he was weighing up whether I might re-join him. I felt honoured that he might consider me. I suppose that's the measure of his leadership.

'I know why you're here, Jake. Nicolas told me. I can get you into the prison. In fact, I've already taken steps to position an experienced operative in the cellblock. He's actually served time for real. By the time you're trained he'll be established. I'll arrange for him to guide you but, and this is important, Jake, you've to be trained first and I'll send you to the States to be trained. Secondly, you'll have to be a member of MI5 Special Unit.'

'MI5 Special Unit?'

'Just a relabelling of what we had before but it now has a separate undisclosed budget.'

'Will it give you any problems to reinstall me?'

'I talked with the personnel people or HR or business partners or whatever they call themselves these days and that's fixed. Is that okay, Jake?'

'I'm happy if Sir Nicolas is happy.'

'He said as long as you come back to him after this job's done. A key issue will be your cover.'

'Yes, well, I think I could go in as me. That means they'll soon find out that I'm an ex-military copper. So I'll be as popular as a pork chop in a synagogue. It also means I can't possibly be undercover and it'll also give rise to the information that I put Jase away and confusion will reign.'

'Jake, that's a very high-risk strategy. Somebody might just kill you for being a copper.'

'Very true but if a false identity's uncovered then I'll definitely be killed.'

'True and there'll be ex-soldiers and probably Family links in there. What will be your crime?'

'Murder.'

'Where?'

'In the States. I reckon that if you can get me transferred from a nice notorious prison in say Oklahoma it may create an impression.'

'So you're an ex-military policeman, imprisoned in, I suggest Mississippi State Penitentiary, for murder of, let us say, an FBI Special Agent.'

'Why Mississippi?'

'Yes, well, I know somebody. Hold on a minute.' Barrow went to his computer and banged a few keys. 'Right. The prison's Parchman Farm. It's the only maximum-security prison in Mississippi and one of the roughest toughest in the States. Well, that's a reputation I'm sure it doesn't deserve.' He came back and sat down again. He thought for a few moments. 'An appeal court hears your appeal and you're given leave to be transferred to the UK. I'll get that fixed with Sir Nicolas.'

'What about the court case?'

'No problem there; I'll talk to somebody from the embassy. Let me see, the Home Office decides where you go. I'll get Mabry onto getting you sent to Peasmarsh. He wants this job done. You were sentenced to fifteen to twenty-five years in the States on a plea bargain and here it's life. Okay, Jake?'

'Sounds good to me, Barrow.' I knew it would go as smooth as silk. It's the network scratching each other's backs and Barrow must have been owed more favours than the rest of them put together.

'One small thing that I know will be all right, you'll have to go through a psychological assessment.'

'Okay.'

'I'll fix that. Assuming everything goes as I expect, you can do something for me while you're in there. Peasmarsh is new. It's a high security prison run on experimental lines that have resurrected some historical ideas. I want your views of it as an incarceration centre for spies and terrorists. I think it would be useful to have an inmate's view.'

'Do I get a consultancy fee for that?'

'I see the private sector has already warped your view of the world. Let me see, the consultancy fee will just pay for your fares, accommodation and training in the States.'

'Touché!' We did a high five just as Barrow's administrator walk in. Consequently, we had a deal and a very shocked administrator. I wonder if they think people turn into something else when they become very senior or get knighted.

5

I left Thames House and walked over Lambeth Bridge, along Millbank into Whitehall and on to the Strand. By the time I arrived there I had my head in order. I would go back into MI5 and sort the Jase thing out. I just knew I was heading for another fine mess. As I walked in, the beautiful Samantha was her normal smiling self.

'Hi, Sam, you glorious vision of womanhood.'

'It's Samantha and Sir Nicolas isn't here.'

'Yes, I thought I'd talk to you about that.'

'About what?'

'About coming to lunch with me.'

'I see. Well, it can't be today because I'm going to a conference this afternoon.'

'Where?'

'Some place called Frimley Hall.'

'In Surrey.'

'Yes.'

'I know it. If we leave here now we'll be there in time to get lunch in the best Italian restaurant in Surrey and it's just down the road from Frimley Hall Hotel.'

'Ha ha, you will have your little jokes.'

'No, I'm serious. I'll drive you down there, buy you the bestest lunch you've had in years and deliver you to your hotel. I'll even come and collect you after you've been conferenced or whatever they're going to do to you.'

'And what do you expect in exchange for your largesse?'

'O cynical woman! I offer you the delight of a lifetime and you believe I've some ulterior motive.'

'Well, if you don't have an ulterior motive I'll not bother to come to lunch with you.'

'I see, well, I'll have to think of one.'

'Okay, I'll just grab my bag.'

The trip was on. We nipped back to my flat and collected my car from the basement garage. We were quickly on the A4 heading west towards the M4, then we crossed the M25 link to the M3 and headed southwest.

'What CDs have you got?' she said as she flicked through the CD controller. 'Oh you've got Dean Martin, Sammy Davis and Frank Sinatra.'

'Yes, I got them from my Gran.' She punched me on the arm.

'No you didn't.'

'I did, honest.' She pressed the button and she started singing, *Come Fly With Me*, and she could sing so I joined in. We worked through about five songs before she found the Beatles and we had a go at those. She did stop me weaving the car in time to the music.

We sang and laughed all the way to junction 3 and into downtown Bagshot, where the all-night café shuts at six o'clock. It was only one o'clock so Bel Vedere was still open for lunch and we parked round the back. Mario, the owner, was still there. He clearly didn't remember me but I wasn't surprised. He gave us a table in the front corner that looked out onto the High Street. Sam looked fantastic. She always looked fantastic, but today, she looked especially fantastic.

'What are you looking at?' she asked.

'You.'

'Is there something wrong? Have I got lipstick on my teeth?'

'I don't know. Let me see.'

'Stop pissing about.'

'No, you've a little black smudge on your nose. Hold on.' I took out my handkerchief, made a big deal of unfolding it and shaking it out, got up, walked round the table, put my hand under her chin, lifted and turned her head and kissed her on the lips.

'You bugger,' she said. 'Do it again.' So I did and she responded. Nobody in the restaurant seemed to mind.

'What would you like?' I asked, moving back to my seat.

'For lunch?' she asked with a cheeky grin.

'Um, yes, for lunch.'

Mario came back and told us the specials. As usual he told us the Italian names. As had always been the case, his specials were very special. After he had gone Sam looked at me and said, 'I'm not sure what he said.'

'Well,' I said, 'I'm going to have the Tagliatelle con funghi di staglione.'

'And what is that?'

'I don't know, it just sounds good.'

She laughed. 'Well, I'm going to have the third one he said.'

'I wouldn't advise that.'

'Why not?'

'It was the chef.'

'I'll have the chef then.'

'Not wise.'

'Why?'

'His wife is behind the bar.' Sam laughed.

'Tell me what you like.'

'Give me a clue.'

'Lobster tail or asparagus with a cheese sauce. They're the best two starters.'

'Okay.'

'And the main course specials are grilled chicken breast, crispy pancetta, sun-dried cranberries and apricots, in Madeira sauce or veal scaloppine, asparagus and seasonal mushroom confit, white wine sauce flavoured with tarragon or duck with the usual stuff.'

'The usual stuff?'

'Yes, the usual stuff.'

'You can't remember.'

'Right, it's my age, you know.' Sam was laughing.

'Okay, I'll have the lobster tail and the duck. What are you having?'

'I'm having the tagliatelle, mushrooms, olive oil, fresh oregano, garlic and for the main course I'm having the sole, with, um, stuff. Now, you have to pick the wine.'

'Good, are you rich?'

'Yes, for you I am very rich.'

'Okay, we will have a white wine, um, Gavi La Lancellotta.'

'My word! I said I was rich but not that rich.'

'Oh, I'm...' She looked concerned. I laughed.

'You bastard.'

We'd been chatting all through the lunch when Sam said, 'How on earth did you find this place?'

'Sandhurst is just down the road.' This clearly didn't mean anything to her. 'The military academy.'

'Oh yes.' Suddenly she fell in. 'Of course, you went there. I'd never really thought about it. Tell me about the army.'

So I did. What surprised me was that she really wanted to know. We finished with sweets from the trolley. Sam had the torta di fragole and I had the tiramisu and as we had coffee Sam said, 'A village like this would be a great place to live.' So we talked about places to live. Time went on.

'I'll have to get you to your hotel.'

She agreed. So I paid.

As we left she said to Mario, 'We'll be back.' I registered the 'we'll' and that, I suppose, was the highlight of my day, the first inkling of an on-going relationship.

'I thought you might,' he said in his lovely Italian accent

31

and kissed her on the cheek, the way Italians do. And I felt like a million dollars.

We walked into the car park and I opened the passenger door and Sam got in. Mario was watching, he smiled and nodded to me. Clearly he approved.

I drove Sam round to the hotel, took her bag in. This was an old building. Fear and loneliness engulfed me. It was like I was seven again on the first day at prep school where I knew my mother was going to leave me. I watched Sam go to reception as I had watched my mother all those years before. She talked and laughed with the woman behind the desk and I felt excluded, lonely, I wanted to run. *'Bloody get a grip, Jake Robinson.'* Sam came back. She put her arms around me and we kissed goodbye. I couldn't speak.

Sam said, 'I'll see you in a couple of days then, Jake.' We kissed again.

'Okay my lovely, four o'clock on Friday.' I think I sounded okay.

Sam picked up her bag and headed for the stairs. She turned and waved and then started up them.

I was already missing her. I got back to my car, put on the same CD and sang to it on my way home but it wasn't the same without Sam.

6

On Friday, I went to collect Sam from her hotel at about four. She was in the lounge waiting.

'I was thinking, perhaps you'd like to go to dinner tonight,' she said to me as I approached.

'Sounds good to me. Where?'

'How about a little Italian place a friend showed me near here.'

'Friday? You must be joking; we'd have to have booked this morning at the very latest.'

'I did.'

'I see. Means one of us can't drink if we're to drive back to London tonight.'

'Oh, that's fixed; I've got a room here.' The message was clear or I hoped it was.

'What time's dinner?'

'I booked for eight.'

'So what are we going to do now then?' I'd something in mind but was unsure whether Sam had the same idea.

'We could go and look at the room,' she said.

'Yes, we could.'

We climbed the stairs.

'We could have a bath,' Sam said. She had one of those card keys that she slipped into the lock and gently pushed the door open.

'Um, yes.'

'You could scrub my back.' She pushed the door closed with her bum.

'Ah, um, yes, I could.'

It was a nice room. Well, the little I saw was; the curtains were drawn. We kissed as soon as the door was closed. Her lips were cool and wet. The tip of her tongue touched the tip of my tongue and it was electric. I'm sure my hair stood up on end. Well, more than my hair. Her teeth were small. Her tongue was agile. It was a great kiss. I'd one hand in her hair and one on the small of her back. She was jammed hard against me and moving round. More than jammed against me; she moved me back so my back was against the door. Her eyes were open. So were mine. We kept that first kiss going for minutes. Her breasts were firm; as they pressed against me I could feel her nipples. We were both adults, all grown-up. Not teenagers. We didn't rush. We didn't fumble. We took our time. We were patient. We took it slowly.

We came up for air and I placed my left hand on her right breast; it was rock solid. She pulled my shirt out of my trousers, undid the buttons and slipped it backwards over my shoulders. She then ran her hands over my shoulders, feeling the scar from the knife wound in my right shoulder with her fingers. She looked up into my eyes.

'Soldier wounds?'

'Aha.'

She kissed me again and I started to undo the buttons on her blouse, from the top. She started to do the same starting at the bottom.

'No, let me.'

'I see. A kinky lady stripper.'

'I reckon. I just love undressing women, particularly a kinky lady.'

'I've watched you undress me a few times in the office.' She gave a little giggle. 'And I admit I've undressed you but this is much better.'

I stepped back, held her hand forward and undid the button on her cuff. She held her other hand forward. She dropped her hands to her sides and the blouse slipped off her shoulders and onto the floor. She put her hands on my chest then slid them up behind my head. We kissed again, for five whole minutes. I was out of breath but I didn't care. 'Killed with a kiss,' it said on his headstone. Another great kiss. Better than the first. I could feel the lacy material of her bra against my chest. I slipped my hands along the back strap to the catch. It was clear of her back in the cleft of her spine and as I unclipped it, it fell forward. She stepped back and it fell to the floor, revealing her magnificent bust. Her breasts were fantastic, round, smooth and firm. The nipples were large brown rings with the protrusions standing proud. I couldn't resist; I just had to suck them. Her perfume came up at me, a mixture of the real essence of her and the subtle aroma of the perfumer's art.

She unclipped her waistband, pulled down the zip at the side and her skirt fell to the floor. Tights are ugly things so I didn't look, just slipped my hands in the waistband and pushed gently downwards, taking the panties with the tights. They collected in a pile at her ankles. She scuffled backwards, naked apart from the knickers, tights and shoes around her feet. She sat on the bed and raised her legs and I removed her shoes and with them the conglomeration around her feet.

'Now your shoes,' she said and her throat buzzed against my lips. She turned me around, pushed me backward and sat me down on the edge of the bed. She knelt in front of me, untied my right shoe and then my left. She eased them off then hooked her thumbs in my socks and peeled them down and off. We stood up again and kissed again. By that point in my life I'd kissed a few girls, but I was ready to admit that Sam was the finest of them all. She was specta-cular. She moved and quivered and trembled. She was strong, but gentle, passionate, fiery but not aggressive, hungry, but not demanding. All these things merged into the essence of Sam. We had all the time in the world – well, until eight o'clock – and we were going to use every last minute of it.

She hooked her fingers behind the front of my waistband and tugged on it then undid the clip with a squeeze. We kept on kissing. She found my zipper tab and eased it down, slowly, slowly, small hand, neat thumb, precise finger. As my trousers dropped she held me through my Y-fronts.

'Oh, you're a big boy,' she said and then pulled my pants down, unhooking them from my erection that she kissed. I stepped out of my trousers and pants. We were totally naked and she pushed me so that I sat on the bed. She climbed into my lap, her legs on either side of me with her heels against my thighs. I lifted her hair away and kissed her ear, tracing its shape with my tongue. I could feel her cheek against mine. I could feel the smile. I kissed her mouth. She kissed my ear. We spent twenty minutes learning every contour above each other's necks. Then we moved lower. I ducked my head, holding my hands behind her back. Her head went back, arching her breasts towards me. They were firm and round and smooth. Her nipples were sensitive. She moaned a little. So did I. She moved and I rolled back onto the bed. She kissed my chest. I lifted her off my lap and rolled her on her back on the bed. Twenty fabulous minutes spent getting to know each other above the waist.

Then we moved lower. She moved lower, her mouth closing around me, sucking and moving. I was dizzy and after some minutes, I rolled her onto her back and she lifted and opened her knees and I buried my face between her thighs, my tongue working her clitoris. She moaned and shuddered then rolled me over so I was on my back with her over me and again she closed her mouth over my penis. It was fabulous and then she moved over me and pushed me inside her.

We started tenderly. Long and slow, long and slow, deep and easy. She flushed and gasped. So did I.

Long and slow.

Then faster and harder. Then we were panting.

Faster, harder, faster, harder.

Panting and gasping.

She was moaning then shouting, 'Yes! Yes!'

Then I exploded inside of her, climaxed and spent.

We lay on the bed, for how long I don't know. A knobbly elbow stuck in my ribs.

'Hey you.'

'What?'

'You have to scrub my back.'

I rolled over and looked at her. She was smiling. A beautiful smile, a contented smile, a possessive smile. 'Okay, what's the time?'

'Just gone six thirty.'

'Okay, no rush.'

'I agree, but I want my back scrubbed.'

'Oh alright then, bully,' I said.

'You can go off people you know.'

We ran the bath, or rather I ran the bath while Sam sorted out her clothes for the evening. It struck me that I had now probably earned the necessary qualification to call her Sam although no actual sleep was involved. We climbed in and soaked, gently washing each other and finding tickly bits. We dried each other, got dressed, prepared to depart and went to Bel Vedere.

I'm not sure how it happened but Sam moved in with me about three weeks later. I really can't remember me asking her to or agreeing that she should. It just sort of happened. The big problem was that soon after she moved in, I received the instruction to go to the States.

7

My invitation to visit the psychologist arrived and two days later I arrived at nine fifteen. A receptionist met me in the passageway, took my name, asked somebody on the phone whether they were ready for me and asked me whether I needed the toilet. That may sound strange but it indicated to me that I was going to be psychometrically tested. I was given a whole raft of tests and one of the personality profile tests I hadn't seen before and there seemed to be one based on the Hare Psychopathy Checklist, which seemed to cover depression and anxiety. These people meant business. On completing the tests I went into a small room with armchairs and coffee. A woman who told me she was a nursing sister asked me a series of questions about illnesses, visits to doctors, hospitals, operations, etc. She told me she had my last medical report that had been done by BUPA about six month before and then asked me some more medical-type questions based on what I'd told her. She explored the knife wound on my shoulder, the knee wound that had been caused by being hit with a brick, and the scars on my stomach below my ribs. She shuddered when I told her small fragments of shrapnel and bits of brick had caused them. The nursing sister left to be replaced by a psychologist, Doctor Thomas Kuhn. He said he was going to ask me a series of questions and ensure I would be able to operate undercover in a prison. Because of this, I felt reassured. I hadn't felt concerned but clearly somebody was.

'Tell me about school,' he started. This surprised me but I just answered.

'I went to a preparatory school when I was seven, as a part boarder staying four nights a week and going home at weekends, and became a full boarder when I was eleven and went to public school when I was thirteen.'

'So you come from a well-off family?'

'I'm not sure what that means.'

'Well, they could afford public school.'

'Not exactly; the Government paid because my father was a diplomat and he and my mother were nearly always abroad.' He nodded and made a note.

'Did you like school?'

'I loved it.'

'Why?'

'Now that's quite difficult to answer. I didn't really know anything else, but I was never unhappy. Some of the boys were. Had lots of fun and challenges, well they were the same thing really.'

'Your school record shows you did well academically and at sport. Did you have any enemies at school?' This was an unexpected question.

'Enemies? Not until the fifth form.'

'That would be year eleven.'

'Yes.'

'Tell me.'

'Well, one of the boys in my form didn't like me for some reason. I don't know why, but he would sneer and make comments.'

'How did that make you feel?'

'I suppose I was upset – no, confused. Yes, confused. I didn't know why he didn't like me.'

'Looking back now, can you think of a reason for his dislike of you?'

'It may have been my sporting success. He was a good

middle-distance runner – not something I was good at. He couldn't swim and in the summer I taught other boys to swim but he didn't come to that. Perhaps my success at schoolwork? Maybe it was just me?'

'What do you mean by "maybe it was just me"?'

'Well, some people just don't like other people.'

'What did you think of him?'

'I didn't think of him.'

'Perhaps he wanted you to.'

'Or perhaps he didn't.'

Dr Kuhn smiled. 'You were expelled in the sixth form: "conduct unbecoming".'

'Yes, yes, I was caught having sex with a girl under the stage.'

'I thought it was a boys' school.'

'It was but she worked in the office.'

'I see. What did you think about that?'

'What, being expelled or the sex?'

He smiled. 'The being expelled.'

'Bit of a pain. It caused upheaval for me. I had to go to a tech college to get my A-levels.'

'What about the girl?'

'She got the sack but my father found her a job.'

'She wasn't a student then?'

'No, she just worked in the office.'

'Yes, you said. What did you feel about her?'

'It wasn't a romance; it was just nookie, like kids do.'

'What did she think about it?'

'I have no idea. I never saw her again.'

'You didn't write or phone or anything?'

'No, I'd no address or phone number and anyway, I'd been advised by my dad not to.'

'So, you obeyed your father?'

'Not really, I just didn't try to contact her, like most boys I suppose.'

'Like most boys? Explain.'

'I just think that boys, and perhaps girls, just experiment with sex. It's not really about anything serious, it's just sex.'

'Was your later life similar to school in terms of relationships?'

'Yes, I suppose it was.'

'Describe relationships for you.'

'I'm very close to a very few people and then there's everybody else that I try to get along with.'

'Are you in a close relationship now?'

'Yes.'

'That is Samantha?'

'Yes.'

'What does she think about this undercover job?'

'I don't really know.'

'Should you know?'

'Yes.'

'But you don't?'

'I will explore it.' Sam knew but had said nothing, we had just sort of accepted it. I was feeling uneasy but I knew Sam understood, I just knew - but did she?

'What about large groups?'

'I don't mind large groups, but if I'm in a group of people who are in cliques and I'm isolated I don't like that. No, let's start again; I don't like being in a large group of strangers unless I have a role within the group.'

'A role within the group?'

'Well anything really, from serving tea to giving a presentation, just a reason for me to be there.'

'Yes, that ties up with your profile. You tend to be a socially competent introvert, which is ideal for this job. That was the only result that I needed to clarify. You've a high level of independence, your history indicates you're unlikely to be cowed in a dangerous situation, equally you're not aggressive but you may sometimes take risks. I can see

41

nothing in your history or your profiles that flags a serious warning. However, there is one issue. On your own, in an alien environment, you may become isolated but this would not give you a problem. In groups there are people who try to include others so you are likely to be included if you choose to be. However, if you do become isolated you'll not be able to complete the task that it seems you've been given. This has been foreseen and you'll have a companion who will create leads for you. Because of your social competence and independence you are likely to end up as a leader. That may be inappropriate in prison but isn't controllable.'

'Not controllable?'

'No, in general terms leadership is a relationship thing, not about position. Leaders can't be appointed, they emerge, but it does depend on the social grouping and interactive requirements. Given your personality, education and intelligence, and given the prisoner society, you could end up a leader or an isolate, but you are unlikely to be a follower; you are too independent for that.'

'Either could be dangerous then.'

'Yes, either, that is leader or isolate, could be dangerous; no, either *will* be dangerous. You are going into a high-risk situation.' He smiled, stood up and held out his hand. I stood. We shook hands. 'Thank you, Jake, it's been a pleasure to meet you.'

It seemed like all systems go then, but if Sam has a problem? Oh let's just find out.

8

The flight to the States and the train journey to the pokey little town of Gears Flats were uneventful. When I finally arrived, it was clear that the group leaving the train with me were heading in the same direction: to a bus with a man dressed in a blue uniform standing alongside it. Very soon, we were heading off along some desert roads – not the most attractive countryside I'd ever seen: flat, brown and arid with scrub trees and sparse grasses, not one of America's fertile plains. The few buildings we did see had those windmill water pumps you see in cowboy films, but there were no cows or at least I never saw them.

An hour and a half later, I took one look at the training centre from the bus and recognised that I was in for a hard time. We were in the middle of a desert in West Texas. The concrete buildings may even have been built as a prison: single-storey buildings of dirty brown crumbling concrete with rust streaks from the reinforcing. It's odd how the concrete here was brown. A double fence of linked razor wire about 15 feet high surrounded the sprawling buildings and between the two fences were coils of loose razor wire.

We approached the double gate, and the first gate opened and closed behind us as we drove in. Then the inner gate opened and revealed our new temporary home. It was clear from the moment we had boarded the bus that the training had started; we were told where to sit and the three men in uniform didn't smile. In fact, the silence became oppressive, although nobody had stopped us talking during the drive in the sweltering heat.

The bus pulled up in front of the first building, but the doors remained closed. Six men in dark, navy-blue uniforms with six-button, single-breasted serge jackets, heavy black shoes and black helmets were in a line. Four of them were armed with 3-foot heavy-duty batons and two had rifles, Smith and Wesson semi-automatics. They were very business-like. The ones with batons swung them slowly by their sides, pointing them at the ground. Menace was the description I would use. If the intention was to make an impression they were highly successful. When the door eventually opened we started to get up, but a voice from the back, the large black man who'd collected us at the station and guided us to the bus, snapped the order, 'Sit down!'

We sat. I was feeling concerned. This may have been training but it was far too realistic for me. It was way over the top. It was frightening and I assumed it was meant to be.

The driver and the other uniformed man got off. One of the guards with a baton then got on the bus. He'd chevrons on his collar.

'Now look here –' one of the two guys nearest the front said, but he got no further.

'Shut the fuck up!' The voice was flat and emotionless. The baton end was 2 inches from his mouth. 'One more word and you'll be collecting teeth from the floor.'

'Wait one –'

The end of the baton smashed into the man's mouth like a pool cue hitting a ball, hard. The guard leaned forward, grabbed the man by his collar, dragged him to the front of the bus and threw him down the step and out of the door. He then turned, faced us, the baton pointing at us, and moving to point to each of us randomly.

'Anyone else want'a fuckin' mouth off?'

Nobody said a word.

This was total immersion training. We were going to know exactly what the worst situation we may face would be like. But there was a real fear; what controls were on these people role-playing? A baton in the mouth is not what I would have expected on a training course, any training course, and I had done the tough tactics course run by the SAS in the army. Yes, it was tough. Yes, it was rough. But it didn't have the direct, physically damaging violence that we had just witnessed. Jake, handle it, I told myself. I watched out of the window as the guy was manhandled across to the buildings. He was clearly in pain and he staggered, as he was harried along. I didn't think we'd see him again and we didn't. I must admit that I thought the consent form I'd signed had been a bit extreme; now I knew why. I'd signed away all my legal rights of redress against anything and I'd done it knowingly. The guy who gave us the forms was introduced as a lawyer and he emphasised the rights we would sign away. He told us he would be the attorney we would face if we were to bring any action against the company. Two people, both Americans, refused to sign and left the room. So seven of us stayed and signed. It was only now that the uncertainty crept in.

The six remaining trainee prisoners, including me, were stock-still and totally silent. All I could hear was my breathing and the creaks from the bus as our guards moved. This was the Milgram experiment writ large. We were role-playing prisoners and they were role-playing the guards. The only difference from the Milgram experiment was that we knew we were in a simulation. We would have to learn and learn fast to be prisoners and then we could do our jobs. It was at times like this that I got concerned about men in white coats – They're coming to take me away, ha ha!

'What the fuck-yer smiling at?' The guard was pointing his stick at me. The end was 6 inches from my mouth.

'Just my total confusion, sir.'

45

'Well just keep your fuckin' confusion to yourself and if I see you grinning again I'll wipe it off your face – right?' He twirled the baton as he spoke. Clearly he'd practised this and it was too much for me; I wanted to laugh so I lowered my head as if I was a supplicant.

'Yes, sir.'

I heard him clump to the front of the bus.

'Okay, all you piss artists! Off!' This man had a nice line in phraseology but it was, perhaps, a little over the top.

We rose and stared to collect our bags.

'No. You bunch of fuckin' arse bandits. Off the fuckin' bus... Now!' This was different; he meant it. I could hear the frustration in his voice.

I pushed my bag back into the overhead rack and progressed through the bus until I was outside. We were then propelled to the nearest building by less than gentle pushes and prods with the batons. There we stripped, our clothes were taken away, and then we were sprayed down with what smelt like Lysol disinfectant spray and pushed into a shower. A female guard gave us each a rough towel to dry ourselves. No genteel privacy here then. We were then taken before a doctor or someone who said he was a doctor who peered up my bum, told me to roll back my foreskin and all he said then was, 'This would be much easier if you were a fuckin' Jew.' This confirmed to me that he was unlikely to be a doctor. Perhaps he was and role-playing a crude version of himself. I said nothing. He lifted my penis with a pencil and peered at it. The female guard watched with faint interest and absent-mindedly cleaned under her fingernails with a nail file. He listened to my chest with a stethoscope while I breathed deeply. He held my testicles while I coughed with my head to the left, checked my reflexes with a rubber hammer on my knees and elbows, took my pulse, declared me fit and healthy and sent me to pee in a tube that had my name on it. I could be deaf or blind, or have a whole range of other maladies, but that was clearly not a consideration.

We were marched to the next building wearing only the rough, now-damp towel. The gritty dust and small stones hurt our feet and where we'd been reasonably clean we were now dirtier than when we'd started this humiliating process. We went into a wooden shack. The planks on the floor were rough and splintered so we trod gently. This was a store and we were issued with a prison suit in bright orange, baggy underpants in a delicate shade of grey, thick grey woollen socks and a pair of heavy black boots one size larger than the size we asked for. We were also given a rolled blanket that, I realised, contained toilet gear and other necessities of minimal existence. Later, I was to find out the most valuable commodity here was a toilet roll.

We got dressed in the ill-fitting garb and were marched into a hall with desks and tables. My main concern was that I was thirsty and my request for water was promptly refused.

On the desks were papers and pens. The papers were personal detail forms that we had to complete. We had two tests, verbal ability and numeracy, and a personality profile: the Minnesota Multiphasic Personality Inventory.

The requirements of the ability tests were obvious: could we read and understand English and could we add up and manipulate numbers? Nobody explained why we had to do them, so I did them as if they were important. When we'd completed these, or not completed them as the case may be, we were given a Rorschach inkblot test and I assumed this was the real test and the others just a blind. It was only at that stage that I started to play games with the forms. We had to write below each inkblot what we thought it was, so all mine became depictions of female genitalia complete with lewd London street descriptors and the spelling I used was phonetic. I knew this test has been employed to detect underlying thought disorders, such as serious problems with thinking, feelings and behaviour, especially in cases where psychiatric patients were reluctant to describe their thinking processes openly. Well they, the ubiquitous 'they', should have fun with the one I had done. They then photographed us with our names chalked on a board held in front of us. I held mine upside down. No one seemed to notice.

We received a welcoming speech from the governor. This was the standard speech likely to be heard in any prison and boiled down to 'you play ball with us or we'll painfully play with your balls'. The female guard was standing next to him; she was cutting her fingernails with great concentration, using a pair of pointed scissors. I gained the impression that it was she who was going to do the painful bit. I was beginning to hate her. Subliminal messages are very telling. They've a strong influence on our behaviour and emotions and these people emitted them perfectly; either we were in a real situation or they were extremely well trained. I could feel the pain of each little snip of her scissors.

When the speech had finished we were on the go again to a dormitory where we were allocated beds. Food we were told would be in half an hour in the dining hall, but we were given no indication where that was or any other information, and it was clear that it would be futile to ask. Also, as we'd had our watches removed and there were no clocks in the room, time was a bit difficult. Again nobody told us not to ask, but the use of body language and the phrasing in what they did say to us made it clear that this would be pointless. The 'them' and 'us' was being reinforced. This was clearly an exercise in disorientation and fear. We were so shocked or disorientated that we were silent and just sat on our beds. But I quickly managed to get my head sorted out and after about fifteen minutes, I decided to take the lead. I knew this was dangerous in this situation from all the social psychology stuff that I'd studied, so I used a suggestion format.

'Do you think we should find the dining hall?'

'Where is it?' somebody responded.

I stayed quiet, so I stayed safe.

'One of us should go and look,' said a slim guy.

'Okay, smart arse, you go an' look,' said a chunky bald man with a New York accent. I stayed quiet and then posed another question.

'Would someone come with me and we can look together?'

'Okay, Limey, I'm with you.' The speaker was a young, blond, muscular man and he sounded Australian. We shook hands then left our dormitory and walked into a yard. Between the buildings we could see a group of four people running around what appeared to be an obstacle course with pull-up bars and steps up and steps down and other training apparatus. They looked tired, very tired. In only a few minutes we found a dining room. In the dining room were a group of six women in blue jumpsuits that seemed to fit less well than our orange suits. They appeared to be finishing their lunch and like any group of women, most were talking at the same time. The female guard was sitting on a windowsill with a look of bored disinterest on her face. She coldly watched us come in. We left and collected our fellow inmates. She was gone when we returned.

The food was served on plastic trays with various-sized indentations. It was surprisingly good. The flat plastic spatula and soft spoon took some mastering, but neither seemed to be much use as weapons or eating implements come to that. I found that I was starving. It must have been all the adrenaline pumping around my system burning off energy. There were large jugs of water and that was my greatest need.

As we were finishing, a man in a suit and a smartly dressed woman came into the dining hall and took us into a room next door.

49

'Gentlemen, my name is Dr Mgdi Yacoub and this is Dr Hayley Hulme. I'm a psychologist and have specialised in the psychology of prison inmates. Hayley is a psychotherapist and will help you cope with anything that stretches you too far.' So here were the people in the white coats. 'So what will you go through? We'll get you physically fit. We'll get you mentally fit.' He looked serious and stared at me. 'Mind you, I've some concerns about you, Jake. Your responses to the inkblot test were such as to indicate considerable mental disorder in the psychosexual domain. Because of that you'll not be allowed to be alone with Dr Hulme.' Big smiles were now on his and her face. 'I must admit that we were concerned until we looked at your psychometric results and read the profile sent to us from your employing agency in the UK.' He looked back at the group. 'I'm your chief instructor and Hayley will spend time with you in regularly programmed sessions and will be available to you if you find that you're having psychological problems. Let me not beat about the bush here. There were seven of you and now there are six. You're here for six weeks. We know we'll lose at least one of you, probably two and possibly three.'

My view that this was going to be tough was being confirmed. I registered the 'will', 'probably' and 'possibly' when it came to the failure rates.

'You'll be pleased to know you've just been through the toughest session of your time here. We wanted you to get a feel of the shock and disorientation of the induction into a prison. It was more extreme than is usual and that was deliberate because you knew it was a simulation, but nevertheless you now probably have some feel of that transition. Our experience is that it's at this early stage of entering a prison that you'll give yourselves away. You have to be able to read situations before they become overt. The person we lost didn't have that ability, all the cues were overtly displayed and he didn't observe them, or his self-centeredness did not allow him to conform. The rest of you did and did it naturally.'

'Let me impress something on you now. If any con even thinks you're an undercover agent you're dead. There won't be any questions, you won't see it coming and you will be killed. I'll repeat that: you will be killed. You are doing perhaps the most dangerous form of investigation in the world bar none. Learn well or die. If you decide at any stage you don't think you are going to make the grade tell us and you're out of here. We won't try to persuade you to stay. This course is about staying alive in prison.' He stopped and looked at each of us. 'I'll say that again: this course is about staying alive in prison. You may be excellent at what you do but that'll be of no use to you if you're dead.' He'd made his point. 'I'm going to tell you one other thing. Nobody on the prison staff will know you're not the genuine article. If any of them find out it may show in their behaviour and if it does you're dead meat.' He looked at each of us in turn. 'Nobody will be tracking you. Nobody will be looking out for you. Nobody will feed you warnings. You are in there on your lonesome.'

It hadn't crossed my mind that when I'm inside I would be on my own. I knew Harry would be in there so we would just have to be very careful.

'This evening you'll have a "getting to know you" session conducted by Hayley so you'll know each other. Tomorrow we'll start you on prison culture and language then we'll move on to fitness and self-defence, etc. This programme is modular so the first modules in each subject area will be relatively simple and as the modules progress they become more difficult, and then the modules will be integrated to introduce the reality of complexity.

'Everything will be as practical as we can make it. By the time the successful trainees leave here they'll behave and sound like old lags. While here you'll analyse your own behaviour and actions, get feedback from each other and from your instructors. If you don't make the grade you'll be removed from the training. Your life will depend on your behaviour when in a real prison. Your life will depend on you being able to read signs that you're in danger and being able to take appropriate action. Your life will depend on your ability to physically defend yourself against tough, determined attack with or without weapons such as knives. Any questions?'

There were a few and we quickly built a picture of the programme and the elements within it.

'You haven't asked any questions, Jake.'

'Um no.'

'Well, ask one now.'

'Okay. We're being put through intensive training to handle prison, but if I were just an ordinary Joe who got sent to prison nobody is going to train me.'

'So, the question is what, Jake?'

'How do ordinary Joes cope and what is different about us?'

'Many ordinary Joes, as you call them, don't cope. They become subservient to experienced prisoners and their life is hell. Some become aggressive and have their resistance beaten out of them or end up integrated. Some become sex slaves of one or more prisoners and if they don't co-operate they're raped. Many do cope and merge into prison life. Many, irrespective of how they integrate or survive, are damaged mentally, though most recover. Now to you, you've a dual role: prisoner and undercover agent. That puts an additional load on you so this training will enable integration and enable you to go undetected in your undercover role.' He stopped and looked at me; my face was blank; I said nothing. 'Well done, Jake, you're a fast learner.' So encouragement to reinforce useful behaviour was built into this programme. 'Any other questions?'

'How many courses are here at any one time?' I asked.

'Yes, we take a course every two weeks so there are three courses at any one time. Female courses are rare, probably three a year, and there is one ahead of you. The smallest course we start with is four and the largest is eight. Normally our courses consist of only US citizens with the occasional foreign national. In this course there are two foreign nationals: Jake who is English and Sean who is Australian. This is an unusual course as there are no Hispanics and no African-Americans. This is disproportionate as while people of colour make up thirty per cent of the US population, they make up sixty per cent of those imprisoned. The implication of that is not hard to work out.'

It may not have been difficult for him to work out but I could have gone down all sorts of routes with those statistics, from bias in the justice system to where poverty lies, to the educational divide – the implications seemed to me to be endless.

9

The days flew by. My body ached, my head ached and I sometimes felt I was destined to fail, but I bashed on. After a week we were down to five, after four weeks we dropped to four, and we were gaining the picture of a prison as a closed world. The true misery of imprisonment was now very real to me. I recognised how the prison authorities can do anything as they have the power, but below that was the very real, informal power structure, ruled by violence. The staff role-played other prisoners or guards. We were learning that staying safe comes down to some basics: stay alert and learn some manners. Prison is a close environment containing too many people close together, so manners are extremely important. The sheer pressure of overcrowding, that you can't avoid, generates irritation and violence, particularly as many inmates have low emotional control in the first place. The worst thing for me was that I was missing Sam. I had an ache like a big hole where my solar plexus should be. It had only been a short time and many couples, from long-distance lorry drivers to international businessmen and women, spend more time apart than together. But this was crippling me, although at least I knew when it would end.

One solution was to be polite to people, treat them with consideration, don't be nosy or impinge on their limited personal space, never borrow things, don't boast or bullshit, never grass anyone up, don't kowtow to those in power, but do show them respect and even more important, avoid drugs and stay away from junkies. Not that we were likely to go native and become junkies, but it was very clear how easy it would be to become one, particularly as up to 80% of prisoners in the USA were drug- or alcohol-dependent, but this was much lower in the UK at about 60%.

I was amazed at the range and variety of tricks of prison survival and power we learned, from how to conceal things from searches, how to pass things unseen, how to communicate, how to bargain, how to do just about anything that aided survival and personal wellbeing behind bars.

After five weeks only three of us survived. We were on the home run now and I was totally acclimatised to the prison regime. My learned behaviour was now second nature and, apparently, matched the required norms of prison life. I renewed my fighting skills, which had, again, become second nature, and I learned some new ones. Paramount was the zero-consideration concept. That is, if you get into a physical confrontation you must have no consideration for the other person; they are a dangerous enemy to be destroyed. If they can recover they may become a threat when you're not looking. I think I was fitter and harder than at any time in my life. Strangely, I felt aware of being both more considerate and more callous of others. They were either a friend or a foe; there was no grey, just black or white.

I sat with McPhee, one of the instructors, on the steps outside the dining area.

'Looks like you made it, Jake, but we knew you would.'

'Can you tell then?'

'More or less. It's a sort of steel in the way a trainee looks at you, the way they move and shift, the way they react in different situations and you can see some of that on day one. Being ex-military helps, you know. Obeying an order even though you know it's stupid and can get you killed, but you were special from the start.'

'Me? Special?'

'Yes you. And you've just done it again. You ask questions but they're soft, non-challenging. You make the other person feel good about themselves without bull like praise and stuff. We don't get many like you here.'

'All the trainers seem very experienced.'

He smiled. 'Half of us have served as prison guards, some of us have been prisoners and we've all been educated in criminology and psychology. Yes, Jake, you'll be okay in there.' He smiled and patted my shoulder as he stood. 'Two more days, Jake, two more days.'

10

My return home was odd. Well, Sam thought I'd become odd and I suppose I had. What I hadn't realised was that I had to normalise to live outside of prison and that was essential before I went back into the prison environment.

I spent three weeks at home and most important was the time I spent with Barrow and with Sam. Barrow was crucial to my rapid recovery because he was my counsellor. He asked me the right question at the right time and gave me jobs that matched where I was in my head. He, being a psychiatrist by profession, helped and I did wonder how people without that form of help recovered their balance. My concern was if the training had screwed me up what would the real thing do to me? Barrow pointed out that there were a number of pressures in the training situation that I was in that were very different from a normal prison situation, if any prison was normal. We weren't only learning to live in a prison but to do an undercover job. He also mentioned a very odd thing; people in prison don't want to be there whereas we, in training, had the threat of being thrown off the course. That hadn't dawned on me. Sam was a rock, she asked, she listened and she understood, and she nurtured me through the bad nights with pure affection.

Too soon, I was back in the States to spend some time as an observer in Mississippi. I had to gather the sorts of facts and figures that the average inmate would be familiar with and the layout, work regime and general ambience of the state penitentiary, Parchman Farm. Not that anybody was likely to have been there but one never knew in this shrinking world.

I decided to focus on Unit 32, mainly because my brief discussions with the deputy warden indicated for the particular crime of murdering a member of the FBI a prisoner would be housed in Unit 32. It turned out that Unit 32 was in the process of rapid change (well, rapid for the prison service). The prison authorities were attempting to reduce the number of prisoners held there. In 2009 there'd been about a thousand but most of them were fairly ordinary prisoners who didn't need special confinement. Unit 32 had now been reduced to those that were considered dangerous to other prisoners or prison staff or were likely to be escapees. The issue was where to house those that should be moved and how to restructure this area to best make use of the facility. The result was that it wasn't quite chaos but each move threw up a myriad of problems. The number of prisoners had dropped from the thousand when the reform started to about five hundred when I was there and the proper number calculated for the high security facility was about two hundred. One wing was empty and being restructured as a death row and prisoners were being employed to do the work so it was a rehabilitation project for them. One of the issues was people who weren't, as individuals, considered dangerous but fitted a category that dictated special incarceration, such as revolutionaries, those with very dangerous mental health problems and some forms of protective custody, the basis of which seemed to be unclear.

The prison as such was unlike anything in the UK and probably unique in the USA. In the old days, Parchman was, and still is, in prime cotton-growing country. Inmates laboured in the fields raising cotton, soybeans and other cash crops, and the production of livestock, pigs, poultry and milk. To some extent that happened while I was there and it was one of the things I felt gave an old-fashioned feel to a prison that, in the main, was run on modern lines.

It had beds for nearly five thousand prisoners. Prisoners worked on the prison farms and in manufacturing workshops, and the senior staff were statistics mad. They were very proud and often said things like we produced this many carrots or whatever and we provided umpteen hours of labour for the local communities. To some extent, the buildings reflected the history of a pre-Civil War plantation of fifteen work camps. Because of the sale of produce and cotton, Parchman Farm was consistently profitable for the state. This was very different in concept to the UK and, strangely, the trade unions accepted this.

Despite its size, Parchman didn't house general female offenders but it was the location of the female death row. That was the general information. I then had to get to grips with the impact of solitary confinement, so I joined a shift to observe the prisoners and the way they were handled. I would have to behave like some of the inmates and it was soon clear that the people transferred out of solitary were, in the main, nutters. This deterioration occurred after a relatively short time in solitary. They displayed agitation, self-destructive behaviour and overt psychotic disorganisation. When they returned to the normal prison regime they tended to be intolerant of social interaction, which is a real handicap to readjustment as the more normal prisoners excluded them. I gave up trying to replicate that behaviour and prayed that it was accepted that I wasn't in solitary, but I did the Unit 32 statutory five days just to understand what it was like.

The staff referred to solitary as 'AdSeg', the abbreviation of Administrative Segregation. Prisoners used two terms: either 'the hotbox' or 'the hole'. The first day wasn't that bad, the main problem was what was I going to do. Clearly I had to have a routine but with no clock, how long I did things for was the first problem I met. What to do was less of a problem at first. I exercised - press ups and sit ups and, well, you name it: with only a bed in a bare cell, innovation was the name of the game. Now what? I decided to sing, that was fine but even I got bored of my singing. I needed to keep my mind active so I went over things I had learned but I needed some writing materials and I had none. By day three I found I was talking to myself. With nothing to read, nothing to write on, no stimulation, life was getting tough. I realised I was sleeping more. So I exercised, sang, slept and thought about things. Being with only me was becoming purgatory. I suppose it was day four when I heard voices for the first time, so it was then I realised I had to stay in control of myself, but a new horror started and that was the fear that they wouldn't let me out. I was also scared that I had lost track of the days; was it day three or four? Or had we actually reached day five and they had decided to leave me in the hole? On day five I was released from solitary and this was a massive relief.

I was learning. Every day I walked in the prison, different parts of Parchman prison, and saw how some prisoners fell into a pit of despair. I wasn't sharing this but I was observing it. I realised it takes a lot of energy not to drop into the black hole and those that coped well were working at it. I talked to some of these prisoners and they, in a kind of embarrassed way, said how they replaced negative thoughts with positive ones. It was something they had learned to do and they knew it was paying off for them. For some it would be years before they tasted freedom again. Some, it seemed to me, wanted to be in prison. They were fed, clothed, protected from anything that was changing in society, if not always protected from the violence of other prisoners. For them release was something to be feared. I learned so much in the time at Parchman, things I hadn't learned on the survival course, and that was the difference. The course taught me about survival and the skills required for it, but Parchman got me in tune with prisoners, what it felt like, the emotional mix that different prisoners faced. A course could not do that, only the reality of a prison can give you that and I was getting a flavour of it without suffering it.

It was soon very clear that if I did run into somebody who knew about Parchman, just saying I was in Unit 32 would register deeply and if the person had been a prisoner it would give me status. I would have to add the rider that I was only in Unit 32 awaiting repatriation. However it was with some trepidation I approached my incarceration in a real prison.

11

I came home and Sam and I knew that soon I would be away again. Sam decided she would like us to go on holiday before I left for my incarceration. It was difficult. I hate holidays but, it seemed, Sam loved holidays. I suppose, for me, disliking holidays started as a relatively young boy when I was sent to aunts who didn't really want me and cousins who I actively disliked. Of course there was an exception and that was my aunt Lil, who had no children and she grossly over indulged me.

Sam wanted to go to Italy. Fine, I would go to Italy but only because Sam wanted to go. Of course if you are going on holiday you have to get there so why not make the travelling part of the holiday? So we went on a 'Great Trains Holiday'. What could be simpler? First class from Waterloo to Stresa on Lake Maggiore, with overnight stop in a four-star hotel in Dijon, France, and through Switzerland to Lausanne and down to the final destination. What could possibly go wrong? After all, the continental trains, we are told, are wonderful. Well, delays, engineering works and strikes meant that we arrived exhausted and in need of a holiday, having had an adventure that I, for one, didn't sign up to. It was with some trepidation that I contemplated the journey home but the next two days in a deck chair watching Sam chatting and organising made me believe holidays are fun.

We had adventures. We went on the lake in a little boat

and, in glorious sunshine, wandered around the streets and alleys and ate fantastic food with names we couldn't pronounce. We bought wine and ended up with little art things that we didn't know what to do with, it was just fun. It was a honeymoon without the wedding. The great one was the language. We bought a guidebook to the Italian language and had great fun attempting to buy stuff and get into places only using Italian. We were walking down a lane and Sam spied a silk blouse in the window and we worked out how to buy it using Italian. We tossed a coin and I lost so I had to do the business. Sam, the shopkeeper and me ended up in fits of laughter but after about half an hour Sam had her silk blouse. She tried it on and she was parading around the shop. The shopkeeper quietly said to me, 'You did real good, mate, an' she is bu'iful.'

I was flabbergasted. It turned out that his father was Italian and he had been brought up in the East End of London. When his mother died he had brought his father home. So the three of us went to his local regular hostelry and had a couple of the finest bottles of red wine.

How I'm supposed to relax surrounded by people who speak a language I don't understand, do things in ways I find totally incomprehensible and who treat me in a kind and friendly way as if I was the local village idiot, I don't know, but with Sam it was just great. When it went wrong it was just funny and when it went right it was just fun. Travelling home went as smooth as silk and I decided I loved holidays but only with Sam.

Now I had to say goodbye and go to prison. I think we both hit the depths. Sam tried but I walked into the bedroom and she was crying. She was hiding how she felt from me and I headed for the phone to resign. Sam stopped me. Tears ran down her face, and tears ran down mine. Sam didn't want me to go but knew it was something I had to do. A big black cloud filled me. I wanted to stay with my Sam. I had lived an independent, dangerous life but Sam had changed that.

Authenticity was going to be vital if my undercover status wasn't to be revealed. I was to be flown back to the States and spend a few nights in Oxford, Mississippi and from there start the route to incarceration proper.

I travelled to Jackson in cuffs. From Jackson I was flown to Washington still as a prisoner. In Washington I was handed over to British prison service personnel and flown into Heathrow with two officers, cuffed to the seat, with a whole row of seats at the back of the aircraft reserved for us – the whole nine yards as the Yanks say.

One of my escorts handed me a *Daily Telegraph* folded to page five. The *Telegraph*'s crime correspondent, Edward Richards, had produced a short column that raised the issue of one Jake Robinson who it appeared had been convicted inappropriately of killing an American federal officer and due to the excellent work of Sir Nicolas Ross QC, was repatriated to the UK. The opposition in Parliament were questioning the legitimacy of this repatriation as the European Court of Appeal had been bypassed, although the shadow Home Secretary didn't go so far as suggesting this decorated army officer had actually committed the crime he'd been accused of.

It was on landing at Heathrow that the whole plan went pear-shaped, as I was transferred to Brixton. Why Brixton? Apparently I was a Londoner and as such I should be in a London prison. Oddly, the nearest prison to my home was The Scrubs but that isn't how the bureaucratic mind works. Well, I'm not sure bureaucrats have minds. So I travelled from Heathrow to the M4, A4, through my part of London, south on the A3220 onto the A3 and to Brixton Prison. You might imagine my concern. I'd heard the reputation of Brixton and it wasn't good and it wasn't meant for long-term prisoners.

My first sight of it wasn't reassuring. It looked like an old factory with chimney stacks surrounded by a 15-foot brick wall. The G4S transport wasn't the most comfortable as I was in cuffs and it seemed like it hadn't been cleaned for months. It stank, in fact. Was I getting special treatment or was this the standard? Later, I was assured that the vehicles were inspected before each job but that clearly wasn't the case. We passed through the gate but it took two tries, so I assumed that the gates were very narrow or the driver was a trainee.

Once inside, I was parked in a cell and left. It wasn't an attractive cell. It also stank. I'd been in much worse places but they were in battle zones; here it was just plain unsanitary inefficiency. My bag and personal effects had been taken so I was without toiletries, even a razor to shave with. I also had a sense of dread. Had The Family taken the opportunity to royally screw me?

After three hours of incarceration, I was taken to see the governor and this wasn't a joyful experience. He was a tall, gaunt man named Wexford with a pallid completion and he needed a shave. He had a rosy red nose and veins showed on his pallid cheeks. I might assume he was a drinker. He sat at his desk and I stood on the other side and anybody in range, as I was, would suffer from his halitosis. I wasn't impressed.

'Prisoner Robinson it says here.' He looked at me expecting a response. He was fiddling with a pen and it was clear that he bit his fingernails; they were painfully short and the flesh of the fingers bulged up in front of the edge of the nails.

'Yes, sir.'

'It says transferred from the United States of America to England.'

'Yes, sir.'

'A murderer.'

'No, sir.'

'Oh, one of those "I didn't do it" arseholes.' His language surprised me, particularly as he was what might be called well-spoken apart from the lisp that I bet was mimicked when he was at school and probably by his staff here when he was out of earshot. He wasn't a happy bunny. 'It says you should be in Peasmarsh but for some reason they don't want you and you've been dumped on me.' He was taking this personally. I said nothing. 'Well?'

'I was told I was going to Peasmarsh, sir.'

'So you want to go to Peasmarsh.'

I did but I hadn't actually said that.

'I want you to go to Peasmarsh but some spotty jerkin of a brainless office clerk has changed your destination to here.'

I didn't know what a jerkin was but I could guess.

'I don't want you here and I expect you don't want to be here.' His exasperation boiled over. 'Well, you have a cell so you'll stay there until this cock-up is sorted out. Any questions?'

'May I have my belongings, sir?'

'No, you can't. I don't know what the world is coming to when a commissioned officer in the Royal Military Police goes around killing American FBI agents. I think the best thing would be to send you back to... Where are you from?'

'Parchman Farm, Mississippi, sir.'

'I suppose your daddy pulled some strings to get you home, ay?'

'Sir Nicolas Ross QC did, sir.'

'Oh and why would he do that?' The voice resounded with sarcasm but there was some uncertainty.

'Because I'm not guilty, sir.'

'Oh, Christ, not on that again. Give him what he needs and we'll sort this out tomorrow. Oh, and you better feed him,' he said to the senior prison officer who had brought me in. 'And shift him to a reasonable cell.' His tone had changed. I had the feeling that the mention of Sir Nicolas's name had created a shift in the governor's thinking; it's wonderful the power that rests in a name.

'May I make a phone call, sir?'

'Yes, if it's to somebody who will get rid of you.' It was a question but he wasn't speaking clearly.

'My solicitor, sir.'

'Good.'

He looked at the senior prison officer, who said, 'Yes, sir.'

I was taken from the governor's office to another office where I was searched and interviewed. I had to fill in some forms and also signed lots of papers that I didn't have time to read. I was fed with some cold, inedible rubbish that I didn't eat, given a breakfast pack and made a call to Keith Todd who wasn't there but I left a message. I was given a rolled blanket, my travel bag and the instruction I got was simple – Cell 24, C-Wing.

I found the C-Wing corridor and set off down it. There were no numbers so I counted the cells with some trepidation. I avoided looking into the cells as I passed them. These were the private living quarters of prisoners. Nevertheless, it's impossible not to have glimpses of the interiors. The cells I did see had posters with nudes, occasionally crucifixes, TVs, some had sheets tenting out the bunks and some were singles. What struck me was that even though the prisoners had cells and weren't in a dormitory, as I'd been in training, they weren't individual cells as in Parchman Farm, so privacy was in short supply. Most of the cell doors were open and nobody was inside, so not only was there no privacy but also no security of possessions. Then I thought; what could you steal from a man with nothing? Then the thought struck me that the little they did have would be even more valuable to them.

I soon found the corridor I needed and Cell 24. The bunk bed was, as I was to find out, typical prison issue: no sharp corners, rusty and cold. The cell was sparse; it had a sink and a toilet, a table and a wall-mounted television. There was even a remote control – wow, modern technology! It was so cramped, however, that standing at the sink my back was against the bed.

In the top bunk was an Afro-Caribbean guy named Lenny who was due to visit the magistrate's court the next day for shoplifting and resisting arrest.

I'd purloined a book when being interviewed (I had a feeling that purloining something is much less of a crime than stealing), so at least I had something to read. It was *South Riding* and the prison officer who watched me nick it didn't mind as it belonged to a female prison officer who had put it on the desk when she went to get the paperwork. I sat on the bunk at the cell door end to get some light and started to read.

'It will be lockdown soon,' said Lenny.

'Okay, and?'

'Oh, nothing.'

So that meant there was something but he wasn't going to tell me. On guard, Jake.

A shadow passed across my book and a very large, fat man stood in the doorway. I looked up.

'Oow-er you?' he asked.

'I'm Jake.'

'Got yer breakfas' pack?'

'Yes, thank you.'

He laughed. 'Give it me.'

'No.'

There was a click as he flicked open a blade. 'Wot cheu say?'

'I said no, Fatso. Put that toy away or I'll stuff it up your arse.'

There was a look of disbelief on his face.

'Wot cheu say?' He took a step forward. Mistake. He had

led with his left foot so he was vulnerable and my right fist was driven upwards and hit him in the testicles. He cried out in pain and clasped himself, dropping his blade. As I stood, driving up through my legs, I hit him in the throat with my fist. He staggered backwards through the door and collapsed, gasping for air and choking in the passageway. I threw the blade down the passageway and closed the door. Lenny was standing hard against the end wall and he was a paler shade of black. He mumbled some words that I interpreted as 'you can't do that'.

Some minutes later I heard a shemozzle outside and five minutes later the door opened. A prison officer stood there.

'What happened?' he demanded.

'When?'

'Ten minutes ago.'

'Ask me another; that one's too hard for me.'

'Smart arse,' he exclaimed as he slammed the door and locked it.

This was not a good prison: overcrowded, two in single cells, long time in lockdown where you eat, drink, wash, go to the toilet, watch TV and sleep. In fact this was primitive, lacking privacy and was unsanitary.

Morning came and I'd slept reasonably well. I'd acclimatised quickly to the odd smell of this prison. I already understood that all prisons have their own smell. This one was just old, the ubiquitous smell of cabbage was old cabbage, the smell of ancient brickwork permeated other smells such as that of sweaty bodies and faeces, but the biggest impact was the draughts. No matter where you went there was a draught. It would cut across the floor and numb your ankles, or slice horizontally across a room and paralyse your back or descend vertically down and give you a stiff neck. The drafts had to have been designed into this building. It was just not possible that they occurred naturally; their temperature was at least 10 degrees below ambient temperature.

At ten in the morning I was taken once again to the governor's office and Sarah Sands was there. I'd heard of Sarah but never met her. I knew she'd done the legwork on getting me back to the UK, working for Keith Todd, my solicitor, and Sir Nicolas. I didn't know if she knew I was undercover but that would be buried deep. I knew her mother was Indian and her father was English. The whole family apart from her were in the medical professions. Father and one brother were surgeons, mother and other brother GPs and a younger sister was a clinical psychologist in the NHS. She was bucking the trend being in the legal profession. She had a beautiful skin colouring, a bronze that shone with health, long black shining hair and a true size twelve, slim, attractive figure. A most unlikely solicitor, but that's my prejudice. She had a reputation for being as sharp as a razor, incredibly detail-conscious and disciplined. Hence, my secret was safe.

As I walked in she stood, held out her hand and said, 'I think we've got this little mishap sorted, Mr Robinson. Some member of a committee looking at the welfare of prisoners had noted the anomaly of you coming back to the UK and being sent to Peasmarsh when you live in London and did her do-gooding bit, and a civil servant obliged her by you being transferred to Brixton.'

I wasn't sure about Sarah's phraseology that a civil servant had obliged the do-gooding woman, but she was from the upper reaches of society.

'They'd overlooked the fact that the American authorities had insisted that you were to be imprisoned in a high security establishment, a friend of yours is already in Peasmarsh and the committee had already approved you being sent there to be with that friend. The fact that he is an Afro-Caribbean seems to have weighed heavily with the committee members at the time so the chairman, who we spoke to, wasn't enthralled that you'd been transferred and he was quite annoyed that such an action had been taken without him being informed. We requested the name of the committee member who instigated your transfer but the chairman preferred not to tell us. However, he said he didn't understand how this committee member would know about you coming to the UK from America. He found this most strange. The governor has put the transfer action in place.'

Well that was that then. I'd said nothing, the governor had said nothing and all was hunky dory.

'Thank you, Sarah. May you live long and prosper.'

She laughed. 'I didn't know you were a trekkie.'

'Well, you have to do something to keep out of prison.'

She had a beautiful smile: white, even, attractive teeth and a beautiful shade of lipstick that suited her skin colouring. She held out her hand and I took it.

'Keith said I'd be looking after your interests and he's given me a deep briefing. Goodbye, Jake.' She turned to the governor, held out her hand and said, 'Goodbye and thank you, Governor.'

He said his goodbye as she headed for the door. Job done.

'Well, Robinson, you're somebody that definitely needs watching. I expected a month of wrangling and your young friend sorted it out in a matter of an hour. I don't expect to see you again and you'll be transferred out of here in about an hour.'

Alarm bells were ringing in my head. Somebody somewhere didn't want me in Peasmarsh and had pulled the prison move. Not a very smart move, as they must have known it couldn't work, so it was a junior person in The Family. What it told me was that The Family knew what I was doing. Well, Mabry knew, but I thought he was on my side in this, so where was the problem? It must have been one of his staff or it could have been Superintendent West. Screwing me would be something he would want to do.

71

'Thank you, Governor.'

I was taken back to my cell, packed my gear and sat waiting for the transport out of there. It was a great relief when it arrived.

12

My arrival at Peasmarsh Prison was similar to the training simulation but nowhere near as traumatic. The approach was along a new arrow-straight concrete road in a bus that had picked me up at the station. It seemed as if this was a normal bus converted to carry prisoners. It was a small bus of ten specially constructed seats on each side, each one carrying one prisoner. I had a belt locked around my waist that had a chain to a lock on the aisle floor. I knew it could be released electrically because the guards (oops, sorry – prison officers) tested it before we left. Two prison officers and a driver staffed it.

My four fellow passengers didn't look any different from any other travellers on a bus. I knew the one forward on the left was very dangerous because he was also bound in handcuffs. I'd seen his picture in the papers: Marvin O'Brian, late of Strangeways, where he killed two prison officers, one of them female, whom he was trying to rape. He didn't look dangerous but apparently he'd a string of rapes and murders to his credit. A medium-sized man, wavy fair hair starting to recede; it was difficult to believe he had killed two adults with his bare hands and it took a number of others to restrain him even after he'd been hit with a Taser. I was under the impression that a Taser causes strong muscle contractions and incapacity but apparently this guy went on fighting. But that was just a newspaper report and it was difficult to believe what they said. The snippet on me in

73

the *Mirror* that morning said that I was a war hero who killed in self-defence and the court in the US was wrong to convict me as the plea bargain was illegally obtained. It seemed that newspaper reports about me were so different to create confusion in the public eye but in each I was a hero.

It was drizzling and the dirty windows of the prison transport were streaked and distorted everything we saw, but still the prison could be seen in the distance across the open moor: a three-storey concrete eyesore. Aesthetics weren't in the mind of the architect when he designed this monstrosity. I could remember the protestors objecting to the prison being an outrage. If it had been browns and greens it would have disappeared, but grey concrete was a blemish even in this bleak, less than attractive moorland. As we approached, I noted that there were no watchtowers and a wire fence surrounded the prison: just a simple wire-link fence about 8-feet high, topped with barbed wire. It seemed to be designed to keep people out rather than to keep anybody in. I was surprised. I thought that an insurmountable outer fence was a requirement of a high security prison, particularly as I'd been briefed that Peasmarsh was primarily for Category A prisoners who were highly dangerous to the public or to national security if they were to escape. Me, I was just a miserable Category B: a prisoner for whom the highest security conditions weren't necessary, but the powers that be just didn't want me to get out. Perhaps the fence was there because the public and protestors were more dangerous than the prisoners. You had to keep the prisoners safe from the local forces of protest, you know.

As we approached the gate I noticed it was open and the grounds inside the fence to the left of the gate were like allotments with men working them. They must have been sodden working in this continual drizzle, but they didn't seem to be concerned. Inside the fence it looked like there was a tartan track and at intervals, there were obstacles such as steps up and down, parallel bars, a high bar and other apparatus, so this was an exercise track. This was like the training establishment in the States. I had also seen them at Stresa in Italy, but I was surprised to see one in a British prison.

There were signs facing the outside announcing that there were guard dogs, so I think dogs were a warning to protesters. There were also floodlights and CCTV cameras at regular intervals, and I was told later that there were movement sensors that triggered the equipment and traced the movement, so technology rather than physical barriers was the security methodology. There was also a helicopter pad. It would be difficult, if not impossible, to cross this boggy moor at night where a helicopter with infrared would find it easy to pick you up.

The induction was just like the training: shower, strip search, peer up your bum, but interestingly none of the prison officers actually touched me; apparently, this was an EU regulation: human rights or some such. If they couldn't see something stuck up your bum they couldn't take any action and, if they needed to, all they could do was park you until it came out naturally – bit different from the States. I had a perfunctory medical that was more questioning than any real inspection, and then received my prison clothing. I was given a natty blue number but Anil Mouratoglou, a terrorist bomber, was in a fetching orange outfit that, I was reliably informed, by overhearing the officer giving him his suit, glowed in minimal light and some form of detector strips were incorporated in it so if he escaped he would have to do it in the nude. It was amazing how some people got their kicks. Each of us also had a tracker. This was a new one on me. Mine was on my wrist like a bulky watch. The orange-suited prisoners had a second one on their ankles. Mine just tracked where I was at any one time, so if I was being looked for I could be found. A record was kept of where Cat A prisoners had travelled in the prison and computer software analysed their movements. I understood that some do-gooding team was conducting a test case claiming this was an infringement of human rights. I have never been quite clear why killing somebody or their family being deprived of a relation wasn't an infringement of human rights.

I was shown to a booth that was about 2 by 2 metres and open on one side, with walls that went up about 2 metres and a ceiling way above that. It contained a table and two chairs, one on either side of the table. Sitting on one of the chairs was a large, tough-looking female prison officer. She was a bit overweight and her red hair was cut like a Second World War German soldier's helmet. It looked solid: probably sprayed with fibreglass resin so that it was a helmet. She wore no makeup or any adornment except a plain prison officer's uniform: pale-blue shirt with epaulets containing a pip and below that a crown, a black skirt, black stockings and regulation laced shoes. This wasn't a lady who had any regard for her appearance; her clothes just sort of sat on her bulky, muscular frame. I'd read that female prison officers had been warned not to appear sexy; no chance with this one. Perhaps she was James Bond's antagonist Rosa Klebb, but she wasn't knitting with poison-tipped knitting needles. Perhaps she'd a poisoned knife blade concealed in those heavy shoes. No, that was wrong; with red hair and a poison blade in the toe of her shoe she must have been Irma Bunt, and Irma Bunt wasn't killed so this is where she had turned up. I laughed at my make-believe and the prison officer looked at me strangely. She may have thought I was nuts and, as I was to find out, a number of prisoners were.

'Please sit down, Jake. I'm Senior Officer James and I'm your personal officer.'

'Yes, ma'am. What's a personal officer?' I could smell her. It was a mixture of carbolic soap and a body spray called

Goddess that the housekeeper who cleaned my flat twice a week used. It came in very large spray cans and I had assumed it was for killing insects. Perhaps I was wrong; on the other hand... Senior Officer James was clearly a practical woman.

'If you've any problems, if you've any questions, I'm the person to ask. If you find yourself in trouble I'll be your spokesperson, if you feel you need a spokesperson. I've your personal file here.' She pointed at a file about half an inch thick. 'And I'm surprised that you ended up breaking the law. It says you killed an FBI special agent, but it's a bit vague, very surprising that. How did this come about?'

'Why do you want to know?'

'So that I've an understanding of you and the reason you're here.'

'Are all prisoners asked these questions?'

'No, it's unusual, but you're very unusual. A commissioned army officer with a psychology degree, served in the RMP with what appears to be a distinguished record, a medal for bravery, seconded to MI5, goes to the USA and kills somebody, not just anybody but an FBI special agent and as far as I can tell from the information here, no motive.'

'And what does that tell you?'

'I was hoping you'd tell me.'

'Will I end up in solitary if I tell you to fuck off?'

'Are you telling me to fuck off?'

'No I'm seeking information. You said if I'd any questions to ask you, so that's what I'm doing.'

We sat looking at each other.

'Are you going to answer my question?'

'Yes. You won't go to solitary for telling me to fuck off.'

'Let me ask a different question then.' I paused, waiting for permission.

'Go on then.'

'Tell me your real role here.'

'I told you I'm a senior officer.'

'And my ol' man's a dustman. Not your apparent role, your real role.'

'What makes you think I'm not a senior officer?'

'Well that may be your rank but that isn't your role, is it?'

'And what on earth makes you think that?'

'One: your pronunciation. Two: your syntax. Three: the structure of your questions. Four: the questions you're asking.'

'Yes, if we've a strange one I'm the person that becomes their personal officer.'

'Just you?'

'No, there are two of us.'

'Your degree?'

'I don't –'

'Bollocks.'

She looked at me. She was evaluating me. She'd a decision to make and she could only make a decision in the light of her role here and her evaluation of me after seeing very limited information about me. This was an educated woman. She was bright, aware, confident, and she had purpose. She had to make a decision. If she lied to me and I recognised the lie then confidence would be broken and she needed my trust if she was going to achieve her goal, but at the same time she knew I knew that she wasn't what she pretended to be. Could I trust her if she told others her doubts about me – and I could feel she had doubts that I was the genuine article? I held her eyes and gently tipped my head to my right. She answered my question.

'My first degree is an honours in psychology and criminology, and I've a master's degree in forensic psychology.'

'Now there's a clever girl. And your real role here?'

'To get inside the head of ambiguous cases.'

'Why?'

'Some people are exceptionally dangerous.'

I waited. She was going to outwait me but I needed information more than she did.

'Am I exceptionally dangerous?'

'We don't know. It says here that you were in Parchman Farm, Mississippi and while there in Unit 32. I understand that's solitary confinement.'

'We?' I'd ducked the implied question.

'There's a committee. The members of the committee review all people that come here. Some are obviously dangerous, some are obviously not and some are ambiguous.'

'And I'm ambiguous?'

'It seems so.'

'I'll tell you what. I'm likely to be here for a very long time so what I'd like is a straightforward briefing and after you've observed me for four or five years you can decide if I'm dangerous. How does that suit you? No, wait: I bet you're one of those fast-track goodies, so in four years you'll be a governor or you'll have completed your doctoral thesis and be in some educational establishment and I'll be a case study.'

She completely ignored what I said. She was cutting her losses. It must have been that I was too near the mark. Interesting.

'I'd like to ask you a question about Parchman Unit 32. Did you do solitary?'

'Everybody in Unit 32 does solitary.'

'Why?'

'It's the routine.'

'Tell me about it.' She'd opened a spiral-bound American Quarto book with a shiny blue and white cover. I knew it was about Unit 32. I'd seen one before; well, I had one. I wondered how she had one.

'What do you want to know?'

'When did you go into solitary?'

'First Monday at nine in the morning.'

'Reason?'

'Everybody in Unit 32 does a short spell in solitary just so they know what will happen if they play silly buggers.'

'When did you come out?'

'Saturday, five days later, in the same order that we went in.'

'We?' She'd just done to me what I'd done to her.

'All the new entries to Unit 32.'

'How many?'

'Five'

'So five of you went in on the Monday morning and five came out on Saturday morning?'

'Yes.'

'What did they tell you before they put you in?'

'The Chief lined us up and told us there were five things to remember.' I wasn't making this easy for her. Why should I?

'They were?'

'The first one was silence is golden, so we could enjoy its riches. Prayer is good for the soul, so we should pray. He said we should eat well because it would give us strength to endure the pain of the remorse for what we'd done. Exercise to maintain flexibility of body and through that, maintain flexibility of the mind. And the last one was to masturbate as little as possible as it's better to conserve our strength, dignity and self-respect. He said we would know not to return.'

'What did they tell you when you came out?'

'Same sort of stuff: learn from your experiences, good actions – no, positive actions – have positive consequences and disruptive actions have negative consequences or something like that, learn and behave yourself. It was like being in school again.'

'What was it like when you came out?'

'What was it like?'

'Yes, how did you feel?'

'Right, um, yes. Immediately I felt relief. After four days you're scared they won't let you out so when you come out you feel relief. Then you feel, or I felt, anger. What right did they have to do that to me?'

'So what did you do?'

'Nothing.'

'Why not?'

'Because I might get solitary or a lethal injection.'

'Okay, Jake Robinson, here is your number. Each number is unique and it'll tie together everything that's to do with you and is done to you.' She droned on: the rules, health care, what I can take to my cell, cell cleaning, what is in the canteen and on and on until she said, 'Anything I've missed?' What a neat trick question. She was testing if I was a plant.

'How the hell would I know?'

'Oh, I just thought you'd know about prisons.'

'I know this is very different from Mississippi State.'

'How?'

'They're very careful in Mississippi. I was an oddity so they stuck me in Unit 32. You probably know from your notes there that Unit 32 is high security and most people in it are in solitary lock down, and some are just in close confinement as I was, so for the short period I was there I saw little and heard little. No cosy conversations like this. I was convicted of killing a federal officer, so by definition I was a dangerous prisoner and I was doubly dangerous as there were people trying to get me transferred out and what was even worse they weren't Americans, so I must also be a terrorist, but as they'd lawyers and politicians looking over their shoulders they just kept me in close confinement.'

'I see.' She was again evaluating what I said.

'Well, there's something I'd like to know.'

'What?'

'Visiting.'

'As a Category B prisoner serving a long sentence you'll be allowed at least two visits lasting one hour or more every four weeks. If you behave yourself and stay out of trouble for the next six months then that may be increased.'

'Wow, I'm going to be overwhelmed by the social round. When will the first visit be?'

'In about two weeks. Just fill in a form and it will be authorised.'

'Phone calls?'

'We've a pin-number system here. You can make calls lasting a total of one hour each month so you can have one, one-hour call or sixty, one-minute calls. You have to be here two weeks before you get your pin number.'

'Are they monitored?'

'Most calls are recorded and may be monitored at any time except if they are made to a legal adviser or the Samaritans. Some numbers are blocked, such as chat-lines.'

'My lawyer?'

'You looking to find a legal way out?'

'I want to see my lawyer.'

'Why?'

'Two things: The first is that I want to challenge my conviction and secondly, I want to challenge the regime in here on the basis of infringement of human rights.'

'Who is your lawyer?'

'You've read my file.'

She opened the file and turned over some pages. 'The criminal one is Sir Nicolas Ross QC. Sir Nicolas Ross, eh? That's a bit high powered.'

'You better believe it, lady.'

'Does he know you then?'

'You know he does. He got me back here from the States so that he could work on my case.'

'He'd be very expensive.'

Oh dear, Jake; you've just made your first cock-up.

'Not really, Senior Officer James. I was a witness in a case before him and he took a shine to me. I was also in MI5 at the time of my arrest and they've recognised the cock-up that got me imprisoned, and Sir Nicolas, as you know, got me back here.'

'It says you've a solicitor, Keith Todd.'

'Yes, I want to start a challenge using human rights legislation. Keith Todd will find me the person I'll need.'

'What human rights abuse are you going to challenge?'

'This thing.' I held up the tracker on my wrist.

'So you think that violates your human rights?'

'I'm not a lawyer but let's see Article 3: Prohibition of Torture. A person has the absolute right not to be tortured or subjected to treatment or punishment which is inhuman or degrading.' I held up my wrist. 'Article 4: A person has the absolute right not to be treated as a slave.' I pointed to my wrist. 'Article 5: The right not to be deprived of their liberty without a proper legal basis in law. The judge didn't mention this thing. Article 11: Right to associate with other people. I reckon somewhere in this lot you are violating my human rights by putting this thing on me.'

'I think you might be very dangerous, but in a different way to how we thought.'

'You'd better believe it, lady.' I thought I'd thrown enough sand in her eyes for them to leave me alone, at least in the short term. 'Can I ask you a question?'

'Is it about telling me to fuck off.'

I had to smile. 'No, it's about me being sent to Brixton and then here when I was told I would be coming here from the States.'

'Now that is interesting; I was going to ask you about that. Why do you prefer to be here?'

'Well, here you get a personal officer and Brixton is, to be polite, a disgusting shit hole.'

'See, two very good reasons, Jake, but could it be that somebody doesn't want you here?'

'You know I thought that, but I couldn't think why not.'

'Yes, Jake Robinson, you can lay more false trails than a Red Indian.'

'You're not allowed to say that; it's racist. You have to say Native American.' I used a prissy voice. She smiled.

'You're good at avoiding answering me, Jake.' She pulled out a pink form, ticked a number of boxes, put crosses in a couple and wrote a little note at the bottom.

'So that's the report?' I asked

'Yes. Despite what I've read about Unit 32 Parchman, you show no evident psychological maladjustment or psychotic disorganisation.'

'Your conclusion?'

'I haven't reached one yet.'

'Don't believe all you read, lady.'

She tipped her head to the left, looking at me; she was definitely unsure about me. 'Well, you've a friend in here and you'll be sharing a cell with him.'

'Who?'

'Harry Mount.'

'Harry Mount? I'm not sure I know him.'

'He says you do and he says he knows you.'

'Give me a clue.'

'He's about six foot three or four, weighs about eighteen stone of solid muscle, ex-Royal Marine Commando. Said you were a hero in Iraq. Pulled you out when you got injured in a riot.'

'Christ, yes – a big, black sergeant.'

She winced: probably the fact I mentioned his colour when she avoided mentioning it. 'That's right.'

'What happened to him?'

'Took some drugs and killed five men over a period of

seven weeks. He's a Category A prisoner. You've nice friends, Captain.'

'I never heard about this.'

'No, you wouldn't. He was a mercenary in Nigeria when he went on his killing spree. When the Nigerians caught up with him they were going to shoot him but the British Government did a deal and he came back here to Brixton as a Cat B, but he was a trifle disruptive and after only a week inside he made a break. That would be about two months ago and a policeman got seriously injured. He was upgraded to Cat A and transferred here. He's been absolutely no trouble since. I'd say he's a model prisoner. Strange that, don't you think?'

'Don't I think what?'

'That someone has a record of violence, was highly disruptive in one prison, comes to another and he's just a pussy cat.'

I decided to tackle this one straight on and say exactly what this very bright lady was thinking. 'Perhaps he disliked Brixton or, I know, he's a plant and it was a way to get him in here.'

'I was thinking the same thing.'

'Yes, I know; that's why I said it.'

'Why might he be planted in here?'

'Well,' I pretended to think, 'he heard that in here is a very sexy red-headed senior prison officer named James who loves to shag six foot four, black, ex-Royal Marine sergeants.'

Her whole being relaxed and she smiled. 'It's going to be great having you here, Jake. Let's go and see him.'

Complete with my roll of gear, I followed her to B-Wing and had my first glimpse of my new living quarters. It was similar to one of the modern American prisons I'd viewed: very open and light due to the sloping glass roof, with wings radiating from a central area. It smelled fresh, open and clean, the way all institutions should smell, but already it was suffering from what all British prisons suffer from – over-crowding. On the first landing the cells were built as singles and already, due to the lack of prison space, most were doubled up.

13

The walkways above the ground floor were cast and wrought iron and scanned by CCTV. This place was very secure, so why was it that I didn't feel safe? I knew. It was the hidden calls that said things like, 'You're a dead man, copper.' Prisoners were making gestures indicating that I wasn't going to survive long. Perhaps my plan to be high profile was misplaced. Senior Officer James ignored this threatening atmosphere.

As we walked onto the first landing she said, 'Most of it's just sounding off to look big and feel brave.'

'Thank goodness for that.'

'You're in danger though.'

'Now she tells me.'

'Just keep yourself to yourself until they get used to you. Don't be provoked and if you do end up in some form of fight, win. If you lose your life will be hell.'

'That's what I like: encouragement. Let me say this, lady, if any of these bozos pick a fight with me I'll kill him if he doesn't succeed in killing me first. There's only one conclusion to fighting with me.'

She looked at me and I could see her wondering whether this was bravado or I meant it. She made up her mind.

'You can address me as ma'am or Senior Officer James.'

I said, 'Gee, right on, ma'am,' in a Southern States accent.

She smiled.

Suddenly, in front of me, was a giant of a man. He was twice the size of his photo.

'Hi, Jake, long time no see.' He pulled me into a bear-like hug then pushed me out to arm's length. 'Still beating up bad boys?'

'Only if they deserve it, Sergeant.'

'God, it's great to be called Sergeant again, Captain. Welcome to our humble abode. You can have the top bunk. Rank has its privileges. I'd hate to fall through those flimsy springs onto you.'

I scanned my new abode. It was intended to be a single cell but was more than twice the size of the Brixton cell I had just left. It had everything that Brixton had except the toilet area was enclosed and the enclosure included the washbasin and an extractor fan. How about that for posh?

Officer James was watching, but there was no indication what she was thinking, so I asked, 'Are you Harry's personal officer as well?'

'Yes, as it happens, I am.'

'So you only pick the good boys.'

She laughed. 'Yes, I suppose that's right. Good is of course relative. Tomorrow we'll look at your work or training assignments; though, we were thinking you might want to teach some education courses. We're not overburdened with people of your educational level.'

'That would be brilliant.'

'We'll see, tomorrow then.'

So I was in and over the first hurdle. Harry briefed me but he was concerned that I'd be targeted. The briefing I received was unlike any that another prisoner might have with his new cellmate. I got the informal organisation run by the cons, who would be dangerous to me, who was in the frame for killing Jase and where the order probably came from. I was surprised that he was concerned about two of the prison officers. Eric Moorby and J.J. Manson. They'd been on duty when Jase was killed.

'What's the problem there then, Harry?'

'It seems to me that they've a relationship with Mr Wharton.'

'The boss man?'

'That's right. Well, sort of, but I'm not sure he really pulls the strings. As I was saying, everybody has to call him Mr Wharton and they do.'

'Why, Harry?'

'It's just easier and safer to do it.'

'This Mr Wharton character, you're not sure he really is the top man?'

'Right, but it's just a feeling.'

'Okay. What do the screws call him?'

'Sam. Remember this prison has a first-name or nick-name policy.'

'Why?'

'It seems some sociologist wrote a book about, well, sociology and it said in the book it would aid relationships or something like that.'

'Okay. Can I just go back? You said that this Mr Wharton might not be the top man, Harry. Who do you think is?'

'That's a difficult one, Jake, but there's a guy named Peter Jackson. He seems to have privileges and around him are a small group protecting him.'

'Privileges?'

'Difficult to put your finger on. He ends up with the best seats at a concert; he is in an area of the prison that seems to be better kept than the rest of the prison. It's just lots of little things.'

'So the governor would be responsible for that.'

'That's exactly the point, Jake. But he exerts no obvious power. Mr Wharton does all the controlling. I've just thought that "sergeant" and "captain" might just be a good pattern to cultivate, Captain.'

'Okay, Sergeant.' We both laughed. 'They didn't kill Jase, though.'

'No, the rumour is that a little shit called Ratty did. Ratty – or Raymond Tidy, to give him his full name – runs errand for Mr Wharton. He got a step up in status from bum boy when Jase was killed.'

'So, Mr Wharton is...?'

'As bent as a corkscrew. Control is through rape.'

'You must be joking.'

'No, as far as I know there's only been a couple of cases but the mythology is that everybody knows somebody who knows somebody it happened to. The thing is the recorded actions only occurred when Moorby and Manson were on duty. Guard your arse, Captain.' He smiled.

I settled in quickly. I suppose I was used to discipline and that was something that most of my new companions were not amenable to. It seemed to me the atmosphere of threat was lower here than the other prisons I had visited. Perhaps because it was a new prison or perhaps it was the sociological experiment with names. Many of those new to prison looked tired. They clearly weren't sleeping. I'd always been a good sleeper. I suppose it came from spending most of my school years sharing a dormitory or multi-occupied bedroom and then sharing bedroom space in private student accommodation at university. The cries, calls and snores, the groans, gasps and moans, and the bangs, footsteps and the creaking movement of the building didn't bother me. For some, this must have been the real punishment of prison, that, together with the lack of privacy. I'd never had a private life: prep school, public school, university, Sandhurst and then the army proper. I suppose officer accommodation was the greatest privacy I'd ever had. No, I suppose, strangely, my privileged life had equipped me for prison. I suppose it must be the mass of people in the middle strata of society that would suffer most with mummy and daddy always around to look after them and their own bedroom and privacy. I assume that those in the top and bottom strata, as children, face a range of life's stresses that toughen a person up to be independent, with the top end involving more parental interest but less parental contact.

14

The next two weeks went fast. I sat in with some of the other teachers and instructors to get a feel for teaching and to try and pick up hints, tips and approaches. Some seemed to me to be really good and others were, quite frankly, rubbish. I went to the library and found some books on teaching and they, at least, gave me some structure. Slowly I integrated into prison life, massively helped by Harry, but my overriding thought was my first visit and I was counting down the days until I would see Sam again.

When the day finally arrived I was walking from the classroom allocated to me, towards the hub of the building, when two prisoners confronted me. This was a 'blind' area of the building. I didn't know them. It surprised me that it had taken so long before I was challenged.

'Got a visitor today then, copper?'

'It seems so.'

'Pity you won't be well enough to see her.' The speaker stepped forward, poking my shoulder with his finger.'

'I would prefer it if you didn't poke me.'

He grinned and went to poke me again, but the grin quickly transformed into a scream when I broke his finger. He dropped to his knees and I still held his finger while he screamed, pain I supposed, and then I kicked his face. I felt his teeth break on the toe of my shoe. His mate turned and ran. I kicked him twice more; his face was badly damaged. I then stamped onto his right hand and heard the bones crunch. I wiped the blood off the toe of my shoe on the downed man's trousers and kicked him three or four more times. Undoubtedly, some ribs would break.

He was still conscious, so I said, 'Okay, sonny Jim, tell your friends the next one I'll kill.' Lesson learned. Message sent. I picked up the books and papers and walked back and into the library. Arthur and Dad, who were in my class, were in there and Jacko the librarian was reading a letter to one of them. All three looked at me.

'I've been in here nearly as long as you.'

They all nodded. They understood; no questions and Jacko restarted reading the letter. The door opened and two prison offices came in, Mary Williamson and Peter Osgood. They stood and looked at us.

'Last one in?' said Williamson, scanning the four of us.

'That would be me I think,' I said. 'Yes, I shut the door. Yes, me, Officer Williamson.'

'How long ago?' Both the officers were staring at me.

'Ten minutes, um, quarter of an hour.'

'Did you see Bert Connolly?'

'I don't know Bert Connolly.'

'Where did you come from?'

'My classroom. Number seven.'

She nodded. 'Okay.' They stared for a few seconds then they left.

I asked Jacko to look after my papers and then followed the two officers down the passageway. The central area was like a tableau; it was quiet, prisoners stationary, looking at the entrance to the passageway, their eyes following me as I meandered towards the reception area. Nobody moved towards me. The repercussions of this little confrontation would be interesting.

Finally, I went into the visitors' room; I was the last one in. It was the first time I'd been in there. The officer on the door checked my name and asked me whether I had read the rules for visitors. No touching was the one that had registered most strongly with me.

Each Formica-topped table was square, facing in the same direction, with two chairs on one side and one on the other, all fixed to the floor in perfect lines so the prisoners were facing the entry door. Video cameras were very noticeable around the room. When seated, prisoners were a long arm-stretch from their visitors and prison staff could patrol in any direction. I was pointed to a table at the back of the room; well, I assumed the visitors' entrance was the front where an officer stood. I could understand the thinking of the designers, low chance of contact, easy viewing of all interactions. There were also vertical boards under the tables, between prisoners and their visitors that went down to just below knee height. Smart these designers: not possible to pass anything even on a shoe, and no hand jobs.

Many of the tables were occupied, some with visitors and prisoners and the rest with waiting prisoners like me, watching the door. You could feel the expectation, or was that just my excitement? I watched as visitors came in and the prison officer on the door took their names and pointed to where their prisoner was. The room was nearly full when finally Sam came in. She was, as she always was, calm, controlled, beautiful and observant. She saw me almost right away, long before the prison officer pointed me out. Her arrival, however, signalled a hush amongst the other prisoners; it seemed that everyone was looking at her and all talking had stopped. Then a breathless voice, filled with awe, said, 'Fucking hell!'

Some laughed at the exclamation that they'd probably controlled and an appreciative growl came from some others. I doubted that many women who looked and dressed like Sam visited people in prison.

Sam smiled her dazzling smile in the direction of the young man who had spoken and he went bright red. Then she looked back to me and walked through the tables to me, all eyes and sighs were following her gently swaying hips as she weaved through the tables and chairs. The air was tingling, awed by her beauty. Perhaps it was the way she carried herself: slender, gracefully and elegantly moving through the tables towards me. She'd the bumps and curves in exactly the right places, exactly the right shape and exactly the size that made any red-blooded male hold his breath as she moved on those exotic, perfect, long legs. I suppose she'd an air of mystery about her. I'm sure that was what dominated the men who came into Sir Nicolas's chambers and these men were no different – dominated, dumfounded by feminine beauty as I'd been from the first time I saw her and I still was. I suppose I'd always just accepted that she was beautiful, never thinking about her beauty, just knowing, but more than that, her inner beauty. But, as she walked amongst the tables toward me, I realised that she was one of the most beautiful women I'd ever seen. I'm sure I knew that already, but it was just in this environment it hit me like a punch to the solar plexus and clearly it had this stunning effect on the other men in the room and put to shame the lesser beauty of their women.

She put her bag on the table, sat, leaned across to take my hand and was promptly stopped.

'No touching,' the female prison officer said.

'I bet you want to touch him,' said Sam with a smile and a knowing look at the officer.

The officer smiled. 'We can't always have what we might want, madam.' She then continued her patrol down the aisles between the tables.

Sam looked at me and said, 'Can we talk here?'

'I think so.'

'Your release is going well. Everything is in place to pull the plug when you trigger it. Your solicitor friend has found a real, live, lefty, human-rights nutter who has linked up with some prisoners' rights nutters and they're starting to create little waves in another prison to test the authorities reactions before tackling this place. Now let's talk about you and me. Tell me what has happened to you.'

'I am now a teacher.'

'A teacher, teaching what?'

'I have this class of non readers and I have to get them to learn to read.'

'Don't they have proper teachers in here, then? Oh, I'm sorry, I didn't mean it like it came out, it's just I never would have thought of you as teaching people to read.'

'I know, it's weird really, but I've learned a lot already.'

We chatted on about my class and then Sam said, 'Barrow came to see me.'

'Oh, yes?'

'He said that Sir Nicolas had an anonymous tip that it was probably an individual called Ratty that killed Jase. Not a very nice name. Anyway he sends his regards. I bought a new picture by Henderson Cisz, *Morning in Westminster.*'

'I bet that cost a few bob.'

'Well, I know you like his pictures.' I noted that she didn't tell me the price so it was probably over five grand.

'Where will you put it?'

'You know where St Paul's, The City is?'

'Yes.'

'Well, I'll move that towards the door and it will fit in there.' I could just visualise it. They would look great next to each other. We chatted on about what she had been doing and what was happening at the chambers. June, in the restaurant, had got engaged at last. She had been going out with a civil servant for five years so that was a move forward towards her ambition. We chattered on and the time just flew by.

The only problem was that half the room was watching us, well, watching Sam. I suppose one of the attractions for our observers was the way Sam used her hands when she was describing things, flowing and expressive, a delight to watch.

Eventually, visiting time ended. The visitors left, Sam with them, and I had a hollow empty feel, a void. I was missing her before she reached the door, where she turned and blew me a kiss. The prisoners were told to leave row by row, except I was told to stay where I was. The room was empty and two prison officers came and sat opposite me. One was Peter Osgood and the other was a senior prison officer that I didn't know.

'Where were you at ten fourteen this morning?' asked the senior prison officer.

'I was in classroom seven or the library.'

'Could you have been in the passageway past the library?'

'Might have been, yes. Probably, I passed the library and then went back.'

'Did you see anybody else?'

'There were three people in the library. They were –'

'No, in the bloody corridor.'

'No, I don't think so.'

'You were there at the same time as Bert Connolly and Charlie Adams.'

'If you say so.'

'You just said that you didn't see them.'

'Well, I didn't.'

'How could you not see them if you were there at the same time?'

'Perhaps I was facing away from them.'

'Did you hear them in the passageway?'

'Um, no.'

Just then, Senior Officer James, my personal officer came in.

'Problems, Jake?'

'No, ma'am, these officers seem to think I saw somebody that I didn't.'

The senior officer and Senior Officer James went to the other side of the room. They called over Osgood then Senior Officer James came back to me and the other two left.

'They don't believe you, Jake.'

'I don't give a shit.'

'Bert Connolly was seriously injured at about ten fourteen in that corridor this morning and you were there.'

'How do they know?'

'Two reasons: tracking switched onto you because you had an appointment and all those who have appointments are scanned to see if they're in the right sort of area. The other reason was that you were also seen in the library just after that time.'

'Well that's right, I told them that, and Officer Osgood saw me in the library. Were they tracking this guy, Bert Connolly, as well?'

'No.'

'So he might have been there earlier or later.'

'Possible, but unlikely. He was on video entering the passageway at ten thirteen.'

'They said somebody else was also there.'

'Yes, and he said he didn't injure Connolly.'

'Did he say who did?'

'You know he didn't. He's not going to grass.'

'So what will he get?'

'Some loss of remission.'

'Good lesson not to pick fights with people.'

'But you didn't kill Connolly, Jake.'

'Then it couldn't have been me.'

Senior Officer James smiled and shook her head. 'He'll take some months to fully recover, Jake.'

'Oh dear. What a shame.'

'Yes, you're very dangerous, Captain Jake Robinson, but I don't think you'll be attacked again in a hurry.'

When I got back to our cell, Sergeant was there.

'You look like shit, Captain,' he said and I told him what happened. 'It's these bloody things,' he said. 'Always carry some silver paper then if you want to disappear, cover the transmitter.' It was so obvious. 'I know what you're thinking, Jake. The screws know, but remember they can't prove a thing.'

15

As I had told Sam, I'd found myself teaching reading and writing to a group of illiterates and, strangely, I was enjoying it. Well, two of them weren't illiterate but they wanted to be in the class with some of the other prisoners so they claimed they were illiterate.

The chief instructor had given me some methods and books but these guys had been subject to these methods for a year, or in some cases a number of years, and they hadn't, it seemed, progressed at all. Initially, they were totally demoralised and only came to lessons because it was the best of the options that they had. Their interest level appeared zero and I had to get control or this teaching number was dead before it had begun and no other instructor wanted this little lot. I quickly found that interest in learning to read seemed of little importance to my class. So, I explored it. The odd thing was that they were, in reality, desperate to learn to read, although they didn't want to say so. They could see all sorts of advantages but the downside was too daunting. The main thing was fear: fear that they couldn't be successful because the subject matter was too hard for them and it was boring and their span of attention was low. They had also found that if they had a half-decent teacher he would eventually give up on them.

I could see one problem almost straight away. How on earth can anybody use a phonetic approach to learn to read when he or she doesn't make the correct sounds when they speak? So we started with learning to say words correctly. The other problem that struck me early on was that English is not a phonetic language, so there is often not a direct relationship between the spelling and the sound. So they were faced with a double problem, but it didn't seem to be quite the sizable problem I thought when I got hold of some explicit sexual magazines and we practised words they could see through the pictures, such as t-i-t. I would then show the picture, write the word and say the letters. They found this fun and related to the pictures and I would take the words they used and we would work on them to get the sounds. It may not have been good teaching practice, but it got some interest and when they got over their embarrassment of doing this out loud, we started to get somewhere. Mind you, I did have some opposition to them using correct pronunciation, as this was posh. A partial answer was to use their words, expletives and all.

'Say after me: shit – sh-ee-t – shit. Sound out the "t" and have the tip of your tongue in contact with the top of your mouth just behind your front teeth – "t".'

As they got used to me, most of the time was spent laughing and some of the professional teachers weren't amused, but I'd interest and my class was working hard, and I was having fun. I quickly understood never to be negative. If something was good I would tell them. I also didn't let them be negative about themselves or the others in the group. We were building a positive culture and it was very hard work and exhausting. They didn't understand at first as they were so used to negativity as a mode of communication and were embarrassed to be positive.

I was surprised by how quickly some of my students, students may be an elevated term, caught on, but some were having difficulties that I just didn't understand. What was more surprising was that, in many other ways, they were the sharpest people in the class. Then I realised that three of them, Johno, Liz and Spider, were probably dyslexic. I needed to talk to somebody and it turned out that one of the old pros was knowledgeable in this area, a man known as Mr Cratcher. Nobody seemed to know his first name and he'd been teaching in the prison since he retired from teaching at the local grammar school when it became a comprehensive some fifteen years before. He was a cold, scratchy old bastard as far as I could see, and must have been at least seventy-five, probably older. Strangely enough, the cons rated him and that was good enough for me. I managed to capture him in his classroom as the classes broke up.

'Can I have a word, Mr Cratcher?'

'Got a problem then?' His response verged on a sneer.

'Yes, I think I've some people who are dyslexic.'

'You think you know enough to diagnose dyslexia do you?' His voice was now definitely dismissive of this arrogant amateur.

'Unfortunately, no. That's why I wanted to talk to you.'

He put his head on one side. The grey stubble on his chin caught the light and his thin grey hair slipped untidily across his head. He then straightened up and his sharp eyes bored into me. 'What do you want to know?' His voice was now more accommodating. Not friendly, but the hostility had diminished.

'Anything that you can tell me.'

'Um, generally, it's considered a reading disorder. Pupils with it can't read so they're disruptive in school and that leads to exclusion and that leads to criminal activity and that leads to prison. Tell me about the ones you think may be affected.'

'Well, there's –'

'Whoa, not their names!'

'Sorry. They all seem very bright – actually, one of them isn't. The two that seem bright have good verbal skills and have good social skills. They participate well in discussions and one of them is very good at thinking laterally and solving problems. He can also see the big picture.'

'What do you mean by that?'

'Now that's difficult. No, he seems to be able to move past the detail and put it in a broader context and he sometimes thinks into the future.'

'That's fairly common with dyslexics. Apparently it's to do with using the right-hand side of the brain.'

'Why can't they read?'

'Now that's a very good question. There are three schools of thought: some think the pupils are just unintelligent or lazy, some think the condition doesn't really exist and some think it's a disorder, the bits of the brain just not linked up properly. There's a new theory that it's about the way the eyes move but I don't really know much about that.'

'Your view?'

'You don't hold back do you?' He gave a thin smile. I was winning him over. 'Mostly it's a disorder but some pupils, very few, are just unintelligent, you may have one of those, and many are just lazy, but the disorder definitely exists.'

'So what do I do?'

'I wish I knew the answer to that one. Look, let me give you some background and then some ideas but what you do with your ones is up to you.' I nodded and he matched me. 'Dyslexia is all about the person's difficulties in processing word sounds. They can say "but", but they can't remember the sound to tie it to any symbols. This may be caused by inefficiencies in language-processing areas in the left hemisphere of the brain. That means it can't be fixed. The person is born that way and will stay that way. Mind you, as you've found out, dyslexics are usually above average intelligence. Many dyslexic people learn to read, but have continuing difficulties with spelling. There are of course people whose difficulties with reading aren't caused by dyslexia like most of your class.'

'So what do I do?'

'There's no easy answer to that question. We suggested that all the prisoners should be tested and a team brought in to help but, well, people in prison aren't considered important and getting people to a level where then can function as non-criminals in society isn't even on the agenda if it costs real money.' The cynicism dripped from his voice.

'So you've no advice for me.'

'Jake, I'll give you some advice. Use a wooden alphabet to teach the names and sequence of letters. Get them to use their spatial ability and feel the letters with their hands as a translation process. They can feel the letter and move it round, hear the sound and see the symbol. Use pictures and memory hooks for sounds. Do what I hear you're doing now; that's make it real and fun. And when you've got them started get them to help each other. Sometimes you will have to go slowly because of the confusion between spelling and pronunciation.'

'Such as?'

'Lets take, um, "read" spelt r-e-a-d and r-e-e-d. But r-e-a-d can be said as red and red is a colour so it's not surprising that reading in English is difficult and spelling is even more difficult.'

The next day I talked to the class and asked Johno, Liz and Spider to explain what it was like for them. Liz was prepared to talk about it.

'Well what 'appens is, the letters move and jumble up and my 'ead fuckin' 'urts. Then sometimes I can see the words and I fink they're gonna stay fixed and they just melt away like they're not on the page and then they come back. But it's different in different rooms.'

'Different in different rooms?'

'Yeah, well, in here it doesn't happen much but in the library or when we were in room 5 it was worse.'

I understood the problem. This room had natural light through the windows but the library and room 5 were on the other side of the corridor and had no external light, only fluorescent lights.

The rest of the class just sat and looked at him. These were problems that were like science fiction to them. It was like science fiction to me but I now could guess at a cause.

Dad said, 'But, Liz, you're great at drawing and can make things and if your eyes don't work you couldn't do that.'

'I knows,' said Liz. 'I can draw fings people talk abart and I can splain pictures but writin' is differen'.'

So this was what Mr Cratcher was saying about the processing area in the brain linking the sounds and letter shapes.

'What about you, Johno?'

'I'm not that bad. I can read easy stuff but when I write it's like Liz says, and I don't know the letter to write and if I'm told the letter I sometimes can't remember what it's like and I sometimes remember and it comes out the wrong way round.'

'What comes out the wrong way round?'

'The letters.'

'You mean a "b" looks like a "d"?'

He just looked at me in pain. He just didn't understand my description and I guessed he was feeling stupid. I could have kicked myself.

'Okay, you lot, what we're going to do is work together. We're going to stick the letters from the alphabet books onto some hardboard and then we're going to cut them out. When we have done that we can use them to make words.' I'd an inkling of where I needed to go but how to get there was my next problem. At least there was now some understanding in the class that not being able to read wasn't all about being thick. I also wondered how many of the problems some of my class had was to do with eyesight

105

and whether there were any hearing problems. These weren't the sorts of men that admit to failings such as these. So I decided to talk to the nurse and set up some testing for all of them.

16

There was a buzz that prisoners could join up for jogging on the moor. I put my name down and it came out in the draw. The system was simple. We had shorts, vests, socks and trainers and then a waistcoat with an identity beacon of some description sewn into it and the waistcoat was locked on. This meant that if any of us decided to abscond, that was the word the notice used, we would be easy to track. Not only that, we would be just outside the perimeter fence initially so that wasn't much of an incentive to run off. We were in groups of twelve and it was noticeable that the twelve I was in were extensively strung out by halfway round the first lap and half had given up by the fifth lap.

A skinny and apparently very fit prisoner jogged up beside me.

'Jake, somebody wants to talk to you.'

'Who?'

'Bennie.'

Bennie was a long-sentence, Cat A prisoner. He was in for a gangland killing but it was said that he'd killed at least eight times. Despite that, he was articulate, funny, easy-going and was one of the group that spent a lot of time with Peter Jackson. They played bridge and chess and seemed to follow intellectual pursuits. There were about eight of them; two or three were always with Peter Jackson and one of those was often Bennie. I'd often seen Bennie in the gym;

he was fast and physically powerful. Not a heavyweight, like Harry, but clearly 'useful', that was the term used.

'What about?'

'No idea,' said the jogger, who I hadn't seen before.

'When?'

'Association tomorrow. Walls have ears and no ears within range.'

Association was a ritual really. The prisoners from two wings were in the yard for about an hour just walking around or sitting on the benches and the benches were scattered around and moved so there were no set positions. Some kicked a ball and some had basketballs and there were three basketball nets so the odd game arose.

'You mean Sergeant?'

'Bennie says anybody.' The jogger speeded up and was soon way ahead of me.

I later talked to Harry about the meeting.

'Should be safe at association with just the two of you. Keep walking, make it slow and we'll track you just in case,' said Harry.

The next afternoon at three we were on association. I was chatting with a couple of guys from my newly formed class with Sergeant and Boy Pritchard from D-Wing. Bennie wandered past and I wandered towards the direction he was heading.

'What's this about, Bennie?'

'You shouldn't be here.'

'What do you mean?'

'Peasmarsh.'

'I shouldn't be in any prison. I didn't kill the FBI guy.'

'Aha, yes, you were supposed to go to Brixton.'

'I did go there and then they sent me here. So what do you want to talk about?'

'A dead major.'

'There isn't anything to talk about. A sergeant shot the

major. The sergeant was found guilty, sent here and exe-cuted by somebody.'

'You were part of the defence in the first trial, why?'

'Because the killing was justifiable; the major was high on cocaine and wanted to take the platoon out of the defensive position. When he was told they didn't have the weaponry to do that he threatened to shoot a sergeant. So the major was shot and killed by Jase Phillips.'

'You know that's shit, Jake.'

'What's shit? It's what happened.'

'He was a killer.'

'Who was a killer? The major or Jase?'

'The major.'

'We were all killers; we were in the army.'

'You're deliberately not understanding, Jake.'

'Then tell me.'

'You really believe that Jase Phillips killed Major Carmi-chael to save the lives of some soldiers?'

'Yes.'

'And why do you think he was killed in here?'

'Because The Family takes revenge.'

'Supposing it was something else.'

'Then tell me and I'll know. On the other hand, don't tell me, but either way if I find out who killed Jase, I'll kill him. I don't care why Jase was killed.'

'How come you ended up in Peasmarsh?'

'I requested it.'

'From who?'

'As part of the deal to get me repatriated I had to go into a high security prison. I was given a list of prisons and this was the newest. There was also the opportunity that if I came here I could find and kill whoever killed Jase.'

'I don't believe you.'

'I really don't care what you believe. I'm here and

somebody has a marker on them and when I see it they're dead.'

'They?'

'Well it may be more than one person and somebody may have told the killer or asked the killer to do it.'

'You would kill the person who gave the order?'

'Oh, yes, but he or she may not be in here, so when I get out I'll kill the co-conspirator.'

'So that person may decide to take you out.'

'Bring it on, Bennie.'

Bennie was thinking. He was a good interrogator but lacked experience. I now knew for certain Bennie was closely connected to the killing but didn't do it. He probably knew who did and who gave the order, so it wasn't random, and he may have known why it was done; it was something to do with Carmichael being a killer and Jase knew about that.

'Can you tell me why Jase was killed?'

'No, but I'll tell you that Jase believed something that may or may not have been true. He thought it was true and that's what got him killed.'

So, I had a bit more information. It was definitely not about the battle situation; it was about something that Jase believed Carmichael had done. A something that, if it leaked out, meant Major Carmichael's name would be blackened and perhaps The Family would be in disrepute. It was about a killing or was it more than one killing? I was only a little further on but I was further on. I'd also put myself at risk because I'd said I would kill the killer and whoever gave the order. I knew it wasn't Mabry and if it was commanded in here I was very vulnerable.

17

Inmates around me were D-Wing; laughing, screeching, kicking balls, bouncing balls and flicking them at basketball nets but most intimidating, they were in groups, all knowing each other, and there was me, separated. I hadn't recognised I'd been separated from my own group. Many around me were black and loud, like the loud black people that I was used to except this wasn't my turf, protected by my B-Wing colleagues. Prison officers were noticeable by their absence. This was their turf, occupied by them like an invading force, and I could sense it with every step I took. For some, association was walking in a large circle and I could feel a hundred pairs of eyes watching me walk back across the large circle of walking prisoners towards where the majority of B-Wing prisoners were. Four large black men, with Afro haircuts and razor-marked tattoos on their faces, left the circle and stood in my path.

'Are yous, Captain?' said the one on the left.

'I am.'

'Yous a frien' o Sergean'.'

'Yes.'

'He raised his hand flat in the high-five indication and we slapped.

'Everyting criss, man,' he said.

'Right on, man,' I responded. I just hoped it was at least somewhere in the right direction. We started to walk together and suddenly we were faced with a group of eight men.

They were white and burly with tattooed arms and necks and shaven heads. The word 'Hate' appeared on most of them. The ones I recognised were from B-Wing but mostly they were D-Wing. There were two in front and four in a line behind them blocking my route through to the B-Wing group. Behind the four were another two facing B-Wingers.

A man joined them and walked to the front. 'You're dead, Captain,' he said. It was Tug Wilson.

'Oh goody, I love new experiences.'

Tug Wilson was surprised by my response but covered it quickly. Two of the Afro-Caribbeans stepped in front of me, facing the now gang of nine, and two were behind me; the odds weren't great and the observing prisoners near us moved back.

'Tell you what; let's make it a fair fight: each of you in turn just against me.'

'Yes, let's make it a fair fight: we just kill you lot.' Wilson held up his hand containing a closed knife and nine knives flicked open. They must have been mad; they were in prison and if I were attacked and killed they would spend the rest of their lives there, but why kill me? So I asked.

'Why kill me?'

'Cos you're a copper and a grass.'

One of the two at the back spoke. 'Trouble, Tug.'

I looked past the group blocking our route to B-Wing at a small advancing group. There was Sergeant, Arthur, Big Fred, Maniac, Robbo, Johno, Liz and Spider. They weren't all fighters but the numbers made the difference – stalemate.

Suddenly, there was turmoil from the main building to our right: the sound of feet coming at us at the double and prisoners trying to get out of the way. Six, no seven, prison officers in helmets and riot gear with shields and batons were coming towards us, two lines of three with one in the lead. Prisoners parted, our opposing forces just melted away and I was left with the four happy Afro-Caribbeans with happy, smiling, tattooed faces. The prison officers stopped. Senior Officer James, who had been in the lead, walked forwards.

'What goes on here then, Jake?'

'Nothing. Just associating with some new friends, ma'am.'

'Oh you were, were you?'

The four Afro-Caribbeans laughed with big friendly grins. There was a pathway through the D-Wingers in the yard and we kept walking until we reached the B-Wing group. It was only then that I realised it was raining. Tension does that; it blocks out irrelevancies. Sergeant certainly had respect here and for the first time the separations in the prison were tangible to me. I went into the prison building, climbed the stairs and walked along the corridor to our cell. Another day done and the picture was a little clearer.

I was walking towards the dining room when I saw Senior Officer James so I went over to her.

'How did you know, ma'am?'

'Know what, Jake?'

'That I was likely to be attacked and I would also be protected.'

'What makes you think we knew?'

'You were in riot gear and that takes time to get into, so you must have been prepared.'

She smiled. 'We do have sources of information and sometimes those are surprising.'

'Thank you, Senior Officer James.'

18

The bell told us that it was time we were doing something else. My class left except for Dad and Arthur. Arthur was built like Arnold Schwarzenegger with the addition of fists like boulders and battle scars on his face and body. He was a Category A prisoner, having killed three men in a brawl with three punches. Unfortunately, one of them was a policeman in uniform. I looked at the two men.

'Yes?'

'Arty, yer know, needs yer 'elp, Capin.'

Now, do I reply to Dad, who has made the statement, or to Arthur? Dad was looking at me with an urgent, pleading look that was so unlikely from a man such as Dad: a competent man, an experienced man, a man in his seventies who would be fazed by very little apart from his failing physical abilities.

'How can I help, Arthur?'

He looked at the ground, clearly embarrassed.

'Arthur, come and sit here, tell me what it's about and then I'll say whether I can help or not.'

'You won't tell, will you?' said Dad.

'Tell who? Tell what?'

'Anybody, anyfin.' They were both looking at me, very concerned.

'No I won't tell anybody anything.'

They still didn't look sure.

'Honestly, I won't tell anybody.'

114

'Go on, tell 'im, Arty,' said Dad.

Arthur shook his head. 'You do it.'

'I'd like one of you to tell me something.'

Dad spoke. 'When Arty was small, 'bout ten or eleven, he could read. They 'ad a new teacher, a woman. She was young and, you know, had tits and everythin'.'

'Aha, so Arthur kind of liked her.'

'Well yeah.' There was a silence.

I looked at Arthur. 'What happened?'

'She give us a new differen' readin' book,' said Arthur.

This was slow. There was a lot of emotion involved. What was surprising was that both Dad and Arthur were showing it.

'And then what happened?'

Tears started to roll down Arthur's cheeks. This giant of a man, this man who many were just plain terrified of, just sat there, head bent forward, hands clasped in front of him and tears running down his face. His nose had a drip on the end that grew and threatened to drop off but determinedly clung there.

'Dad, stand by the door and don't let anybody in. Better still, wedge it with a chair.' Dad just looked at me as if he didn't understand. Then he saw the tears and moved fast. I moved my chair in front of Arthur so our knees were a couple of inches apart. 'Okay, Arthur, I'm going to help you. You must look at me.'

He raised his emotion-torn face.

'Look me in the eyes.'

Arthur raised his head and looked at me. His eyes were large and watery and the tears ran down his cheeks. He looked totally forlorn.

'I'm going to get you to tell me some things. They may seem a little strange but there you go. I'm a little strange.' I'd kept my voice light and I smiled. Arthur tried to smile. 'Okay, tell me something that happened a week ago.'

Arthur looked at me as if I were nuts. He wiped his face

with the heel of each hand pushing up over his cheeks and he sniffed, lifting his head a little with each sniff like a twitch. 'What sorta fing?'

'Anything. Just something that happened.'

He told me about an incident at the servery. His hands moved to his right as he spoke.

'Did you notice where that memory came from?'

He looked blankly at me.

'Point to where last week is.'

He looked at me as if I were daft.

'Just do it.' A simple clear command.

He nervously pointed to his right.

'That's great, Arthur. So the past comes from over there.' I pointed. 'So when you get out of here in the future where will it be?'

He nodded and pointed to his left. I could read the confusion.

'That's good. So, you have like a road in front of you from the past to the future. When you were born is over there and your next birthday is over there.' I pointed to his right and then to his left. I could see he was pleased and a little more confident. I handed him my handkerchief and he wiped his face. He smiled. A less than confident smile but at least a smile. I stayed quiet. He was thinking. He looked at me and nodded. I had his confidence.

'Shut your eyes.'

He obeyed. I took him step by step back into the past. Sometimes he froze and sometimes he was frightened but I'd gained his trust and he answered my questions and gave me information that was clarity for him. We got into the school classroom.

'I've the book open.'

This was the crunch. This was make or break. I controlled my fear. Hang on in there, Jake, have courage you can do this.

116

'Can you read the words on the page?'

'Yes.'

Relief flooded through me.

'So read them.'

'I can't.'

Christ, we've hit the problem.

'Tell me why not.' My voice was encouraging despite my fear.

'I might make a mistake.'

He's said it – great. 'So what?' He had to make his decision and I couldn't help him.

'The other kids will laugh at me. So I'm scared and I can't speak and the other kids will laugh and say things. And Miss will tell them to be quiet. So I don't read and the other kids laugh and say things and Miss tells them to be quiet.'

'How do you feel?'

'I'm angry an' I'm all 'ot and I wanna pee.'

'Why are you angry and hot?'

'Because they're laughin' at me and Miss can see them laughin' and Miss thinks I can't read and ... and ... and I can.' His last three words came out with determination. He knew.

'How do you know what Miss is thinking?'

'Well, cos...' He stopped. He was thinking. 'I don' know what she's finkin'.' His back straightened. This insight was a revelation to him, I could hear it in his voice.

'That's right, Arty. You didn't really know what she was thinking.' I stopped. He was nodding. 'You're back in the classroom and the other kids are laughing. Tell me about it.'

'I wanta punch them and I wet meself and, and...'

'Hang in there, Arty. So what have you learned?'

'I got angry because they were laughin at me' and I didn't need to be angry cos, you know, Miss didn't fink I couldn't read, well she might 'ave ... an well...'

'What have you learned about your reading?' I needed to reinforce his earlier statement.

Arthur was quiet for a long time, perhaps a minute. 'I can read.'

I wanted to shout, 'Yes!' I was emotional and I had to think and control.

'That's right, Arty. You can read. You know you can read and I know you can read, Dad knows you can read and I bet Miss knew you could read.' I let him think for a moment or so. 'What have you learned about the way you feel, and about Miss?'

Arthur was still quiet. He sat there, his eyes closed, thinking.

'I wanted Miss to like me and when I couldn't read out loud I fought she woulden like me and ... and ... and' – he started gabbling, the words just tumbling out – 'well it didn't mat'er if I made a mistake and I didden need to be frigh'end. I can read now and I won't wet myself now.'

'Yes, Arty, you can read. What about wanting to punch them?'

Again, he was silent for a long time. 'It don't matter.'

'What doesn't matter?'

'Them laughing.'

'Good. Now I'm going to bring you back to now and on the way back we'll do some more things. Is that okay?'

'Yes, Captain.'

I brought him back to now. I waited; time went on. It seemed like a long time. Suddenly he said. 'I'm over the classroom.'

'Now, come down slowly, very gently into the classroom. Tell me when you're sitting in your chair.'

I waited and a couple of minutes ticked by.

'I'm here now.'

'Okay, in a minute I'll ask you to open your eyes and when you do I'll be here and Dad will be here. Tomorrow

118

I'll ask you to read out loud to the class and you'll be able to do it. Is that okay?'

'Yes, Captain.'

I waited. His breathing slowed. 'Okay, open your eyes.' Arthur opened his eyes and looked at me. He smiled.

'How do you feel?'

He blew out with bulging cheeks. 'Fucking great.'

'Good. Wipe your face and when you're ready you and Dad best get to where you should be.'

They left the room; I was exhausted, totally drained. I followed them and they went into the toilets. They always went into the toilets as Dad had a weak bladder and didn't want any accidents. I hadn't done any timeline therapy since I was at university but I thought it worked okay. I knew we would find out tomorrow. It was one thing to be okay about reading out loud today, but he had a night to think about it and it might be different tomorrow.

That night I lay looking at the darkness, unable to get to sleep. Daft really that one small thing in a childhood can do so much damage. The next morning was the crunch and I went to the classroom tense. Arthur and Dad came in with the other members of the group. I looked at Dad and he nodded. Relief flooded through me.

I settled the class then said, 'Shall we do some reading out loud?'

There was a silence; I could feel the tension. This always happened when it came to reading out loud. You could sometimes actually feel the fear.

'Okay, perhaps not.' I was chickening out. Perhaps Arthur couldn't do it.

'No,' said Dad. 'Let's try.'

The rest of the class just looked at Dad. They all knew that he was terrified of reading out loud. Then Arthur stood up. I was trembling but I hid it by sitting on my hands. This was just stupid. I knew it was stupid but I was proud of Arthur, proud that Arthur was going to try.

'Go on then, Arty. We're all ears.'

'I'll read page twen'y-one. It ain't a hard page so I should be all right.'

'Well done, Arty. Page twenty-one of Book 1 it is.'

He started, 'Little John.' He stalled and started again. 'Little John ran into the park. He liked the park. He liked best kicking a ball in the park. Little John had a red ball. Little John kicked the ball and it went into the pond.' He looked at me and smiled. No, he didn't smile; he grinned. A beautiful big grin spread across his battered face and I just had to grin as well.

'That was great, Arty. I think that you need to move up a book with some longer words. A clap for Arty.'

The class were clapping and I was relieved. Arthur could read and he would now be able to help me with the others, particularly Dad. We pushed on and some volunteers struggled through pages they'd practised. More of the class read that day and performed better than they'd ever done before. It was breakthrough day. They now knew they could do it if Arthur could do it, but they didn't know Arthur's secret.

That week had been tough. My class was driving me now. I'd been working at pushing them and pulling them and now they were driving me. The challenge was terrific. It was in many ways a good week and I was exhausted. The downside was Ratty. He was in a parallel class and him and his mates tried to provoke me at every opportunity and because I didn't retaliate I was in danger of losing credibility with the wider population and even some of my group.

Ratty was a skinny, rat-faced little idiot with a shaved head that had symbols tattooed on it. He swaggered and was thoroughly disliked. No, more than that, he was held in contempt and he seemed to revel in it. He probably only weighed nine and a half stone and it seemed he'd stabbed Jase from behind. I just couldn't believe a soldier as experienced and as physically powerful as Jase could have been stabbed by this contemptible little shit even if it was from behind.

As I left the classroom on Friday, at the end of what had been a tough week, the rat-faced, poisonous gremlin was in the passageway with his four friends. I was exhausted. The tension and emotion from the work with my class and the additional session with those that had dyslexia had drained me and seeing Ratty didn't help.

'Hay, capin', sir.' He made an exaggerated salute and his mates laughed. 'Was you a tough solger? We 'ad a tough solger in 'ere; 'ad a medal an everyfink. 'E weren't that tough, though. Ended up dead, diden'e.'

I had to act.

'He were a sergean' like yer big, black-arsed fren'.'

We were in the passageway from the training centre. I was tired, emotionally drained and the provocation made me angry. I was usually very slow to anger but he'd now, at last, pressed my buttons. He then set off swaggering and pretending to march. He was in front of me. He was crudely singing some obscene military ditty. I was outnumbered.

I could hear two fellow prisoners were behind me. I realised they were Dad and Arthur. Arthur walked past me followed by Dad and past Ratty. He faced the four, raised his arms and just pointed down the corridor. The four disappeared at a rate of knots followed at a steady walk by Arty and Dad.

Ratty just grinned at me and started to march, swinging his arms and singing. 'Fuck 'em all! Fuck 'em all! The long and the short and the tall; fuck all the sergeants and W.O. ones, fuck all the corporals and their bastard sons.'

Opportunities like this were rare. I took my silver paper and wrapped the transmitter on my wrist then came up quietly behind Ratty. I placed my left hand on the top left side of his head, my right palm under his chin and my fingers closing his nose so he couldn't breathe. His hands scrabbled for my wrists, he rose on his toes, stretching upwards in search of air and straightening his spine – lift, push and twist, all in one smooth movement. This was the second time I'd done it for real. The last time had been in combat in Iraq. I felt his neck break and I dropped him, stepped around his twitching body and kept walking. My head was screaming, don't hurry. Nonchalant. That's the way, Jake. Don't look round. I was trembling and fighting for control of my breathing. I emerged from the passageway and it was then that I realised I would be on one of the CCTV cameras in the central area.

I walked to the spiral stairway that went up to the first landing. This was my normal pattern. I took off the silver paper and slipped it in my back pocket. Old-man Peters was at the bottom of the stairs. He was always there and I always spoke to him.

I took a big breath. 'How's it going, Petey?'

'Fine, Captain Jake, just fine.' He smiled and nodded. He didn't know what day of the week it was and wouldn't remember if you told him. Odd thing was, I was one of the names he remembered and for some arrogant reason I was proud of that.

'Good, good. Don't let the bastards grind you down, Petey.'

He nodded in that sage way he had, although everybody knew he was suffering from dementia. Why he was in here I just didn't understand. He was a Category B prisoner, well over seventy with dementia and physically frail. He should have been in a home with medical care.

I climbed the spiral stairway heading for my cell. At the first twist I looked down. Arthur and Dad, were watching my ascent. I nodded to them. Debt paid but tomorrow would tell, and by tomorrow everyone would know I killed Ratty. The tracking computer, if switched onto me, would have seen me disappear and then later reappear but they'd have no evidence. I'd killed close up and personal before but avoided deliberately killing in a close encounter. I'd never killed in cold anger before and, strangely, I was now calm about it. No, I was exhilarated that I'd killed Jase's killer. Step one. Now I would go up the hierarchy.

That night I felt like shit. I was tired, listless and decided to get an early night. There was no joy in killing, how can there be? I was ashamed of myself but at the same time the reasons to do it crowded in on me. I pulled my skinny blanket over me to shut out the light. Harry was quiet; he let me be how I was. I knew Harry understood. In the next cell Tommy Richards was playing his CDs. The music drifted through the open cell doors. It was Bette Midler singing *Wind Beneath My Wings*. I could remember Sam singing it. I remember thinking that was how I felt about her, the wind beneath my wings, so I could fly higher than an eagle. Not now. Without her I couldn't even struggle along the ground. I was crying. I just wanted to be with my Sam. I needed her to tell me it was all right. I needed her to smile at me across the table and then put some crap on the TV that I didn't want to watch so that I could be close to her on the settee. I heard Harry leave and close the door. I buried my face in the pillow.

19

The police arrived and there was a roster of people they wanted to see. I was right at the top of the list. I wasn't surprised really. The whole prison was filled with a rumour that I'd done it and the rumour was fairly accurate: he'd annoyed me so I just twisted his head and broke his neck. I was in the segregation unit in a solitary confinement cell and Harry had had a word with Dad and Arthur, telling them to keep it shut. I just hoped that it had done the trick.

Nine o'clock on the dot I was in an interview room. On one side of the table were two men and over to one side of the room was a chair for Senior Officer James.

One of the police officers spoke. 'Sit down there, Robinson.' It was a discourteous order. He had a northern accent, a round, sweaty, red face and he was overweight. He looked scruffy. His jacket was creased, his shirt was grubby and his tie hung loosely around his neck.

I stood at ease and ignored him.

'Sit down, Robinson,' he commanded. This man did not recognise that he had absolutely no authority over me.

I turned to Senior Officer James. 'Is this, um, this person speaking to me, ma'am?'

'I'm afraid he is, Jake.'

'Will you ask him to address me civilly and correctly then please, ma'am? Or I will leave.'

'Look, you, sit down.' His tone was aggressive. I didn't move.

Senior Officer James spoke to the policemen. 'Detective Inspector, if you address this prisoner as Mr Robinson, Captain Robinson or Jake Robinson or just Jake he may comply with your *request*. You could of course use prisoner and his number. Oh, and it may help to say please, like you would with any other innocent person or witness at your police station.' The last sentence was said slowly and precisely, emphasising the words 'innocent person or witness'.

The policeman was boiling. His colour had gone up at least two shades. 'Mr Robinson, I'd be eternally grateful if you'd sit in that chair.' His voice had a tone of sarcasm. He indicated the chair opposite him.

'This one?' I asked, pointing at the only chair not occupied. I was actually concerned that this less-than-fit police officer would have a heart attack considering the reaction my simple question had on him. I'd heard the phrase 'through gritted teeth'; this was the first time I'd actually observed it.

'Yes, that one, Mr Robinson.' He paused. 'Please,' he ground out.

In the psychological battle, I was already way ahead on points.

'What can you tell us about the death of Raymond Tidy?'

'Who are you and why are you asking me questions?'

In his anger he'd forgotten the protocol necessary for an interview. Another point. Prisoners: lots of points; police: nil. I was actually enjoying this. Here was a police officer, probably a very good police officer, that had come into a situation with his head full of assumptions and had found them wrong. Perhaps not wrong but prejudiced.

He put his head in his hands with his elbows on the table. The silence went on for about thirty seconds. He looked up. I noticed his breathing was now under control and his colour had returned to its original shade of dull red.

'I apologise, Mr Robinson. I'm Detective Inspector Elliot

and my colleague is Detective Sergeant Ayres. The observer is Senior Officer James. We're looking into the death of Mr Raymond Tidy. We're hoping you can help us with our enquiries. We'd like to ask you some questions.' His speech had been controlled and clear. You want war, Inspector; you're going to get it.

'I'd like a solicitor.'

'This is only a preliminary investigation.'

'I have been put into a segregation cell with absolutely no charges against me. I want my solicitor and I want him now. I think you will have to have me released or arrest me.'

His colour started to rise again.

'Any particular solicitor?'

'Yes. Mr Keith Todd.'

'And where might we find Mr Todd?'

'In London.'

'Specifically?'

'Oh no, I've never heard of a place called specifically. His offices are in Westminster.'

I could see out of the corner of my eye Senior Officer James looking at the ceiling and fighting to keep a straight face.

'Would it be possible to question you with a local solicitor?'

'Let me see.' I pretended to think. 'Um, no.'

'Why the hell not?' The irritation in his voice and his facial expression could have been collected in a black plastic bag.

'The police screwed me in Mississippi so I ended up in prison for something I didn't do by having their bent lawyer. It won't happen to me again.'

'Thank you, Mr Robinson. We'll interview you at a later date.'

I didn't move.

'Come on, Jake. I expect these police officers want to interview somebody else,' said Senior Officer James.

126

'I want an assurance that I will not be segregated again.' Elliot turned to Senior Officer James.

She responded, 'Unless you have specific instructions, Detective Inspector, it might be wise to release this prisoner.'

'No, I believe it is best to hold him in segregation.'

It was three days before they saw me again. Three days I'd spent in a cell. I understood they'd interviewed Dad and Arty. Dad had played the dementia card and Arty said he hadn't seen anything and then just 'no commented' to every other question.

I was pleased to have Sarah Sands with me. She was good: newly qualified, but as sharp as a needle. We'd had a quick chat and the plan was to cooperate with zero information. Sarah, of course, had a strong suspicion that I'd perpetrated the dastardly crime but she certainly would never have dreamed of asking. It would be unethical and she, in her legal capacity, had to assume I was innocent (well, not guilty). I knew Keith would have briefed her.

At half past nine we went into the interview room. DI Elliot and DS Ayres were at the table as before and Senior Officer James was to the side of the room. As we walked in, Elliot said, 'Who are you?' staring at Sarah.

'Sarah Sands, solicitor.'

'But you're a woman.' He sounded mystified. Then I realised he'd expected Keith Todd.

Sarah put down her bag, looked down, placed her hands under her bust, lifted them and said, 'Oh, I wondered what these were.'

DS Ayres smothered a laugh, as did Senior Officer James and I said, 'Wow! You must be a detective, Inspector Elliot.'

'I'm sorry,' grouched Elliot. 'I was expecting a man.'

So, it was the same as before except for the addition of Sarah. DI Elliot started with all the correct procedure, by the book, including the statement that they were interviewing me as a witness.

'Now onto –' he began, but got no further.

Sarah interrupted, 'I am informing you now, Detective Inspector, that I will be making a formal complaint against your instruction to detain my client in segregation and also against the Governor.'

'That is your prerogative Miss Sands.'

'I'd like this recorded, Detective Inspector.'

'Yes certainly, Miss Sands.' Resignation seeped through his words. He was definitely on the back foot when it came to Sarah.

'It's Ms Sands.'

You could see the frustration building. His hands clenched into fists. A tape machine was brought in and set up. The inspector went through the routine again.

'Jake, what do you know about the death of Raymond Tidy?'

'Nothing. Can I go now?'

'But you were in the passageway at that time.'

'Was I?'

'Yes.'

'How do you know?'

'We've got you on tape coming out of the passageway into the atrium.' He showed me a still from the tape, complete with time. It was me.

'That must have been before he was killed then. That should help you narrow down the search. It's Wednesday.'

'What is?'

'Today.'

'No, today is Thursday.'

'Oh, you see, it's so easy to get things wrong in here.'

He looked totally confused then got himself back in balance and focused on me with a hard glare. 'Let me try again,' he said. 'Where were you on Tuesday the eighteenth of May at eleven thirty?' His words were precise and deliberate.

'In prison.'

I could see the exasperation. 'Whereabouts were you in the prison?' The teeth were gritted again.

'I've absolutely no idea.'

'But I just told you that you were coming out of the passageway into the atrium and showed you a photograph.'

'That's what you say, and that's what's on the photograph, but I don't remember. So I can't say I do remember when I don't.'

'There's a rumour that you killed Raymond Tidy.'

Sarah began to intervene but I stopped her with a hand signal.

'There's a rumour that I'm shagging Sarah here but it's not true, worse luck.' I felt Sarah stiffen beside me and then relax and Senior Officer James shifted; she'd turned to the wall.

'If you didn't kill Raymond Tidy who do you think did?'

'Don't answer that.' Sarah cut across me as I was about to answer.

'Sarah, if the nice policeman wants speculation then perhaps he should be allowed to listen to unsubstantiated speculation.'

'Okay, Jake, speculate,' said Sarah then she addressed the police officers. 'My client will answer your question. I point out that what he says is pure speculation and has no basis in evidence.' She looked at me.

'I think it was Moorby and/or Manson.'

'Who are they?' asked Elliot. The two policemen were looking down their notes. I said nothing. The sergeant pointed. 'But they're prison officers.'

'Yes, they were on duty on B-Wing and they were also on duty when Jason Phillips was murdered. That's what the rumour was and you lot didn't find out who killed him.'

129

'But they didn't come out of the passageway into the central area.'

'So they went up the stairs in the training area and onto one of the landings.'

'There's another way out of the training area?' He turned to Senior Officer James.

'Yes. There are the fire doors to the outside but they're alarmed and there are the stairs to the area above the training rooms, but only staff can use those stairs.'

Sarah cut in. 'So your assumption that the perpetrator of this crime came out into the central area is misguided, Detective Inspector.'

'Hell.' He turned and looked at his sergeant. Could it be that these two bozos hadn't done their basic homework? He turned to Officer James. 'Could a prisoner use that route?'

'Only if he had a key,' she answered

'And could a prisoner get a key?' This policeman was blinded by the fact that he was working in a prison. Why the hell should it be a prisoner that commits murder? I know it was but if you don't consider all the possibilities then you're going to miss something obvious. Thank God for half-blind policemen.

'Detective Inspector, this is a prison full of highly experienced criminals. What do you think?'

I thought she was on my side. There was definitely more to Senior Officer James than met the eye. I decided to rub salt into the wound.

'So, let me get this right, Detective Inspector Elliot. Without exploring the crime scene and checking routes in or out, you want to question me because I came out of a route that has surveillance; you also assume the killer was a prisoner.'

The sergeant pointed to a page in a file and said, 'That route was checked and nobody used it around that time.'

'Who told you that then?' I asked. They were both looking

at the file page and from the looks on their faces I realised I'd hit an unexpected bullseye. 'It was Moorby or Manson wasn't it. Oh dear, oh dear!'

Elliot's colour deepened by a couple of shades again. 'Interview closed at nine forty-two,' he growled.

'Can I go now please, gentlemen?' If looks could kill I would be dead.

Senior Officer James said, 'Return to your place of work please, Jake.' I believed that the gentle approach of using first names and 'please' and 'thank you' was having a strong calming effect on me, and getting up the nose of the inspector. Sarah and I said goodbye and Senior Officer James took her away.

20

The next day I went down to breakfast as usual. Harry, Arty and Dad wanted to know how it went and I said nothing really except that the police thought they had some evidence but it was crap.

One of the officers, Moorby, walked across and told me I was to remain in my cell after breakfast. There was something about the way he said it but I couldn't quite place it. My expectation was that I would be called should Inspector Elliot arrive with the damning evidence, and my expectation was (well, my hope was) that he wouldn't have that evidence. I could see the concern in the faces of the people at the table; two of them had watched me kill Ratty. Dad looked particularly concerned. He flicked his head to one side, so I walked around the table and he got up and we walked to the window and looked out.

'You're going to be glassed, Captain. You've seen it. When you come away from the tray rack Tug will do you.'

'Advice, Dad?'

The old man smiled. 'Because of the way the tray racks are, everybody turns right. Turn left so you've an edge then do what you can.'

I looked around the dining room; there were no officers in sight. I went back to my seat and sat. Sergeant was alert. 'I'll come with you, Captain.'

'No, Sergeant, it would send the wrong message.'

I left the table and took my tray to the disposal. I scrapped the debris from my tray into the pig bin and placed it in the rack then threw the plastic tools into the rubbish bin. Out of the corner of my eye I saw Wilson approaching me. I was alone and to some extent in trouble and there were a few hundred observers watching. What a place for taking me down. I couldn't help smiling to myself and that must have shown. I turned left then spun to face him. He went to launch an attack on me and I came off the back foot with a thrust, whipped my head forward and smashed my forehead into his nose. I'd shattered his nose and hopefully his cheekbones. He staggered back, off balance and my knuckles stabbed into his throat. He went down coughing onto his knees and my boot smashed into his ribs: more damage. I stepped over him to walk out and a prison officer was running towards me.

'I think he's having a fit, Officer. I think he needs help.' I thought about Sun Tzu, who said in *The Art of War*, 'Those who are skilled in producing surprises will win.' Yes, I was involved in a war.

The officer was in a dilemma; should he grab me or go and help Wilson? Maniac arrived. 'I'll handle this, Captain,' he said and turned to the officer. 'I think he slipped, sir. You can see where he bashed his nose. Shall we get him up?' Maniac was in sane mode.

I didn't hang around. I just slipped through the door, walked up to our cell and Harry joined me on the way.

'What have you done to Maniac?' he asked. 'He was quite sane.'

'I think the therapy is working, Sergeant.'

'What therapy?'

'A new psychiatrist has some sessions with him. He's put him on some medication and a psychotherapist has started working with him. At good times he becomes Joe. Sometimes Maniac and Joe talk to each other.'

'Christ, he shouldn't be in here.'

'I know that and you know that. Joe knows that but it seems Maniac doesn't and nor do the prison authorities so I have to cope with him.'

I just lay on my bunk after that, looking at the ceiling. The excitement was over. The issue of what the prison authorities were going to do about the murder and what they would do about the incident in the dining hall was to come but my guess was that they would do nothing and my guess turned out to be correct. Explanations as to why no prison officers were there in the dining hall would be awkward, but any explanation was going to be awkward for them. As for the murder, my only concern was whether Elliot had my fingerprints from the body. So I turned my mind to other things. I thought about Arthur, a big, intelligent giant of a man. Mr Cratcher was right; Arthur couldn't read so he dropped out of school. Being on the street meant trouble, trouble in the form of crime, and eventually he got caught. How on earth could he get out of the system if he thought he couldn't read? What else can people do if they can't read or write? How do you apply for a job? Companies have application forms. Even if you do get a job most jobs require some training. How do you find somewhere to live if you can't read the accommodation adverts? I lay there and for the first time, recognised the absolute horror that the prisoners in my class had faced and surmounted. Even though it wasn't an ideal solution, crime solved many of their problems. At least it provided independent survival as opposed to the dependent survival of relying on the state. The state solution required obedience to bureaucratic rules. I wanted even more to help these people who had become my students and now my friends. This was a revelation to me, that the elementary ability to read and write was the foundation of independent, honest survival. I now understood why they liked me. I was one of the few people that had tried to genuinely help them instead of treating them as if they were mere victims or had something wrong with them or were just evil. I was no saint. I was offered this teaching job and I did it and I enjoyed doing it. I wouldn't have selected it. It just happened that I was good at it. It's a funny old life.

No call came and I was told to go back to work, so I joined my motley crew, most of whom weren't there because they thought I wouldn't be, but Maniac was there and now he was Joe. I hoped it would last.

21

Three days went past and on the Saturday morning I received a summons from the governor. I duly arrived at the appointed place at the appointed hour and saw that it was all very formal. My personal officer, Senior Officer James, met me in the waiting area.

'What is this about?' I asked.

'I was hoping you could tell me,' she replied.

'Do you get paid overtime?'

'I will for this as it's outside of my shift pattern.'

'See, I even get you extra pay.'

'I'd prefer it if you didn't. I was supposed to be watching my boy play football in half an hour.'

'Let's see if we can escape quickly then, shall we?'

We waited; half an hour went by. I looked at the cracks in the plaster on the walls. This must have been the most boring waiting area in the world; less to see than on the tube and people often fell asleep when travelling on the tube despite the noise. The boy's football would have started. Oddly, I was upset by this and, clearly, so was Senior Officer James.

I could hear the voices through the wall and they didn't seem to be agreeing but I couldn't hear the words. Then the governor's secretary invited us in. A man in a suit and tie accompanied Inspector Elliot, who was as red-faced and dishevelled as before.

The man looked like a funeral director apart from the fact that he had brown shoes that didn't go with his

136

pinstriped suit. He also had a comb-over to try to hide his bald patch, which didn't work. It just looked ridiculous. The governor invited me to sit, which was a surprise, and introduced Inspector Elliot and Mr Brian Benton from the Crown Prosecution Service. Neither offered me their hands to shake. Mr Benton then took over.

'Mr Robinson, you've been questioned in relation to the death of one Raymond Tidy.' He stopped. Clearly, he expected a response. I said nothing. 'Is that correct?'

'I want my solicitor.'

'A solicitor is unnecessary.'

'Then she can tell me that.'

'I see. Yes, I understand you may have concerns. Let me outline a small problem that the police and the CPS have encountered. Fingerprints have been taken from Raymond Tidy's face. A check of those fingerprints on the national database indicates access is denied. Would access to your fingerprints on the national database be denied for any reason?'

'You have an insufficient level of clearance.'

'We have the highest level of clearance.'

'Clearly not.' There was a thoughtful look on his face. 'I want my solicitor.'

'They could eliminate you from the enquiries.'

'I want my solicitor.'

'In circumstances such as this we can request access to the person in question if access to the information on the database is denied without the name of the person being revealed to any other person.'

'I have a sneaking feeling you would have to go through a legal procedure to achieve that.' The look on his face told me I was right. 'I want my solicitor and I've the impression you're denying me access to legal representation and I think that comes within the Human Rights Act and PACE, so I suggest we stop this harassment now.'

'I see. Have you anything you can tell us?'

'Yes, one thing; you've revealed information to all the people in this room, two of whom are not cleared to have access to such information, that fingerprints found on Raymond Tidy are on the national database and the police have been denied access to the name of that person and that I, Jake Robinson, have been questioned about that. A leak of that information inside this prison may lead to speculation that my fingerprints are on a national database and the police cannot access my name. That form of speculation can put my life in danger. I'll be taking action through the courts should there be any indication of an information leak. Not only that, if any legal action is taken against me I've witnesses in this room that I was denied access to legal representation, which I think you'll know, being a barrister, would cause any prosecution to be thrown out.' I wasn't sure this was true but it was worth a try, as I knew I had the right to legal representation.

Mr Brian Benton shook his head. 'Given the situation Inspector Elliot now faces, I'll grant him permission to arrest you for the murder of Raymond Tidy and take your finger prints.'

'In the unlikely event that those prints are mine, you know why you cannot have access.'

'Do we?' said Benton. Surely he couldn't have been stupid enough to come here without doing some background checks.

'I was and I still am, until I'm dismissed, a member of MI5. I was transferred here from the USA due to a miscarriage of justice there and I expect to be released from here and again to resume my service.'

'All that is immaterial given the facts that are presently in evidence.'

'Mr Benton, you're on very thin ice. I've two or three witnesses in this room to this conversation and irrespective of the findings with regards to fingerprints, any competent judge will throw them out and legal proceeding will be taken against you.'

'I think not, Mr Robinson.' He must have known he was breaking the law and more serious action could be taken against him.

'And my protection against leakage?'

He shrugged his shoulders and shook his head.

'You're setting a precedent and you know this is a breach of procedure and as such, it will render any court proceedings, should any result, null and void.'

His square-cut, rimless glasses flashed in the light of the sun coming through the window as he raised his head to look at me. He then looked at Elliot and the governor and licked his lips. I read this as concern. He was operating under instructions and he knew what he was doing was wrong; not just wrong – it was illegal. He was no hero just a gofer and he couldn't refuse the instructions given to him.

'Sir, I'm an MI5 officer; I was an RMP captain. I know how to follow procedure. I know you're breaking procedure. That means you've a reason to do that and you probably also know that that breach can get me killed in here. Tell your Family contact to talk to Mabry.'

Benton looked at me. He was unsure and had a decision to make. I was struggling with who it could be and then it came to me. 'Ha, it was Superintendent West, wasn't it? Tell him if something happens to me in here and I survive, he'll be dead and you better lock your doors.' West and I had crossed swords on more than one occasion. He was a creature of the Family.

'Robinson, I'll not have those sorts of threats in my prison to an officer of the crown,' said the governor.

Elliot was just sitting watching this exchange, clearly not understanding what was going on.

Benton said, 'Oh, I think we'll cross any bridge if any

comes up.' His voice didn't reflect the words he was using. The man was a dolt.

Elliot then arrested me, telling me I'd the right to remain silent, to have a friend or relative told of my arrest and to speak to a lawyer. I was also told that I was being arrested for the murder of Raymond Tidy with other details of date and place. My fingerprints were then taken. I knew I was in trouble as a match would be easy, worse still I was dead meat in the prison and I knew that was West's little game. He was protecting The Family and none of this would ever see the light of day.

Elliot said, 'You may go now and I'll interview you tomorrow with your solicitor present.'

'I don't think so, Inspector,' I answered and left the office, accompanied by Senior Prison Officer James. She looked around and we walked on. She looked around again and then pressed a telephone in my hand.

'I just knew you'd be trouble, Jake Robinson, and I think you need to make some phone calls or you might just spend the rest of your very limited life in here. Just let me have my phone back when you can and don't get caught with it.'

I just knew I'd been born under a lucky star.

'I'd like to go to the library, ma'am.'

'I'll just escort you there then.'

We walked into the library and Jacko the librarian was there as normal.

'You, out, and nobody comes in, right?' said my personal officer.

Jacko's eyebrows went up and it dawned on me what he must have thought. I had to smile and Officer James was about to disabuse him of his thoughts when I shook my head and her lips compressed.

'You, out, and say nowt,' she said.

He left and she leaned against the door. I phoned Barrow and got Pauline. I told her the problem quickly and simply.

'What do you suggest, Jake?'

'One, the post mortem prints are replaced both at the police station and the mortuary. Two, any prints that might be on the body are cleaned off so the exercise can't be repeated.'

'Timescale?'

'Immediate. Ideally tonight.'

'Okay, Jake.'

'Please get Barrow to ring Mabry to muzzle West and block a guy named Benton from the CPS. Meanwhile, I'll just try to stay alive.'

'Good as done, Jake.'

'Thank you, Pauline.'

I gave Officer James her phone back. 'I just knew you were trouble, Jake Robinson. I just didn't know how much. It's okay. Mum's the word.' She now had the confirmation she wanted that I was undercover.

'You better undo the top button of your jacket.'

'Why?'

'Bit of confirming realism for Jacko.'

'Fuck off, Jake Robinson,' she said as she undid her top button and we waited ten minutes. We were both laughing when she opened the door and said to Jacko, 'Say nothing if you want to retain your balls.'

'Yes, ma'am,' he said, looking quite concerned.

'You may be in time to see the second half, ma'am,' I told her. We then parted and went our separate ways.

22

Maniac was still in my class. He was still switching between personalities. I understood why his classmates called him Maniac; he did have some weird ideas and they were fairly consistent. He would talk to Joe, though. I had asked him who Joe was but then Joe sometimes disappeared and Maniac could become aggressive because I had driven him away. The other class members had learned not to talk to Maniac at all when he was with Joe. I now felt it was a multiple personality syndrome but apparently the psychiatrist didn't think so. Correction: the HMP psychiatrists didn't think so but the guy currently treating him did. I had witnessed a couple of episodes when Joe apparently controlled him and at other times Maniac just wasn't there in my classroom at all, but Joe was. The fascinating thing was that Joe could read better than Maniac, was co-operative and logical. He would respond to questions and participate in discussions more logically and with better thought-out arguments than Maniac. In fact, I, and the class members, liked Joe better than Maniac, but Joe would only appear about twice a week and his appearances were random. It seemed that Joe sometimes controlled Maniac. It was, or seemed, that they were both there. It was odd watching and listening to two personalities in one body arguing. Usually, Maniac would be disruptive – he would shout and argue, become angry and throw things – and Joe would turn up and a battle would ensue between them. Sometimes Joe won and Maniac would settle down and become Joe and at other times, Joe would leave and we had to cope with Maniac being unreasonable or sulking or storming out and we might not see him again that day, or he would return as the 'normal' Maniac. Mind you, normal Maniac wasn't a normal, rational person. He would hear things that we couldn't hear, or he would just lose interest or if asked a question he would argue about it or argue with another class member. He also had or seemed to have hallucinations. I imagine that all classes have a difficult person but this was way outside of difficult.

My conversation with the doctor wasn't a lot of help. The medics had tried him on drugs since our first discussions but they'd apparently been worse than not drugging him. The HMP psychiatrist was even less help. He smiled and nodded and gave the distinct impression that I was the one with the mental problem not Maniac. I talked to a couple of the other instructors who had had Maniac in their groups and they just told me to get rid of him, but that was easier said than done as he had turned up in their classes until he decided to move on, which is how I had ended up with him.

He had now started the new treatment and I was supposed to keep a record of his behaviour. It did seem to have changed, but not a lot. It seemed he had bonded with my class, so if there was a group of them he would just join them; he didn't seem to recognise that he wasn't wanted. This had the effect that my class members became close, as other prisoners would leave them when Maniac turned up. Teaching was tough enough but with Maniac in the class it could sometimes be purgatory, but things were improving. I had a feeling his behaviour was improving and I was on the point of reporting the improvement when it all went pear-shaped.

It was a Wednesday. Wednesdays for me were usually the day of the week where if things were going to go wrong they usually would. I was with the usual crew at our table when Maniac came up to the servery. I just knew things were going to go wrong. I could read him. It was the way he looked, his eyes, the way he moved, nothing exaggerated, nothing specific just little indications. Pansy was serving soup. As you might guess, he was called Pansy because he was a pansy. Maniac snatched the ladle from him and hit him on the head. The duty officer went to Pansy's aid and he was attacked. Prisoners moved back; why should they get involved with a nutter? I looked at Arty and we went to sort it. I tried talking to him.

'Come on, Maniac, we need the ladle for the soup.'

'Fuck off, Captain. They've poisoned it.' Here we go into delusion land again.

'Have they? Who poisoned it?'

'That Pansy. He wants us to catch HIV and die of AIDS.'

'Who told you that then, Maniac?'

He shook his head. 'I don't know.'

'What does Joe say?'

'Joe ain't here.'

'Shouldn't you ask him?'

Maniac stood still; he was puzzled, lost. Two prison officers moved in and he just surrendered to them. He was escorted away and so was I. I sat in a waiting room for about half an hour then Senior Officer James arrived and I was wheeled in to see the governor. The doc was also there and the two officers who had turned up and led Maniac away.

The governor asked what I had done to provoke Prisoner Arkwright. I outlined what had happened and that Maniac was under control when the prison officers arrived. I also suggested they talked to Pansy and the downed officer. This wasn't greeted with enthusiasm. However, after a few more questions, I was dismissed. Senior Officer James came with me.

'You can be a real dick, Jake,' she said.

'Why? What did I do?'

'One: you got involved. Two: it seems you sorted the problem or at least took the sting out of Maniac. Three: you told it how it was.'

'How's that wrong?'

'Jake, this is a prison. You're a prisoner. You aren't supposed to be capable of taking initiatives let alone successful initiatives.'

'But Maniac could have done a lot of damage with that ladle.'

'Yes and he has done things like this before and we've handled it using brute force and beaten Maniac to pulp, so you've made the system look stupid.'

'But he's mentally ill.'

'You know that, I know that, the bloody doctor knows that, we know he shouldn't be in here but the law doesn't understand that, so the governor plays the game and you come waltzing in and bugger the whole thing up.'

'You have to be joking.'

'No. Maniac killed two women and a kid. He was tried for murder and found guilty but the docs don't know what's wrong with him. He was just a bit weird at his trial so he got fifteen years, as he pleaded guilty, because Joe told him to. He was regarded as responsible for his actions.'

'Christ, there has to be a better system than this.'

'No, he is, as far as the law is concerned, as sane as you or I, but I'm not too sure about you and I must be nuts to do this job, but the psychs said he knows right from wrong so he's sane. Christ, you know the law, Jake; you were a policeman.'

'Yes, you're right.' I did know that in criminal and mental health law sanity is a legal thing not a medical thing; therefore, a person can be acting under profound mental illness and yet be sane, and can also be ruled insane without an underlying mental illness.'

'So what happens now?'

'Now we forget the whole thing.'

'And Maniac?'

'He'll turn up tomorrow. You'll run your class tomorrow and hopefully, he won't hit anybody with a ladle and if he kicks off and you're around you'll walk away. We'll beat seven bells out of him, stick him in the sick bay to heal and recover and turn him loose on the rest of you again, got it?'

'Yes, ma'am.'

'Good.'

23

Harry and I were receiving too much deference. The inmates of this prison knew I'd killed Ratty and they knew I was going to get away with it. It also seemed that the information about my prints hadn't leaked or the reaction to me would be very different. What I hadn't recognised was that the killing gave me a lot of respect and I'd gained that respect without exerting any violence to force compliance of my wishes. I'd also successfully gone up against Tug Wilson in front of a large audience and that had knocked the prestige of the present power regime. I hadn't of course expressed my wishes but there were a lot of prisoners who wanted the reign of Mr Wharton to end. The problem was that Mr Wharton was becoming concerned. The fact that we were now known as Captain and Sergeant was also a threatening factor for Mr Wharton. Tug Wilson guarded him. Tug was nearly as big as Harry with a reputation as a sadistic, homosexual bully. I was surprised I'd taken him. In fact, surprise had given me the edge. Mr Wharton had now recruited two other minders, Pete Costello and Marty Clifford, probably because of the dining room incident with Tug. These two had been muscle for hire in the prison but now they were aligned with the current power structure. Yes, I thought, Harry and I were vulnerable.

It was a Friday morning. Harry and I went to breakfast. Seemed a normal day. We joined the end of the queue to the servery. Then the two guys who were chatting in front of us went quiet and moved out of the queue, and in behind us. One of the group of three now in front of us then became aware that we were there. He brought that to the attention of the other two and all three moved out of the queue and joined behind us.

Harry said very quietly, 'Say and do nothing, Captain.'

We moved rapidly down the queue and we were served with very generous helpings of the things we chose. Some people, like Mr Wharton and Tug Wilson, always walked to the front of the queue, as did one or two others like Dad. Dad was the oldest prisoner and wasn't only respected because he was an old man, a fine man, but he was also a frail man. I was determined we wouldn't adopt the arrogance of the few like Mr Wharton and Tug Wilson who regarded it as their right to queue jump. I had an urge to thank the people who moved aside for us but I recognised Harry's instruction to say and do nothing was a wise one. If we said nothing then it hadn't happened and if it hadn't happened then there was no reason to say anything.

As we left the servery with our trays, Mr Wharton and Tug Wilson were standing looking at us. I presume it was supposed to be some sort of threat.

I smiled and said, 'Good morning gentlemen.' Tug went to step forward but Mr Wharton just put his arm in front of him.

'Good morning, Jake.' He had a quiet voice.

This was the first time I had been up close to him. He was in the usual orange suit but he was, as always, wearing a brown trilby hat set towards the back of his head like Frank Sinatra. He wasn't a tall man but bulky with a large head and fat lips. On the wrist of the arm he had put in front of Wilson was a large gold watch with a heavyweight gold wrist strap. He held out his right hand to be shaken. I took it and we shook hands. On this wrist he had a very heavy gold chain. His brown eyes held mine. He smiled.

'I think we may need to have a conversation soon, Jake.' And he let go of my hand and turned away.

We went to the table where we usually sat. There were three spaces.

'Can we join you?' I asked. This had been my routine learned in the States. Always be polite. One of the seated men went to leave.

'Flash, you haven't finished your breakfast.' I smiled.

He sat down again. They were all looking at me. There was uncertainty in their expressions.

'Fellas, today's Friday and it isn't really different from yesterday and tomorrow will be much the same as today. I'm the same, Sergeant's the same and you're the same so let's do the same things as before.'

They were all thinking, mulling over what I'd said.

Flash Gordon smiled. 'Thank you, Captain.'

'You're very welcome, Flash.'

Haltingly the conversation on the merits of betting to win as opposed to betting each way was resumed. I had to prepare some stuff for my class, so I had to leave soon after.

'Excuse me please, gentlemen,' I said and the people at the table responded as they normally did to me leaving. At least some things were still normal. As I left the dining room I could feel over a hundred pairs of eyes watching me or was I becoming paranoid?

On the landing outside of my cell was Tom. Tom was a finder. He could find anything that you wanted. He traded in everything except drugs and he would have traded in them except it was, as he described it, 'heavy shit'.

'Morning, Captain, I just wondered if you needed anything.' He'd never approached me before but I knew that Harry had dealings with him.

'I don't think so, Tom.'

'I've left you a few items as a token of goodwill.'

'Thank you, Tom. Can you get me some information?'

'Information can get heavy, Captain. It depends what it is.'

'I just wondered what visitors Jase had before he was topped and what visitors Mr Wharton had.'

'I reckon I might be able to do that. Would be a pleasure. I liked Jase.'

'What will that cost me?'

'You're a very special customer, Captain. I'm sure you'll reward me when I'm in need.'

Leadership is a very funny thing, as is respect. Leaders in prison were the same as leaders elsewhere. They were just people who had followers and like elsewhere, they were only real leaders if the people wanted to follow them. Respect in here could be odd and was different from outside. I'm unsure what it was for any one person to respect another but I clearly had the respect of many convicts in here. Perhaps being a killer and getting away with it was a core. It was also clear that Harry had emerged as the leader of The Brothers. Their leadership had been fragmented, although the factions were cooperative towards each other. Now the factions seemed to be coalescing under Harry. I expect that would be seen as a threat by some in here. Black power was bound to be seen as a threat. There were still three groups: the Afro-Caribbeans, the Africans and the Asians (mainly Indians and Pakistanis; they were two subgroups. The difference was religion, so the Pakistani group was Muslim and had some other Middle Eastern individuals in it).

A power struggle was emerging and, unlike the political scene, the contestants hadn't generated it; it was coming from the prisoners and it was pitching Mr Wharton and Tug Wilson against Harry and me. We hadn't chosen this confrontation; it had just happened and I think the catalyst had been me killing Ratty, underpinned by the incident with Tug Wilson in the dining room.

150

24

I wandered down to the classroom. I suppose I just wanted to clear my head and be alone and I knew that the classroom would be empty on a Saturday, but it wasn't. Maniac was sitting in it. I'd never been alone with Maniac before.

'Hello, Maniac. What can I do for you?'

'My name is Joe, Captain, Joe Nokes.' The alter self, that was an advantage as Joe was far more in control. As he answered I mused on the fact that prisons must be super study grounds for academics: all these people with something strange about them all under one roof and nowhere to go. That was not quite true; they probably had somewhere to go, they were just not allowed to go there.

'Okay, Joe, what can I do for you?'

'You have this great thing of being all about the other person, Captain.'

'Thank you, Joe, and?'

'And you helped Arthur and I want you to help me.'

'Explain please, Joe.'

'Well, he had some sort of hang up and you unhooked him.'

I had to smile. It was a neat visual description.'

'So tell me, Joe.'

'I bumped some people off, women, and thought that if I tried the mentally incompetent bit I might get a light sentence in a mental institution.'

'I thought you killed two women and a small boy.'

151

'No, I now think the woman I killed had killed Mary and little Pauley; I just killed the murdering bitch. Yes, I thought I'd try the spilt personality thing but, well, it didn't work. Got fifteen years so I thought I'd keep it up and they would transfer me. Still, it did have a payoff; nobody has ever tried any of the sex stuff on me or any other stuff. They try to stay away from me.'

'So, what do you want from me then, Joe?'

'Well you helped Arthur, so I wondered what you might do for me.'

'If you are sane, Joe, and not suffering from multiple personality syndrome why not just behave normally?'

'If I do, won't they smell a rat and bang me up for longer?'

'No, Joe, you're in here for a crime, a crime you have been found guilty of. They can't retry you but you may have grounds for appeal.'

'Appeal?'

'Yes appeal, it depends on the reason you committed the murder of the one you did kill.'

'I didn't have a choice.'

'Explain.'

'I walked in and Pauley and his mum were dead, stabbed, the woman went for me and I took the knife off her and killed her.'

'So it was a struggle for the weapon and you killed this woman in the struggle.'

'Yes, well, I suppose so.'

'You suppose so?'

'Well, I think I killed her. There wasn't anybody else there or I don't think so.'

'You don't think so? Is this what you told the police?'

'I don't know.'

'You don't know. Let me take you back. There are two women and a child dead, stabbed. You are covered in blood. What happened next?'

'I don't know?'

'Do you remember stabbing the woman?'

'Yes.'

'Tell me.'

'Well, it was like I said. Pauley and his mum were dead, stabbed, the woman went for me and I took the knife off her and killed her.'

'You took the knife off her. Were you injured?'

'Yes. My hands and arms were cut and my face. See?'

He had a scar that ran from above his temple, jumped his eye and started again on his cheekbone.

'Let's go back again. Where were you?'

'At Mary Collins's house. We'd been going out and she found out that I had, well, done a couple of jobs and she broke up with me so I wanted to explain and, well, you know... I remember her answering the door. She was all upset and she left me there and told me to stay there so I did. I remember going into the kitchen and she and my kid were dead; there was blood everywhere and this woman had a knife and I stabbed her.'

I registered 'my kid' but just stored it.

'How?'

'The police said I stabbed her fourteen times.'

'What do you say?'

'I don't remember.'

'If you were to remember what would you remember?'

'That I stabbed her and she hit me with something and she kept hitting me and I kept stabbing and she stopped hitting me and I kept on stabbing her.'

'Were you injured?'

'Yes my left arm was broken and my left collar bone.'

'What did she hit you with?'

'I think it was an iron.'

'Were you treated for those injuries?'

'Yes.'

153

'Where?'

'In the A and E of a hospital.'

'Where?'

'I don't know.'

'Did you stay in the hospital?'

'I don't know.'

'You were questioned by the police?'

'Yes.'

'When was that?'

'I don't know?'

'Did you have a solicitor?'

'I think so.'

'But you're not sure?'

'Look, it's all a blur. The police told me what happened and so I tried the nutty trick.'

'Did you kill Mary Collins and Pauley?'

'I don't know. I don't think so, but the police said I did. I must have done but then sometimes I think this woman did it.'

'What was the woman's name?'

'Mable Nokes. She was my wife. Well, we were divorced.'

'Let me get this right. There is some confusion in what you tell me. You went to Mary Collins's house. She told you to wait at the door. You went into the kitchen and Mary Collins and Pauley were dead. Mable Nokes attacked you with a knife that you took from her and you stabbed her with it and she attacked you with an iron. You had defensive knife wounds, a broken arm and collarbone. Is that correct?'

'I think so.'

'At the time you were arrested were you clear what had happened?'

'Well, not really. At the trial I was clear but since then I keep remembering things and I don't know if they're real or not.'

'Do you remember killing little Pauley?'

'No, not really?'

'Did you or didn't you kill him?'

Joe started to cry. He was sobbing. I let him settle.

'Tell me, Joe.'

'He was my boy. I wouldn't kill him, but the police said I did.' That cleared up the question I had stored.

'Did the police know he was your son?'

'I don't know.'

'So you didn't tell them?'

'I don't know.'

'Did you see a psychiatrist before the trial?'

'Yes. He said I was fit to plead but he said some other things like I was sick in some way.'

'What way?'

'I think he said I suffered from dissociative identity disorder and post-traumatic stress disorder.'

'Joe, do you know what those things are?'

'I think so. I am me and I lose time and I know I have done things, but I don't know what those things are. I've never been a soldier.'

'Does it matter that you haven't been a soldier?'

'Well it's soldiers that get that post-traumatic stress disorder.'

'I see. Before you killed and were arrested what did you do for a living, Joe?'

'I was a gardener and tree surgeon, worked for a company called Garden Care.'

'Did you lose time then?'

'I think so, Captain.'

'I'm confused again. You have just said that you think you lost time before the killing, then when it came to the trial you said you tried the mentally incompetent bit.'

'Yes, it's like I've always lost time but it didn't matter so if I told them it might help me.'

'When did it start?'

'I don't know really. I must have been small.'

'Did anything happen to you when you were small?'

'Well, my mum died and I went into the home.'

'Do you know when you are going to lose time?'

'Sometimes.'

'Do you try to stop it?'

'Yes, it's all sort of confused.'

'Have you seen the psychiatrist recently?'

'I don't know. I think so.'

'Why did you come to see me, Joe?'

'To get help, Captain.'

'Help to do what?'

'I don't know really. Just to get better I suppose.'

'Joe, only a psychiatrist can get you better. I can't.'

He was looking at me and he seemed confused.

'If you get better you may find out you did kill your son. What do you think about that?'

'I don't know, Captain.' He sat looking at me then he said, 'I suppose it would be better than wondering. I know sometimes I'm crackers, Captain.'

'Go on.'

'Well, I'm always me but then I want to be Maniac, so I am.'

'Okay, just try to be the real you and I suppose I'm talking to him now. I will talk to somebody who knows about the legal stuff and we'll see what she says.'

That evening, I phoned Sarah and outlined the issue as I saw it. Basically, here was a suspect, probably a guilty suspect, who was in no condition to be interviewed and in a suggestible condition, probably post-traumatic stress syndrome or a similar condition. The result was that they put together a case and he's in the can for what amounts to life. The present result was mental illness.

Her response was, 'Okay, what are you suggesting, Jake?'

'You talk to him and see if you get the same feeling as me. Go over the stuff done by the police, his solicitor and the CPS.'

'If it's dodgy, what do you suggest, Jake?'

'Have him treated by EMDR or some similar therapy.'

'What is that, Jake?'

'Eye movement desensitisation and reprocessing. It can help remove the blockages to his memory and he may be able to say what actually happened and why he killed his wife and child.'

'I'll get back to you, Jake.'

A week later, I got a phone call. Sarah was taking this on and she had fixed a project with her old university as a case study for some module or for some qualification.

The next week Joe, Sarah and I were in an interview room with the psychiatrist Professor Roland Quinby and the prison doctor. Sarah had been through the CPS notes with Andrew Miles, a QC who worked for Sir Nicolas. Joe had seen a psychiatrist from the NHS and the prison service. They agreed that there was some form of memory repression. Roland Quinby explained the process that Joe would go through. He talked it through and they discussed what they would attempt to achieve and the main symptoms that were apparent, such as the lack of memory of the event of the murders, and also some previous loss of memory. He also talked about the discussions that he and Joe had about things he knew to be true and he felt safe with. Then he explained that EMDR stood for eye movement desensitization and reprocessing, and is a psychotherapy that alleviates the symptoms of post-traumatic stress disorder and is used for individuals who have experienced severe trauma that remains unresolved. The idea is that it overwhelms the normal cognitive and neurological coping mechanisms. It is these coping mechanisms that block the memories. Joe would be asked to follow a light that moved backwards and forwards from left to right and talk about negative ideas he has and then make positive self-statements that are preferable to negative thoughts. This took some explaining as Joe didn't understand some of the ideas, but he got the picture that he would remember things and some of them would be disturbing and he would become emotionally upset as he recognised what he had done, but within that he would recognise the positive actions that he took and the reasons he did what he did. It was also pointed out to him that this may not lead to anything that may help his present situation and it could take months.

Joe sat and thought about all the stuff he had been given. He looked at me and said, 'What would you do, Captain?'

'Not my decision, Joe. You have to decide.'

'Yes, I know, but if you were me, what would you do?'

'Me, I suppose it may not make any difference or it may make some difference. Either way, you'll know more about what happened. The question is: do you want to know?'

'I could do all this, go through a lot of angst and still be in here?'

'Yes, Joe, you could.'

'But I would know more about me?'

'Perhaps, Joe, and if you do you will have to live with that.'

'I know you would do it, Captain.' He sat looking at me. I think he was trying to read my mind. 'Oh fuck it! I've got fuck all else to do.'

'I take that as a yes,' said Sarah.

'What about the multiple personality thing, Professor?' I asked.

'That may be related but would be much more deep-seated. It may be that the stress suffered at the time of his son's death we can tackle but the childhood trauma may be something we can only treat.'

That was me out of the loop and what would happen I really had no idea.

25

I was teaching when Boy Pritchard stuck his head round the door of my classroom.

'Can I have a word, Captain?' Boy was a very pretty homosexual who sold oral sex.

'Hey hey, Captain! We didn't know you were into that!' said one of my class members.

'Silence or I'll sit you in the corner on the naughty stool wearing a pointy hat. Now finish the exercise,' I told them and left the room.

'Captain,' Boy began, his voice quivering, 'they're going to rape you today to take you down.'

'Tell me more, Boy.'

'I don't know but, well, they'll do you in the showers.'

'Who are they?'

'Mr Wharton and Tug Wilson. Mr Wharton will do you first and then Tug Wilson. It's horrible.'

I didn't ask how he knew, but the message was interesting. He said 'Tug Wilson'; normally only first names were used here in conversation. I didn't know what it meant but it was different.

'Will you go and tell Sergeant, please?'

'Okay, Captain.'

It's amazing how power and respect grows. I'm sure that two weeks ago Boy would never have told me, let alone run a message for me.

Ten minutes later, Harry slipped into the room and sat at the back. You could feel a change in the room.

'Are you in trouble, Captain?'

'I don't know, Arty, but I could be.' He looked around the room. There was no oral communication but a series of nods.

Maniac spoke. 'If it comes to trouble, Captain, we're with you.' His voice was as it normally was but sane with purpose. Were the psychiatrists right and he really was sane?

'Thank you, fellas. If I need help Sergeant will enrol you.'

'I can spell that,' said George. 'E-N-R-O-L – enrol.'

'Thank you, George.'

George wasn't the sharpest knife in the drawer. He was big and soft like a teddy bear and usually missed what was going on around him, but he was a trier. He'd avoided being used as a bitch for some of the experienced prisoners because somebody with a conscience and some muscle would always step in and protect him. He should never have been in prison; he needed care and guidance not confinement. He'd been tortured and goaded for months. Then one day he'd exploded and killed four younger boys who were bullying him. He went into hiding or rather somebody hid him but he was seen and he was frightened and killed two women and a policeman. In fact, he was as gentle as a lamb but he was just scared by threat, and threat made him violent. I'm sure with appropriate psychiatric treatment he would recover and be okay in some form of sheltered accommodation. I'd once heard a recording of a woman who I think was named Joyce Grenfell. I found myself doing her thing with him: 'George, don't do that'. George used to smile, a shy smile, and stop doing whatever it was, usually with his hand in his pocket.

Dad, who was well over seventy, knew all about Joyce Grenfell. He thought I was a magician. He'd been trying to learn to read for about ten years and he was now nearly through Book 1 after only a few weeks with me. It's funny really. I don't know what I did but whatever it was had unblocked something that was stopping him learning to read and the Arthur thing, I was sure, had helped.

As we walked along the landing, Officer Moorby was waiting.

'Jake, you've a medical this afternoon. Go for a shower now,' he said.

I didn't like Moorby, or Manson come to that, but I'd be hard-pressed to explain why. On the face of it they were like any other prison officers but my sixth sense said these men were slippery. When they told you something it was as if they were doing you a personal favour for which you should be grateful and their utterances were full of innuendo. When they gave you information it often lacked clarity or a vital piece of information so you were pushed into a position of seeking clarification.

'Senior Officer James didn't tell me.'

Harry had slipped into our cell while I was talking to Moorby.

'She's off today so I'm telling you.'

'What time?'

'In half an hour.' He still gave no time and no answer to my question.

'Okay, I'll be at the blue room in ten minutes.'

That was another odd thing about this place; the bath and shower rooms were called the blue rooms.

When I walked into the cell Harry said, 'Sit. Listen good now. Go into the shower room, B-Wing doorway and straight down the first leg. Turn the fifth or sixth shower on, on the right side. Go to the end of the row and along the back row to the fifth shower. Get stripped, turn the shower on and leave your gear there. Go back to the first shower that you put on. Here's a chiv and a shank.' He handed me a cutthroat razor; the blade was taped open. The shank was

161

a five-inch ice pick. 'When they come at you do your best. When you're successful go to the shower on the back row. Have a shower. Make sure there's no blood on you. Leave the showers, get dressed and come down the far side past the baths to the A-Wing side door so you don't pass the damage you've done.'

I loved the 'when' and not 'if'; he left the unsuccessful unsaid.

'What about the blades?'

'Yes, the upper window at the end of the first line of showers is always open. Drop the blades out of there. Wash them first, no blood, no prints; The Brothers will pick them up. Oh, and turn the first shower off before you leave it. No prints, though.'

26

I wandered along to the blue room. Moorby and Manson were leaning on the landing rail outside. Clearly only I was going into the showers. I could feel the expectation in the wing or perhaps it was just my raised level of adrenaline. The blue room served two wings, A and B, and all the levels. The A-Wing door was on the left and the B-Wing door on the right. Mr Wharton and Tug Wilson were in A-Wing, so they would probably come in through the left door. I followed the instructions Harry had given me and wondered how he knew what to do. But mine was not to wonder why; mine was but to do and hopefully not die.

I was in the first shower row, the fifth shower cubicle along, and I heard someone approaching. Suddenly Mr Wharton was standing in front of me, naked and erect. He was still wearing his hat.

'How about that one, soldier?' His hands were above his head and his hips were thrust forward.

I swung the razor upwards, right to left, across his body, cut deeply into his pride and joy, and blood spurted everywhere. His scream died as I slashed sideways again from right to left, aiming for his throat. More by luck than anything else, the blade sliced into his neck and forward into his windpipe. I had to pull it free. An artery must have been cut or perhaps a major vein as the blood pumped and poured out. My stomach tied into a knot; I was horrified at what I had done and was fighting to breathe and at the

163

same time, my thinking was clear, ice cold. I stepped across the body into the opposite cubical and heard the sound of running feet above the whoosh of the two running showers opposite. Tug appeared. He was naked apart from the plastic faceguard they had fitted because of the facial damage I had inflicted, looking like the phantom of the shower room. He was facing the first running shower, looking down at his master. I picked my spot and stabbed him with the ice pick between the shoulder blades. I held him on the spike as I reached around his body and used the razor to cut his throat. His knees folded, he tipped forward and the long, slim pick in my hand pulled free from his back. He was dead before he hit the ground.

I froze, looking at my hands and the weapons in them. For the first attack I'd had the razor in my right hand and the pick in my left. At some point I'd changed hands so the razor was in my left and the pick in my right and that aided my attack, but I didn't recollect doing that.

The two naked bodies were at my feet face down. Wilson was draped around Wharton and slightly over him. Wilson's right arm was around Wharton's chest and his chest against his back like two lovers dreaming. I shuddered at the gross image and the realisation of what I'd done. I was trembling and my breathing was shallow and rapid. I'd killed before, more than once, but this was different, very different. I wanted to be sick, gagging. But I daren't as this might identify me through DNA. I swallowed with that revolting acid taste left in my mouth.

I washed the blades and stepped into the still-running second shower. Blood flowed into the first one, the spots of blood on me washed off and I gargled and spat. I turned off the second shower and used my wet flannel to clean the shower valve. The first shower was still running, washing the blood down the drain. I cleaned the shower valve and I wonder why Harry wanted me to do this shower routine.

Then I was confused, did he actually tell me to do that? I walked to the end of the row, wiped the blades with my flannel and rolled them in a rag that was on the window ledge. Luck was with me and I dropped them through the window. There was a hose dribbling at the end of the line of the second row of showers. I turned it on full and washed the passageway between the showers so that if I'd dripped any blood from me it would be washed away.

I went to my still-running shower, along the back of the blue room, washed myself down quickly just in case any blood was still on me, dried myself, dressed and walked out of the showers, past the baths to the A-Wing door. The two prison officers were opposite. Their surprised reaction could be seen. Moorby put his hand onto Manson's hand and they didn't move. What could they do? I caught their eyes and did a little nodding tweak of my head in a greeting. I could see the confusion in their faces and in their stance, and I wandered nonchalantly back to my cell. I could hear a very quiet buzz just above a deathly silence. The atmosphere was electric. Expectation hung in the air. I was so relaxed I could have sung or danced but I held myself in, quiet and controlled; no rush, just the usual wander. How strange: from shuddering horror to happy relaxation in a few minutes.

Harry was waiting and when I got back to our cell, he hugged me and said, 'Thank God for that, Captain. Are they dead? Of course they are; now you better go to your medical. You've an appointment.' He was proud of me. How strange. I could hear it in his voice. He hadn't doubted me for a minute. This is what sergeants expect – no, want – from their officers, to be listened to and then for the officer to do the job excellently as their leader.

I walked along the landings, down the stairs, through the passageways to the medical centre. It seemed to me that everybody knew something had happened; it was in the very

165

air that we breathed; it was in the creaks and bangs and scrapes of the very fabric of the building and voices of the prisoners. The 'what' wasn't known but the fact that something had happened or was about to happen was there – an intangible knowledge.

27

Medical departments are all the same. They have specially designed, uncomfortable chairs and they leave you sitting for a minimum of ten minutes after your appointment time just to get you frustrated and raise your blood pressure. They also have the sort of pictures that nobody wants to look at on the walls. I'm sure that it's all part of a cunning ploy by the NHS to create an environment of non-expectation so that the non-thinking section of the general public are pleased with the poor service they actually get. No, that's far too clever for the NHS; it's just 1948 socialistic bureaucracy carried on to the present day.

I was shown into a treatment room and I was trying to explain to the sister that there was nothing wrong with me when the hoo-ha broke out. An alarm sounded followed by a Tannoy message for all prisoners to return to their cells. The phones in the medical centre were ringing and a message came over for medical staff to go to the A and B bathroom. The sister shot off and I wandered back to my cell. As I did, prison officers were shouting at me to get a move on.

There followed a lock down, the second one in two weeks and for the same reason – murder. This time a double murder. I was feeling differently about this one. It was self-defence. No longer was I elated; I just had a sense of relief mixed with a sense of horror of what had happened and what could have happened to me. My hands were now trembling, my mouth was dry and I felt sick. I realised that for the first time in my life I felt fear and it was after the event. I'd had apprehension before when in action. I'd concerns that my men could be injured but it was never me. I'd always assumed I would be okay. No, that's wrong; I'd never thought about me and I'd always been okay, well, more or less. Yes, I'd been injured and wounded but never what I considered seriously. I wonder why that was. I'd seen men terrificd and thought I understood but I didn't because I'd never experienced what they were experiencing. Now I understood fear: a black illogical dread that you couldn't prevent. Something so awful it had no name happening to you and yet this was after what could have happened was past. I realised if I'd felt like this in the showers I couldn't have done what I did. Thank God for Harry's little mind game. For the first time I understood the suffering some people had through fear and made a resolution to never let fear incapacitate me.

We sat and waited. I was reading a John Grisham novel, *The Summons*, and Harry was sticking some bits of cardboard and wood together for some kid's party somewhere. The door opened and we were hurried out of our cell. The search team went in and took the cell apart. Everything – the cupboards, the drawers, even the misnamed sponge bag (who the hell has a sponge in prison?) – was scattered on the floor. For what purpose? Perhaps just to relieve their stress and anger. Needless to say, they found nothing in our cell. After all, we'd been trained so that if we had anything we shouldn't have had, they wouldn't find it. They then locked us in and just left us to clear up the mess. Harry wasn't a happy bunny. The bastards had smashed the toy castle he was making. What petty mindedness. He started again.

28

I'd been dreaming that I was drowning, drowning in blood, the blood of Mr Wharton and Tug Wilson. They'd been pulling me into their blood. A big stinking pool of blood; I could feel its cold clammy stickiness and its contraction as it congealed on my skin and turned from red to chocolate brown, and the iron metallic taste in my mouth and the smell – that smell. I don't think I've ever been so scared; no, I'd never been so scared. I was soaked in sweat and had difficulty breathing. I just lay still and controlled my breathing. I ached. I tried to lift my head but my neck was like rock. My eyes were open but I could only see the dim outline of things in the glimmer of light from the blue safety lamp over the cell door. It was so dark it must have been the middle of the night. I could feel my hands trembling and my heart pounding. I lay on my bunk looking upwards at the grey area above me as the darkness was hiding the ceiling from me. I could feel the sensation in my right hand of the cutthroat razor slicing into Mr Wharton's throat and see the blood flowing across the bathroom floor reflected in the greyness above me in curling streaks, like a modern abstract painting. I could see his face reflected in this bizarre picture, surprise, shock, horror, floating in the cold darkness. I could see his grey, dying body in the light of the blue safety lamp. I could feel his coldness in the chill of this cell – cold, very cold in death – and the greyness of the dead body that had pumped out its blood from the severed arteries and veins in his throat and penis. I could hear him choking and whispering in the scraping and rattling that pervades the bareness of the prison, in the cries of other prisoners, but most of all in the soft rasping of Harry breathing in the bunk below me, whispering with a voice that I'd cut from Mr Wharton. I pulled my skinny blanket up to my throat in an attempt to shield myself from that, that from which I couldn't hide. No warmth, no hiding place from what I'd done.

'Are you okay, Captain?'

'Not really, Harry.'

'Bad dream?'

'Yes, a bad dream.'

'The killings?'

'Yes, Harry.'

'But you've killed before, Captain.'

'Yes and I've had nightmares before but not quite like this one.'

'What was it?' It was a simple open question.

'Blood, Harry. I've never stabbed anyone before.'

'Messy stuff blood: shooting at a distance or breaking someone's neck is kind of clean but blood is messy stuff.' I could hear the understanding in his voice. An understanding that none of the counsellors had had when I'd spoken to them in the past about killing people. Odd isn't it: organisations send people to counselling with people who have never actually been engaged in the real situation. They may have attended the lectures or read the good books but they've never actually killed anybody or been stabbed or shot or lost a leg or a child. How would they know what it feels like, the horror, the fear, and the self-loathing? Yet, I'd done it, I'd been a counsellor and not really known what the poor bastard I was supposed to help was going through and because of the enormity and the personal nature of the problems, they couldn't really tell me, but Harry had been there, done it and suffered from the results.

170

'You had nightmares, Harry?'

'Oh yes and nights when I couldn't get to sleep, but not now, not anymore. You'll be okay, Captain. Those bastards deserved to die.'

The strange thing was that his words relaxed me. Harry knew; he'd been there. He was something special. My shakes stopped, the stiff neck evaporated and I felt tired. I was going to be all right with Harry guarding my back. I even started to giggle. I could see the two bodies like lovers and could imagine the images on the police photos.

'What is it, Captain?'

'Oh, it's nothing, Harry. I'm okay now. Thanks.'

Then I must have just fallen asleep. Well, I knew that I had as I had a dream.

It was raining, I could hear the rain and we were in my car. The rain bounced off the roof with that drumming noise and the rain splashed off the windscreen and we were looking through the streaky windscreen across green fields and there were cows. We were talking and I knew it was Sam with me and I felt wonderful but I couldn't see her.

'Where are we going?' she asked.

'To the village.' She was pleased.

'Can we go to the restaurant?'

'Yes,' I said but the car wouldn't start and she got out and she walked away and I couldn't get out because the door was locked. And I was shouting for her, it got dark and I could hear her calling me.

Then we were home and she was in the bath and calling me and I said I was coming and Harry woke me up.

'You okay, Jake?' he asked.

'Why?'

'You were shouting.'

'Sorry.'

He got back in his bunk.

171

29

It was dawn. The sun was coming up and shining through the window of our cell. It was our cell now, it had always been our cell, Harry's and mine; we were a team, an unbeatable team. I was lying on my back with my hands behind my head looking at the ceiling, grey-white cracked plaster, and thinking, reviewing what might lay before me that day and working out how I was going to slide from under the avalanche of corruption that was about to fall on me. I worked out step by step what I would do if I was investigating this killing; what would I want to know and what would I want to find? The whys, the whens, the hows, the whos and wheres. Some were obvious but the obvious for me, as an investigator, would beg other questions. Now, how could I screw the investigators?

'Okay, what is it?' Harry asked.

'I was just wondering.'

'And what were you just bloody wondering?' said the voice from the bunk below me.

'How'd you know I was lying here wondering?'

'I can tell from your breathing when you're awake and you only ever sleep on your side so you're lying on your back stock still, so you're bloody thinking and when you start thinking, somebody, probably me, is in the crap.'

'Harry, you've people who have access to the prison officers' offices, locker rooms, etc.?'

'Uh-huh.'

'So they might know where particular prison officers' lockers, desks and things are?'

'Uh-huh.'

'And they've the razor and ice pick?'

'Uh-huh.'

'So they could put them somewhere that wouldn't be in view but if a search was made they might be found?'

'Uh-huh.'

'You're big on the "uh-huh" this morning, Sergeant.' I was smiling but Harry couldn't see that.

'Why on earth would the screws' offices and locker room be searched?'

'Because I'm going to suggest it when I'm interviewed, probably this morning.'

'Christ, Captain, you don't give us much bloody warning do you? Moorby and Manson?'

'Uh-huh.'

'Now your bloody uh-huh-ing.'

'Uh-huh.'

I heard him chuckle.

'Harry.'

'Yes, Captain.'

'What was all that palaver with the showers?'

He laughed. 'Two reasons, Captain. The first was to keep you focused. You were so busy buggering about with showers you didn't have time to freeze. The second reason was that the police are going to find wet showers and running showers and it'll just create confusion as they try to figure out the murder scene. They'll come up with a theory to fit the facts but it won't make sense.'

'How do you know this stuff?'

'Because I've been a criminal longer than you've been a copper, Captain.'

He was right and the conversation had made me relaxed enough to fall back to sleep.

That morning, Harry and I walked to the dining room for breakfast and other prisoners cleared away from us. If they couldn't be clear they pressed themselves against the walls. We ignored it as if it wasn't happening but the screws saw it and the screws knew. The prison was silent. No, that's an over-statement; it was quiet. The rumour mill was grinding away. Again, I was in the frame, but it was all much more speculative. It varied from suggesting that I'd set a trap for them and murdered them to the nearer reality; they had tried to rape me and failed. The spilt was also interesting; the ex-acolytes of Mr Wharton were supporting the trap and murder theory and the uncommitted and The Brothers were supporting the rape theory. My concern was civil war in the prison. The prison authorities and officers were edgy.

Harry slipped in next to me at breakfast. I was eating a classic, a meal I thoroughly enjoyed that went under the extremely unappetising name of shit on a raft. The cooks of course call it sautéed kidney. It was chopped up kidneys cooked in a thick brown sauce and served on a doorstep of crisp deep-fried bread. Well, the fried bread was crisp until the sauce started soaking into it. It sounds disgusting but tasted wonderful. It also did wonders for bowel movements, which is probably why it was only served once a month.

'I don't know how you can eat that shit,' he said.

'It's great. Try some.'

'You've got to be kidding. I'm pleased to see you've recovered. You'll be okay now. Anyway, the project is underway and from what The Brothers say, they think this is a great scam and have a couple of really good places to position the treasure for the treasure hunters to find.'

Arthur, Dad, Flash and Boy said nothing and I knew they would swear on a stack of Bibles they'd heard nothing. Boy Pritchard had started to sit at our table – security and protection, I suppose, for warning me.

30

I was sent for at about ten o'clock. My class was in full swing and we were all, shall we say, less than happy at the interruption. But the summons came as no surprise. The surprise was that it was the governor and it was in a small room that he held his court for miscreants. I was marched in by a principal officer and stood to attention before a lectern behind which stood the governor on a slightly raised dais, so he could look over the top of the lectern and down upon me. Oh, the games people play.

The sun was shining through the window at the side of the room through the venetian blinds, throwing bars of light and dark across the carpet up the side of the lectern and giving the governor writhing stripes of his own as he moved.

As well as the governor and the principal officer, Senior Officer James and a couple of other senior people were present. It was more like a military disciplinary procedure than anything carrying the weight of criminal law.

'Prisoner Robinson: eight-seven, eight-four, five-two, for enquiry, *sir*,' the principal officer snapped out in a Scottish accent as he led me in. I bet he'd been an NCO in the army. I had to smile as I thought of Mr Mackay in the comedy series, *Porridge*. He even looked like Mackay with the jerking of his head backwards and forwards as he spoke.

'Robinson,' the governor said. The 'let's all play happy bunnies' was suddenly gone. 'You were in the showers at twelve fifteen on Tuesday of this week.'

'Yes, sir.'

'Why were you there at such a strange time?'

'I was ordered to be there in preparation for a medical at twelve thirty.'

'Who ordered you to be there?'

'Officer Moorby, sir.'

'Who arranged the medical?'

'I don't know, sir.'

'What was the purpose of the medical?'

'I don't know, sir.'

'The record shows you booked it.'

'The record is wrong, sir.'

'It says you were suffering severe lower back pain.'

'Then the record is wrong, sir.'

'You went to the medical.'

'Yes, sir.'

He clearly didn't believe me and looked at the ceiling; the tips of his fingers were touching in front of his chest. He tapped them together as he looked at me. He had visibly made the decision that whatever I said was of no consequence to him; self-evident was his condescension or was it contempt?

'Whom did you see?' That was a bit pedantic – 'whom'.

'Nurse Carstairs, sir.'

'What happened when you got there?'

'I waited and as I saw the nurse, an alarm went and I was directed to return to my cell.'

'Who did you see in the showers?'

Oh, no 'whom'?

'Nobody, sir.'

'But two people followed you in.'

'I didn't see them, sir.'

'I'd like you to explain something to me. After all, you were once a policeman. You go into the bathrooms and you see nobody there. Two people follow you in. You leave the

176

bathroom by the entrance the two people entered by. Nobody else goes in or comes out. The two people who'd followed you in are found murdered. What conclusion would you draw from that?'

'Quite honestly, sir, there are some elements of *that* story missing.'

'Explain.'

'There may have been somebody in the bathroom when I entered that I didn't see. That person left without being seen or was seen and nobody's admitting to seeing him or them. Or the killer left after the bodies were discovered and left under the cover of confusion or waited an hour or so. Or the person who found the bodies did the killing. Or the information given to you is incorrect.'

'So you don't accept the simple explanation that you killed two men?'

'Sir, how on earth am I going to kill two men?'

'By stabbing them.'

'What with? I've no weapons.'

The Governor stopped; he looked bemused. 'The police will interview you later this morning, Robinson, when your solicitor arrives. Until they clear you, you'll wear a tracker.'

'Am I now a Category A prisoner, sir?'

'Yes.'

'May I see the judgement or tribunal report from the Category A team, please, sir.'

'No you may not.' He hadn't followed procedure, again. Oh dear.

'Then I will challenge your ruling, sir.'

'You do that, Robinson.'

'Will I be confined in the segregation unit?' I was rubbing salt into a wound. I knew he had received an admonishment for confining me before.

'No, return to your activities, Robinson.'

'Yes, sir. Thank you, sir.'

When we left, Senior Officer James took me down to the reception suite.

'You know the rules then, Jake?'

'Yes, ma'am; they prevent the abuse of power such as sticking trackers on me.'

She pursed her lips in a grim smile; she knew the proper procedure had not been followed to make me a Cat A prisoner.

We went into the reception suite and there a tracker was fitted to my left ankle. We then went into the surveillance room, which had at least twenty screens and two officers watching them. My tracker was matched into the computer and from then on, wherever I went would be recorded.

'So now we will know where you are, Jake,' said Senior Officer James.

'Only till my solicitor arrives, ma'am.'

She shook her head. 'I best go upstairs and get the ruling changed then, Jake.'

31

As I was in limbo, so to speak, I decided to go to the library and play around with some texts and ideas for my class. I was really getting into this teaching bit now. I got a real kick when any of them cleared a hurdle and they really appreciated my help. I was also learning a lot about the English language and about teaching: simple things like parts of speech and tenses. In fact, incorrect tense usage and adverbs annoyed me when I was listening to football pundits and they said things like, 'And he run quick up the side line.' I would find myself saying, 'No! He ran quickly.' Silly really, the guy on the TV couldn't hear me. Because of this misuse of the English language I longed for the time my gran used to talk about, when the announcers on radio and television were posh. Well, she knew and I knew they weren't posh; they just used correct pronunciation, and grammar. It's amazing how teaching highlights little things that start to make a big impact on you, or perhaps it's being in prison that does that.

In terms of teaching, I found that it was better to never 'tell' when you can 'ask'. I would never tell my students when they were incorrect; instead, I would ask them what they'd done correctly and what they would do differently next time, reinforcing what they could do and targeting to correct the things they knew they didn't have correct without me stuffing it down their throats as had often been done to me at school. This was stuff I'd learned in Behaviourist Learning Theory at university and it worked.

179

As I passed down the passageway into the library, I heard the toilet door behind me close. I was being followed. I turned to find myself facing Pete Costello and Marty Clifford. This wasn't good. Pete was facing down the passageway, I suppose to stop anybody coming down, and Marty was facing me.

'Good morning, gentlemen. Can I do something for you?'

'You're a smooth bugger I'll give you that, Captain,' said Marty.

'Thank you, kind sir, but I don't think you were waiting for me to tell me that.'

'No, we've been asked to teach you a little lesson.'

'And what's that, may I ask?'

'The first lesson is coping with pain and the second lesson's for you to learn to do as you're told.'

I'd expected an attack but not until after the police had left. The tactics here were just plain wrong. Both of these highly fit and powerful men outweighed me by at least two stone.

'I see. And if you're successful in the first part of your endeavour do you think there won't be repercussions?'

'We can handle Sergeant.'

'That's what I like: confidence.' This sort of situation is a very scary place and fear is the thing that defeats most people, not the strength and power of the opposition. 'Okay, which of you is going to try me first?'

Marty was looking over my shoulder and the expression of confident antagonism changed. Was it surprise? I then heard a movement behind me.

'Fought you might like a little 'elp, Captain.' It was Arthur. Help in these situations doesn't come much better than Arthur.

'I probably do, Arty.'

'That's good.' It was big Fred. So we now outnumbered them.

Sergeant came round the curve and faced Pete. Now, that was an encounter I'd like to see.

'I think we've stalemate, gentlemen. What would you like to do, Marty?'

'I'll fucking get you, you stuck-up prick.'

'Okay, Marty, just you and me. Here! Now!'

He'd all the apparent advantages: he outweighed me, he was stronger than me, he'd massive street-brawling experience and we were in a small area so my manoeuvrability was limited.

'Wrong place, Captain,' said Sergeant.

'You're right, Sergeant. I'd be taking advantage to fight Marty here.'

'I'll fucking kill you, you stuck-up prick.'

'Oh dear, Marty. You're repeating yourself and using wicked words.' I spoke like a disappointed mother talking to her small child.

He then did exactly what I expected him to do. He rushed me. He charged forward and threw a massive right swing that I ducked, turning to my left and stepping into his body. I grabbed his right sleeve, pulling down with my left hand and pushing my right hand under his jaw, twisting my body and using his momentum to throw him over my right hip. He somersaulted over me: a perfect throw. I released. His head and shoulders hit the concrete floor hard. He wasn't moving and blood trickled from the damage to the back of his scalp; blood was also coming from his left ear, now that worried me, and there was a trickle at the corner of his mouth. He was unconscious.

'Hey, Pete,' I said, 'I think you better help your mate. He seems to have fallen over.'

Pete was gobsmacked. His mouth just hung open and his

eyes were twice their normal size. This was the last thing he'd expected.

'Thank you, gentlemen,' I said, looking round. 'Your support is much appreciated.' I could tell by their reactions that they were pleased, supportive and more than a little surprised. Me? I was just relieved.

Sun Tzu said in *The Art Of War,* 'The key to victory is the ability to use surprise tactics.' He also said, 'He who is prudent and lies in wait for an enemy who is not will be victorious.' No, Marty was not prudent. I once again knew what Sun Tzu said was right and once again I'd reason to thank Li Tie, my martial arts instructor at school. I could hear him deep in my head: 'Don't think, young Master Robinson. Just let it happen. Your subconscious will take the action.'

32

I was a little out of breath after that, recovering from anxiety rather than physical effort, but I was eventually able to settle myself down in the library. As I quietly worked Peter Jackson came and sat at my table. He said nothing; he just sat there and I suddenly realised that we were the only ones in the library. I looked around – nobody. Through the patterned glass panel of the doorway I could see the outline of somebody leaning against it. But I wasn't concerned; Peter wasn't a thug. He was in his fifties, and he had the look of a middle-class gentleman. His orange prison suit seemed to have been tailor made for him and he had a pair of rimless spectacles with fine gold arms. They just looked expensive and sophisticated. I suppose that is an odd thing to say. He never even worked out in the gym and in the exercise yard he was normally surrounded by a small group of acolytes who ran errands for him. He seemed to have a separate existence from the rest of the prisoners and he never demonstrated control or power, just independence.

'Thinking of joining my class, Peter?'

'Actually, I was rather hoping you'd join mine. On the other hand, I've to make a decision about whether to have you eliminated.'

'My word, that sounds a bit drastic.'

'Having killed my front men, Wharton and Wilson, I need a replacement and you and Sergeant seem to be the ideal couple.'

'Why did you send the other two goons after me?'

'Yes, they made a mistake. They thought I'd want you disabled, but that isn't right. I think somebody told them I wanted you disabled, but I think they learned a lesson and I'll arrange for the two who told them to also learn a lesson.'

'Oh I see. That wouldn't be a couple of prison staff would it?'

'Yes, I think we could work together very well, Captain. The only problem I have is you appear to be an enemy of The Family.' He was watching me closely.

'I think you should talk to Randolph Mabry.'

'Yes, I was warned you were probably a Mabry man.'

'Well, he's a boss but not my boss.'

'At the moment I agree, but I'll keep my options open till all's clear. I just find it odd that you ended up here when there are many other prisons where you might have been sent, particularly as you're from London. I find it odd that another military man known to you is here to look after you, also from London. I find it odd that a man you arrested was killed in this prison and he came from, um, yes, London. I find it odd that you killed the killer of that soldier. Not only that; I find it odd that you're such an accomplished fighter. I'd never have dreamed that you could take Marty. I'd even have given odds on him against Sergeant.'

'So, what's your conclusion?'

'Either Mabry placed you in here for some reason that I can't get my head around or somebody else put you in here to gather information about what I've no idea, or it just may be that the world is full of extraordinary coincidences.'

'So why did you order your lead goons to rape me?'

'Oh, that was purely domestic. You were gathering a following and Sergeant is gaining control of The Brothers. With you diminished I thought I could bring over The Brothers and have a nice big happy family.'

'You thought Sergeant would desert me?' I had to smile and Peter Jackson nodded his understanding.

'I did think that might be a problem but one never knows.'

'So did I spoil the party?'

'Not really. I just underestimated you and now I want you as an ally.'

'Supposing I want to replace you?'

'Oh dear! That would be a shame. What I suggest you do is think about my offer.'

'Just out of interest, why did you have Jase killed?'

'Orders and don't ask me who from.'

'Was it just to stop the enquiry?'

'Yes, well, that was my assumption but now I'm not too sure.'

'So what might that have shown?'

'You don't know! Now it never crossed my mind that you didn't know why Jason Phillips killed Michael Carmichael.'

'The evidence showed it was to stop him killing Sergeant Cooper.'

'Yes, Jase was a sharp cookie. But Munro had that covered didn't he? So you didn't really ask why Jase also had a pop?'

He was right. Could Jase have had another motive?

'Are you going to let me into the secret?'

'Well I could but then I'd have to kill you too.'

'That's not very friendly.'

'Let me just say this: It wouldn't have done the Carmichael family any favours, as the bad smell would again pollute the air The Family breathes.' With that, he rose and walked towards the door. He turned, nodded and said, 'I think Jase Phillips did the world a service that day. It was a shame I had to have him killed.' He then turned away and tapped on the door. It opened and he left.

So, Jase knew something and had to be silenced. But what? I would definitely have to start from scratch and look

185

at Carmichael as a killer. But it couldn't be a normal killing; it had to be something that would show him in a very negative light and something that Jase wanted to prevent continuing; something that if exposed would discredit The Family, but why would Jase care? I was sure that he wouldn't care about The Family's reputation so it must have been something else and that something else would also impact The Family. But what? My mind twirled around with lots of ideas but I needed more information.

33

Jacko the librarian tipped me the wink that I was wanted in the interview room. It was the same room as last time. I knocked and entered. The same Sergeant Ayres was there but the inspector had changed. Senior Officer James sat where she'd been before and Sarah was sitting at the table.

'Have a seat please, Jake,' the new man said, indicating the empty chair.

I sat.

'Thank you for agreeing to see us. My name is Redfearn, Detective Inspector David Redfearn. Let me confirm you're Jake Robinson.'

'Yes, I'm Jake Robinson.'

'It is Jake and not Jacob or some other name?'

'Yes, it's Jake. My mother had a thing about liking short names.'

'I think you know all the other people here. You've met Sergeant Ayres before I believe.'

I nodded.

'Jake, I'm going to interview you under caution. I must emphasis you're not under arrest and are free to leave at any time. Do you understand that?'

'I haven't been served with notification of this until now and I've not had time to consult my solicitor. Not only that, the governor has taken action against me relating to the reason you are here and changed my category from B to A. I will refuse all co-operation until that abuse is corrected.'

'Do you wish to take some time to consult your solicitor?'

I looked at Sarah. It was clear that this was in my ballpark so I said, 'Yes. As I have not been found guilty of any offence I wish my solicitor to take action on my behalf.'

Senior Officer James said, 'Please stay here.' She unhooked her radio and was speaking into it as she left the room. Five minutes went by before she returned. 'Please come with me, Jake, your temporary category change has been rescinded and we have to get the tracker removed.'

I left with Senior Officer James and it was removed. We then returned to the interview room.

'I guess we need to start again. As I said, I am Detective Inspector David Redfearn and it appears you have not had the opportunity to consult your solicitor. Do you wish to do that now?'

'Not at the moment, but I reserve the right to consult her at any time before answering any question you may ask me.'

We then went through the whole rigmarole of the caution, the setting up of the tape machine, the time the record was made and everybody saying who they were for voice identification. We then got started.

'Two prisoners have been killed and you're suspected of carrying out that crime. Have you anything to say about that?'

'I've heard that Mr Wharton and Tug Wilson were killed.'

'Jake, please tell me about the events of the twenty third of April.'

'Let me check. That was the day they were killed?'

'Yes.'

'It was midday, the bell went and I finished the morning session with my class.'

'How many in your class, Jake?'

'Let me see, that day there was Arthur, Maniac, George, Dad, Robbo, Johno, Liz, Spider, Little Fred and Big Fred. That's, let me see, ten.'

Sergeant Ayres was making notes. 'Jake, you said Liz?'
There was an enquiry in his voice.

'Yes, Liz.'

'You had a woman in your class?'

'No, no, Liz's name is David Horton. Apparently he
played Elizabeth the First in a play at school and has been
called Liz ever since.'

'Thank you.'

Inspector Redfearn continued. 'So, ten people can vouch
that you were in the classroom at twelve.'

'Well no. Big Fred went to the gym at about a quarter to.'

'So nine saw you there?'

'Yes, Inspector.' He was going to build up a blow-by-blow
picture of my day.

'What happened next?'

'I went to my cell but Officer Moorby was waiting for me
on the landing. He said I've a medical and I had to have a
shower then have the medical that afternoon. It was odd.'

'What was odd?'

'Well, there's nothing wrong with me and if it had been
some routine thing, I'd have been told ages before by my
personal officer.'

'Your personal officer is?'

'Senior Officer James.'

He turned to Senior Officer James and she responded
without being asked. 'There was no routine or special
medical requirement for this prisoner, Inspector.'

'But you booked the appointment, Jake.'

'That's what the governor said, but I didn't.'

'I don't understand. What has the governor got to do
with this?'

'He interviewed me this morning.'

'So you've already been interviewed about this incident?'

'Yes, Inspector.'

He looked pissed off; no, he was pissed off. 'Interview

189

suspended at eleven twenty. Detective Inspector Redfearn leaves the room.'

We waited and it wasn't long before Redfearn returned with a folder and we went through the start procedure again.

'Let me just pick up the theme, Jake. You were told to take a shower because you were due to have a medical. What happened next?'

'I went for a shower.'

'What, straight away?'

'Well, no; I collected my washing gear and got myself ready and went for a shower.'

'Did you speak to anybody else?'

'I'm not sure. Yes, I did. I spoke to Harry, my cell-mate. I think I told him I was going for a shower and I had a medical, I think.'

'You're not sure?'

'Not really. I know I spoke to him so I suppose it was about the medical or the shower.'

'Why did you go for a shower?'

'Because I was told to.'

'Who by?'

'Officer Moorby.' God, this was tedious but thorough. I don't know if he realised it, but he was nailing Moorby.

'You went to the shower room. Did you see anybody else?'

'Probably. It's a bit difficult not to in here.'

'I suppose it is. Can you think of anybody you saw?'

'Oh yes, I saw Russ Hotten. He was with Quinny. And I saw Officers Moorby and Manson. They were leaning on the landing rail outside the blue room.'

'The blue room?'

'Yes, the bathrooms.'

'The bathrooms are called the blue room?'

'Yes.'

'So, they watched you go in?'

'Yes and they watched me come out.'

'Hadn't they moved then?'

'Oh, yes, they were on the landing on the other side of the cellblock looking across at the bathrooms. Like they were waiting for something.'

'Did you see anybody else when you came out?'

'Only about twenty people. Do you want me to try and name them?'

'No, not now, but perhaps later. We'll also talk to a whole range of people and build the picture. You told the governor this morning that you saw nobody else in the showers.' He was reading the governor's notes. 'You stand by what you said to the governor?'

'Yes.'

'You don't mention the scream.' I wondered how he knew about the scream. It hadn't come up in the governor's interview.

'I wasn't asked about a scream.'

'So, I'm asking you now.'

'I heard a scream.'

'And?'

'And what?'

'Didn't you go and look?'

'Are you completely daft, Inspector?'

He looked at me, working it through in his head. 'No, given the environment, I'd probably ignore it too. So who do you think killed Wharton and Wilson?' He'd made a change in his questioning that was unexpected.

Sarah moved forward in her seat and I signalled that it was okay. She leaned back again. She now trusted me.

'I think it's obvious.'

'Obvious?' He clearly didn't comprehend anything obvious.

'Officers Moorby and Manson.'

Redfearn smiled. 'Obvious. Why don't I find it obvious?'

191

'Because you're ether suffering from myopia or prejudice.'

'I see; I'm a short-sighted bigot.'

'I wouldn't be that impolite.'

'Tell me about the myopia and bigotry.'

'You, like your previous colleague, assume the murder has to have been done by a prisoner here. Then he found out that Officer Manson had given him information that wasn't one-hundred per cent correct.'

Redfearn looked at Sergeant Ayres, who nodded.

Inspector Redfearn was a very bright and socially aware man. 'Let me try again. Why would Officers Moorby and Manson murder Wharton and Wilson?'

'That I don't know, but you seem to have a reason for me killing Wharton and Wilson.'

'Only because you were there.' He stopped and shook his head. 'And Moorby and Manson were there as well.'

The sergeant had opened another file and pointed at a page that the inspector read. It had to be the file on the killing of Ratty.

'Your conclusion, Inspector?'

'If I remove my prejudice you may be right. I'll have to check it out. What would you do?'

'I'd check it out.'

'How?' Strangely enough, at that time, it didn't seem odd that he asked me that question.

'Let me see. My cell was searched. My training room is probably being searched now. A couple of your officers are probably building a picture of my movements on that day and today, probably by interpreting the computer records. They say they're not recorded but I don't believe that and anyway there are the CCTV records. It might be useful to do to Moorby and Manson what you're doing to me.'

He looked at me hard and long. He was wondering and I knew what he was wondering. Was I just wriggling? Did I know something? Was I trying to set these officers up? But he knew as I knew that he was going to act and he would have to act fast.

Minutes later, he closed the interview. I asked to stay and talk to my brief and Senior Officer James agreed to that and took Sarah and me to another room. I assumed that the two prison officers would be interviewed now and the search carried out.

34

As soon as the door closed Sarah said, 'What game are you playing, Jake?'

'I need you to do a couple of things. Get hold of Barrow – '

'You mean Sir Barrow Jones?'

'You have it in one. I want information on Peter Jackson – who has contacted him and his visitors – and his relationship to The Family?'

'Do I need to know about his family?'

'No, not *his* family, *The* Family. I best tell you but remember this is strictly confidential. Not just client privilege stuff; this is really secret. It'll be good for you to know what you may be up against or just involved with. Okay?'

She looked intrigued. 'Okay, Jake. Secret it is.'

'But, when I've told you and perhaps you want out then that's okay, but you don't tell anybody because it could cost you your life and perhaps mine.'

'Are you just trying me on, Jake.' I started to laugh.

'Has Keith told you anything?'

'Well, he sort of said you're into some pretty dodgy stuff. Okay, I'm in.'

'Let me sort this out for you. Talk to Keith; he might be a bit annoyed at me for telling you these things but I don't think I've a choice. There's a high-powered criminal family and it has members right across the ruling elite of the UK. I've only had contact with a small and very powerful part of it. Let me go over what we do know. Mike Munro and Jase Phillips killed Major Carmichael and that was how I got involved. The case was thrown out due to evidence tampering. Double jeopardy was invoked and there was a retrial. Jase Phillips got sent here and Mike Munro was dismissed from the service. Jase Phillips was murdered here. Okay so far?'

'Yes.'

'The case was a stitch-up.'

'Yes, I know about the court martial and the double jeopardy. I expect it'll become a classic case study. Are you sure it was a stitch-up?'

'Is the Pope a Catholic?'

'How?'

'A better question is by whom and why?'

'Okay. By whom and why?'

'By The Right Honourable Antony Bray, the cousin of the major.'

'Oh, do come on, Jake.'

'They were brought up together, went to school together, went to university together and took the same degree. Then the brainy one went into politics and the sporty one went into the army. Bray was a minister in the Home Office.'

'Yes, I know, but you don't do this just because he's your cousin.'

'Right. You do this to stop the information getting out that your cousin was a drug addict and a crap officer.'

'But he was a hero; everybody says so.'

'Yes, everybody says so, so the image has to be maintained.'

'I'm struggling. Why does the image have to be maintained?'

'Because they're members of The Family.'

'So they're in the same family; I still don't understand.'

'No, not just in the same family; members of The Family.'

'You're baffling me with words. *The Family*?'

'Right. Rupert Carmichael is the Earl of Charnforth and the present head of The Family. I won't go into history but it's a close-knit, very powerful, political, economic and criminal family.'

'Whoa, just wait one minute, Jake. Do I look green? You're telling me that Rupert Carmichael, one of the most respected men in this country, is head of a criminal family?'

'Yes. Alongside their legitimate businesses of natural gas, tin, insurance and banking, they're into some iffy stuff, part legit and part criminal, such as silver, diamonds from the Marange, diamond fields in Zimbabwe, gambling and, at the extreme, money laundering and drugs.'

'By drugs you mean...?'

'Cocaine and heroin.'

'But they can't be.'

'Try this for size; Rupert Carmichael introduced Penelope Whitehaven, the daughter of an American billionaire, to George Mabry. The Mabrys and Carmichaels have previous family links. The next Mabry to be produced was Randolph Mabry. Rumour has it that Randolph Mabry is actually Rupert Carmichael's son. He runs the drugs, silver, immigration and commodities.'

'You're saying that Randolph Mabry, the Home Secretary, is his illegitimate son and also a criminal?'

'More than that; he's half-brother to Michael Carmichael.'

Sarah was looking at me and I could see the wheels turning. 'So, Phillips and Munro kill Michael Carmichael, they get off, Antony Bray, Carmichael's cousin, cooks the books, there's a retrial and Phillips goes to prison. Munro shoots Bray and is shot by the police at the scene. Sir Nicolas Ross, Keith and you are going to challenge the case against Phillips and that will open a whole can of worms so Phillips is killed here.' She stopped and was thinking again. 'Sir Barrow Jones; you work for him?'

'I do.'

'So you're undercover here?'

'Yes.'

'I thought so, the way Keith talks about you. And The Family tried to kill you? Is it Mabry who ordered that?'

'No, not Mabry, he owes me some favours.'

'Christ, Jake, what for? No, I don't want to know.'

'I'm just giving you an overview so you understand the depth of stuff we're into, okay. You have the message. The Family man in here is Peter Jackson. He intimated that Carmichael was not killed to save the platoon. Well, he was but that was just an opportunity for Jase Phillips. Jase wanted to kill Carmichael for some other reason, but I don't yet know what.'

'Got it. Can I ask some other things?'

'You can ask.'

'You said that Mabry owes you some favours.'

'Yes.'

'Can I ask what for?'

'I'll tell you but if you ever leak what I tell you I'll have to kill you.'

'You're not joking are you?'

'It may sound like that, but no.'

'Keith said I would be the key liaison to Sir Barrow, so I best find out.'

'Are you sure?'

She nodded. 'I know you were the one that actually killed Bray; Munro couldn't. This can't be worse than knowing that.'

'Okay. I rescued Mabry's daughter in Bolivia.'

'But he's not married.'

'True.'

'So he has an illegitimate daughter.'

'Right.'

'That's not so bad.' She stopped and said, 'That isn't it. Was it rape then?'

'Good Lord, no. It's much more damaging than that.'

'What, for goodness sake?' She was irritable, probably the stress of having her picture of the world turned upside-down.

'His daughter is a nun and her mother is a Mother Superior.'

'This is no time for silly bloody jokes, Jake.' She was looking at me. 'Oh Christ! It's true, isn't it?'

'Just imagine what his enemies and the press would do with that information.'

'Christ, Jake, why the hell did you tell me this?'

'Ah, sexy solicitor, you now know what you may be in the middle of and won't talk to anybody, will you?'

She shook her head then tipped it on one side, thinking. 'Can you prove this?'

'Um no, the public evidence is circumstantial.'

'How do you know then?'

'I got involved with the Mabry's part of The Family when in Bolivia. It was all about gas contracts, silver and drugs and I know that what I've outlined is fact.'

Sarah was just looking at me with wide-open eyes. 'You were involved with a criminal gang in Bolivia. Are you pulling my leg? In the past couple of minutes I've heard enough stuff to make Ian Fleming's *Goldfinger* sound like a second-rate criminal turd and you like a James Bond.'

'I'm just telling you like it is.'

'You're just telling me that most of the people ruling this *Sceptred Isle* are criminals, and nuns have babies and the father is the Home Secretary. Jake, I want you to be sane.'

'Look! Powerful people look after powerful people. Honest, powerful people need allies, particularly those with political clout.'

'I don't believe it. No, I do believe it, I just don't want to.'

'Okay, let's look at another wing of The Family. Harvey Cannon, the city guy; have you heard of him?'

'Vaguely. My brother was at university with his son or maybe it was his grandson.'

'He married Rupert Carmichael's sister, Bethany. This guy, Harvey Cannon, is Duke of Bartonshire. He's a big wig in the financial world of investment, venture capital and the like. He currently manages the financial and business end of The Family. Mainly legitimate but the rumour is they've a large holding in gambling throughout Europe and the Far East and he does a little money laundering and banking for various syndicates.'

'But he's not in the government.'

'He's in the House of Lords.'

'Why did you just tell me about Harvey Cannon?'

'Just to give you a feel of the extent of The Family.'

She was shaking her head and at the same time, her powerful intellect was processing the information. I stayed silent.

'Christ, Jake, Mabry can't be a criminal.'

'I was in Bolivia with Frances; she was our section head. Mabry was in Bolivia. Remember, Mabry is the political and muscle end of The Family. He's the link with the Mafia and the Bolivians. In Bolivia he was doing a big deal with the Bolivians and the Mafia on oil, gas and drugs. It was his Mafia contacts that killed Frances by injecting her with some weird disease.'

Sarah was shaking her head.

'Okay?' I asked.

She nodded. 'How close are you?'

'To whom? To what?'

'This Family lot.'

'As I said, some members owe me favours.'

'Including two nuns?'

'Yes. The way I see it they owe me favours.'

'No wonder you're in prison, Jake.'

I just couldn't help smiling.

199

'But Mabry is the Home Secretary.'

'My word, Sarah, you've good general knowledge and are repeating yourself.'

She smiled. 'I mean, you're saying that the Home Secretary is a criminal.'

'Well, what I'm saying is that he has a lot of very dodgy people working for him, but I bet you'd be hard pressed to tie them in directly. From his political position he can, of course, ensure that the empire is well directed and he has some senior police officers who, shall we say, do little jobs for him.'

'But this is outrageous.' She was now bristling.

I laughed at her naivety. She misread my laugh and said, 'You're pulling my leg.'

'I wish I was. Now cut along and see Sir Barrow Jones for me. Remember, I want information on Peter Jackson: who has contacted him, his visitors and his relationship to The Family.'

'Yes, okay, you bastard.' There was a slight edginess in her now. She rang the bell and Senior Officer James came in to escort her out of the prison.

35

Senior Officer James came in. 'You're going in the hole I'm afraid, Jake.'

'The hole?'

'The governor has concerns so you'll be placed in a cell close to the sick bay and put on suicide watch.'

'He thinks I'm a suicide risk?'

'No, it's just a way of isolating you, keeping an eye on you and avoiding putting you in the segregation unit.'

'What you mean is it avoids the proper recorded process.'

'That's right, Jake.' Sarah took a step forward.

'No, Sarah, it's okay.' I turned to Officer James, 'Wonderful; do I get fed first?'

'Haven't you eaten?'

'No and I expect the police haven't eaten either and nor has Sarah here.'

'Let's get that fixed first then, Jake.' She made a call on her radio.

Officer James led the way to the dining room, stomping along in front of us. There was no way that she could walk; her legs were made for stomping. We followed her towards the dining hall and I was humming the tune to the Nancy Sinatra song, 'These boots were made for walking'.

Sarah gave me a poke in the ribs, and said, 'I know what you're thinking, Jake Robinson,' and she laughed quietly.

We arrived just seconds before the police officers, and they joined Sarah, Officer James and me. They really should have sat at another table but they seemed quite happy to sit with us. Well, I was the one they shouldn't sit with.

It was odd how all institutional kitchens smelled of boiled cabbage. I don't suppose they boil more cabbage per cubic metre of space than the average house but by some mysterious, institutional means, boiled cabbage permeates the atmosphere and then is wafted through the whole building.

'How's the investigation going, Inspector?'

'You know I can't tell you that, Jake.'

'No, I suppose not.'

'What's the food like here?'

'Toni's on at the moment so it should be fantastic.'

'He's a good cook then?'

'Toni was one of the best chefs in London. He was at The Langham when they arrested him. He can make baked beans taste heavenly.'

With that, a couple of trustees arrived with sausage and mash with onion gravy and baked beans.

'See, he's even done beans for you.'

Each plate was identical and a delight to observe. In the centre of the table was placed a mustard bowl.

'He also makes his own mustard,' said Officer James.

We all ate in silence until one of the officers said, 'I know I shouldn't ask but what's he in for?'

'Multiple homicide; he was a serial killer. You'll be pleased to know he hasn't killed anyone since he's been in here. Well, perhaps he has but nobody's been able to pin anything on him.'

'Oh,' said the constable.

Another asked, 'How did he kill people then?'

'You really want to know?'

'Um, Yes.' He didn't sound too sure.

'Toni poisoned his family, his wife's family and a lot of people related to him and friends of his dad.'

There was a shocked silence. You could feel the tension

in the air and everybody but Officer James and me had stopped eating. They were all wondering if I was telling the truth.

'You're joking, right?' said the young police constable.

'No,' said Officer James. 'Toni can make poisons out of innocuous ingredients.' Officer James and I continued to eat and Sarah was tentatively picking at her food. The others were silent, looking at me, when Toni came out of the kitchen. He looked around the table.

'Jake's told you why I'm in here then.'

There was a silence.

'Well, they did ask, Toni.'

'Let me tell you folks, Jake probably told you the truth but not the whole truth. I only killed those who abused me as a child and those that knew and did nothing. What you have folks is the best sausage and mash you're ever going to get and the other thing I bet he didn't tell you was I only poisoned puddings.' He laughed and went back towards the kitchen.

'Is it true he only poisoned puddings?'

'I'm pleased to report that's what he says and what the evidence says,' said Officer James.

'Ah well,' said the inspector, 'it's too late now and he's right; this is the best sausage and mash I'm ever likely to have.' With that, he tucked in and the others continued to tentatively eat what was in front of them.

'We don't let him make puddings, though, just in case.'

'That's a shame. I was going to have some treacle pudding,' said the inspector, pointing at the menu board.

'Oh, you can if you like. Mac made that. Dab hand at treacle pudding is Mac; Toni taught him,' I said.

'Sod it,' said the young constable. 'I'll have some; it's got to be better than the stuff at the factory.'

Officer James got a call on her radio. 'Jake, it's been decided that you can go back to your cell.'

203

I looked at the inspector. He shrugged his shoulders. 'It's amazing what a search can reveal, Jake.' He smiled a wry smile and shook his head. He still wasn't sure he had the information. His instinct was telling him one thing and the evidence was saying another.

'Thank you, Inspector.'

I was walking back to my cell when Tom, the finder, appeared at my side. He'd a way of coming up to you sideways so it looked like he was just walking past but was in fact closing with you. He spoke out of the side of his mouth, a trait I associated with borstal and the like.

'You wanted to know about visitors, Captain.'

'Uh ha.'

'Jase had some normal visits but only one of interest: a woman, named Celia Foley. She's a "Ms" and the address was Bulford, Wiltshire: a military address. I asked a friend to do some digging. It would seem the address indicated that she was a military cop. She visited him twice.'

'Might be a girlfriend.'

'Might be, Captain. The other visitors for Mr Wharton were just his normal routine ones. You want to know why Jase was bumped off don't you, Captain.'

'Yes I do, Tom.'

'If I was you, Captain, I wouldn't try to find out.'

'Why not, Tom?'

'I've a feeling that it's pretty heavy.' With that, he wheeled away from me. I just wondered if there was information available or whether Tom was reading between the lines.

36

A couple of days later, I climbed the stairs to our cell and was knackered. And why shouldn't I be? I had worked hard with my group of ne'er-do-wells and they were doing just great. The difference in such a short time from their disinterest, was amazing; interest was something they hadn't previously dared to show through the distrust; I had been a policeman so distrust of me was natural – what convicted criminal would like a policeman, even one who's in prison? Some clung to their old tried and tested views, but some shifted their views as they noticed the dissimilarity with other approaches and they discerned that they were actually learning. Then they discovered that I was actually human in their terms. Now they gave me great difficulties. They were demanding of me to help them and I was struggling. Yes, I could read and write, but how to help them? I had developed an approach and a plan but I lacked teaching experience. They knew that and some were actually making allowances, but it was hard, very hard, as I hadn't studied English since I was at school and while I knew what to do, almost as an instinct, explaining the English language was difficult. So, back to my cell to plough on through *The English Way*, a book I had found in the prison library first published in 1925, but I had the 1958 edition. Mind you, I did have *Strictly English* by Simon Heffer, which I had selected because in the preliminary notes it had a heading that said 'A word about sex'. In my ignorance, I jumped to the conclusion that this would interest my sex-starved students only to discover that it was all about gender in the English language. Still, I found it a great book and I found *The Penguin Guide to Punctuation* a godsend, not for my students but for me. I had never really thought about punctuation until I was faced with the problem of whether to use a comma or a semicolon and how to explain it. I know that probably sounds daft but until you have to explain something you just do it, often without knowing why.

When I got to our cell Harry was sitting on his bunk and we had a visitor who was introduced to me as Mo. I had seen him around but never actually spoken to him, but I knew his name. Mo (I assumed his name was actually Mohammed as he looked to be of Pakistani decent; well, more likely than Indian, given the assumption about his name) was a lawyer; well, he had been. Apparently he'd been offered the teaching job I had inherited but the Caucasian and Afro-Caribbean prisoners had rejected him so that was that then. I understood his problem, as I was also an untouchable as an ex-policeman.

Mo was tall, dark, bald and skinny. He wore large glasses perched on his nose through which his black eyes peered under thick eyebrows and over his long hooked nose.

Harry explained the situation. Mo wanted advice. He was in Peasmarsh as a Cat B prisoner. He claimed he was innocent, set up by some CID detectives because he'd been the solicitor for a series of groups of Pakistanis accused of a range of crimes, including drug offences and sex offences, as well as the procurement of young girls, and they'd been defended successfully so the CID had him on conspiracy. He'd been a pain to the CID and as the accused had different barristers it had to be him putting in some form of fix, so they fixed him. Seemed unlikely to me, as I had only ever been a military policeman, but I had been involved with the Jason Phillips case and that was in my view a grave miscarriage of justice. Well, the second case was, and the first one would have been if I hadn't been around as the investigating officer and acting for the defence. I could have been in serious trouble if Corporal Mike Munro hadn't pleaded guilty at the second trial and as part of the deal got me exonerated even though I'd done nothing wrong. However, from the evidence I had, neither had Mike.

'Mo, you're a lawyer and I was a policeman; I can't imagine how I can help you.'

'Perhaps not, Jake, but I want you to listen to me so that I can get my head around the problem.'

'Why me?'

'Oh, simple: you kill people. It's obviously you, yet the police can't nail you. The guys in your class say you listen to them and I need that. I've tried talking to other people in here, to my solicitor and to my barrister, and they aren't helpful to my thinking. I just want to think clearly but my thinking is muddled and one of your guys says you can do tricks with the mind and it helps thinking.'

I really wasn't sure about that but Harry was nodding.

'Mo, you can't believe all you hear. I'll listen but I won't even pretend I can find solutions to whatever problem you have.'

'I understand that.'

'Okay, fire away.'

'I was charged and found guilty of conspiracy. The conspiracy I was accused of was to, with others, produce false evidence in court so my clients would be found not guilty. Also, to conspire with others to intimidate witnesses for the prosecution and in one case suborn a juror and another was the kidnap of a child. I didn't do these things.'

'It would be easy to have you charged with those things, but did they happen in practice even though you'd nothing to do with them?'

207

'Probably.'

'You don't know they did, you just suspect they did?'

'I suspect they did but I think that in one case the police were the ones who arranged the perjury and then accused me of conspiring and then stating that the person's child had been kidnaped and got the person off.'

'Remind me of what conspiracy is.'

'Under section one of the Criminal Law Act 1977, it's an offence if a person agrees with any other person or persons that a course of conduct shall be pursued which, if the agreement is carried out in accordance with their intentions, results in the commission of an offence.'

Okay, he wasn't a rubbish lawyer; he knew his stuff.

'So the offence in this case is perjury.'

'No, well yes, but it goes further. The conspiracy I was accused of included the suborning of witnesses.'

'Am I right in saying that is to persuade someone to tell lies in a court of law or to do something else that's illegal, especially for money?'

'Yes, I was accused of bribery, and witnesses for the prosecution claimed I had done that and the police claimed I had agreed to do that in conjunction with my clients who were on remand, and that's conspiracy, but real evidence isn't required for conspiracy. I didn't do these things. Lies were told against me. You don't have to be seen talking to a co-conspirator or taking part in any action as is normal in a criminal case; it relies on common sense deductions that the jury can accept. I was lied about.'

I was confused. I wasn't sure whether it was because I didn't fully understand or it was the way Mo was telling me things. Let's have another go. 'So, some witnesses claimed you tried to bribe them or did bribe them. This would have occurred at some regular meeting such as your conversations with your clients or defence witnesses, so nothing odd would appear such as meeting in a pub, for example. One of the instances was the kidnap of a child.'

He nodded.

'How were you stuck with that one?'

'Well, a child was supposedly kidnapped. I was accused of telling the child's mother that unless her brother changed his evidence the child would be killed.'

'Was the child kidnapped?'

'I don't know.'

'Did the uncle change his evidence?'

'Yes.'

'Do you know why he changed his evidence?'

'No.'

'What do you think?'

'I think there were two options. Either there was a kidnap and the guy was got at and changed his evidence and the police got him to say that I told him what to say in the first place or it was some scam to get me by the police and there was no kidnap.'

'What about co-conspirators?'

'They were my clients according to the police.'

'So they were charged with conspiracy?'

'Yes.'

'Convicted?'

'Yes.'

'All of them?'

'No. One of them got off.'

'Why?'

'He gave evidence against me and the police claimed he worked with them. He was found guilty but got a suspended sentence.'

'Sources of evidence?'

'There were three; all had convictions and all were said to have talked to the people I was acting for and had been given information by the accused.'

209

'There must have been an enquiry into this when you used it as your defence.'

'Oh, there was and the police came out whiter than white.'

'Why do you think that was the case?'

'I was a pain and I had been eliminated; if anything had been found against the police officers they would be in here and I would still be a pain out there.'

I believed him. On a number of occasions I had rock solid evidence and then one of the prosecution witnesses became flaky and the case started to slip away and some of the solicitors and occasionally barristers were kind of dodgy, but you'd never be able to prove it.

'Were there any other things you were accused of?'

'Yes, they said I had hacked into a computer and stole information.'

'Do you have those skills?'

He looked at the floor.

'Problem?'

'Yes, I've those skills, but I said I didn't and the police witness showed in court that I did.'

'So, you didn't tell the truth under oath?'

'Yes, I didn't tell the truth.'

'I can understand why, but you must have known that to be found out would guarantee your conviction.'

'Yes, I was stupid.'

'Let me now see if I can help.'

'Thank you, Jake.' He looked so pleased I thought he was going to cry.

'Tell me what you see as the problem.'

'Well, I can't get anyone to believe me.'

'So you believe you're not believable?'

'Well, yes, I suppose that's the basis really.'

'Why aren't you believed?'

'Well, because I was found guilty.'

210

'And?'

'And I lied under oath.'

I had met this so often: people who don't tell the truth because they think it will go against them, so they lie and then it definitely does go against them.

'You can't change that.'

'No, but that's what I want to change.'

So, Mo was caught in an emotional bind and he thought it was about him as a person. Let's make things concrete.

'So, what is it you want to achieve?'

'To be believed.'

'To achieve what?'

'Get released?'

'So, your goal is to get released, and what will you need to achieve that?'

'Be believed.'

'And what rock solid thing will mean that people will believe you?'

'Get evidence, I suppose.'

Great, he got there.

'And what have you done so far to do that?'

'Nothing really.'

'Tell me about "nothing really".'

'I don't know.'

'Do you know the names of the people who gave evidence against you?'

'Yes.'

'What else?'

'I know the evidence they gave.'

'What else do you know?'

'I know the names of the police involved.'

'So, I'm hearing you've a load of information that we've just scratched the surface of. We know that's part of an evidence chain and that you've much more information towards your goal of being released. I'll give you one simple piece of advice at this stage; stick to that goal. Don't go for any revenge goals such as having police charged or other stuff. Stay clean and focussed. And forget about trying to be believed; belief is an emotional thing, facts that can be verified and chains of evidence are the only way out of your problem.'

He nodded; he understood. I saw a spark of clarity that revenge would just get in the way of his goal.

'So, what else have you done so far towards your goal?'

'Nothing really.'

'Nothing really?'

'Well, I've talked to some people.'

'For what purpose?'

He sat and looked at me. He was thinking; he shook his head. He'd understood something. 'I wanted them to believe me.' He stopped and thought about what he had said. 'I need a plan, don't I?'

'Yes. You need a plan to take you to your goal. A plan that uses the resources you have. And what are the resources you have?'

'I've information but I need more and I've people who will help me.'

'Who?'

'My family, friends, some colleagues.'

'What else?'

Again, he just looked at me. He shook his head.

'What about you?'

'Me?' He thought for a moment. 'I'm a lawyer, I know the law, so I know what information I need and I know who can get some of that, and...' Again he just sat and looked at me.

'And?' I queried.

'I need a plan.' He was nodding. 'I have a clear goal so I need a plan to get there.'

Good, he knew what he wanted to achieve and he knew he needed a plan to achieve it and he knew he'd the resources available to him and I hoped he realised that his

212

negative emotions had been getting in the way of achieving that.

'And the outcome of the plan will be what?'

'Getting out of here.'

'Tell me about a plan.'

'Well, I need a goal and I've got that. I need to specify what I have to do by when.'

'You doing that?'

'Ah, yes, and I need other people to do things, so I have to find those people and what they have to do by when.'

'So what is the main thing you are doing at this stage?'

'I suppose it is gathering information.'

'What information?'

'Who was doing what by when? So that tells me I have to have researchers and, yes, like detectives. What the results of that are? Structure it and that will tell me the action points. And the order of those action points and who will do them.'

'As soon as you move into action what will happen?'

'They will know and they will counter attack.'

'Who are they?'

'The police and the people who support them.'

'So what will you need?'

'A better attacking force.'

'Who will your force attack?'

'Ah, yes. I need to identify my enemies.'

'And I need a cup of tea.'

'Thank you, Jake.' He laughed. 'Your guys were right; you do have a clear way of looking at things. I'll get released and I'll repay you for this half hour. I'm sure you've saved my life. Thank you.'

I thought that was a bit over the top but there you go.

He got up and shook my hand then headed out the door with his head high and his shoulders square; he knew he had something to do and he had a massive amount of drive to do it. Harry was looking at me.

213

'Well?' I asked.

'You're just something else, Captain. I'll put the kettle on.'

37

'Hello, Micky.' I didn't really know Micky, I'd just seen him around. He was clearly in emotional pain. Should I ignore it or ask him? Well, he was sitting in my classroom, so I suppose he wanted to talk to me. Oh, shit.

'What's the matter?'

'I was talking to Mo and he said you could help.'

'With what?'

'It's my wife.'

'What's "It's my wife"?'

'She's having a baby.'

Now I knew he was in trouble. I'd have to take care what I said next; he had been in here for at least three years.

'Tell me.'

'It's due, well, soon.'

'Can you get compassionate leave so you can be with her?'

'It's not mine for fuck's sake.'

I knew I would have to be careful and I'd cocked up already.

'Tell me more.'

'Like what?'

'Do you love her?' I can ask some really daft questions sometimes.

'Yes, I fucking love her.'

'Does she love you?'

'I s'pose. She says she does.' He was now looking down with his shoulders hunched, looking at his clenched hands

215

in his lap. 'She writes to me, she visits me, she makes DVDs and sends them.'

'What's on the DVDs?'

'Well, the kids and stuff.'

'Do you write to her and talk when she's visiting?'

'I don't write; I'm not good at writing. I see her at visiting but I don't know what to say. She tells me about her work and the garden and the kids and my mum.'

'So you have other kids?'

'Two of them: Sue and Gill?'

'That's good.'

'Before you ask they're mine and, yes, I know they are.'

'That's good then.' I didn't know what he wanted from me, perhaps just to talk to somebody. 'She loves you.'

'Yes, I said so, didn't I? She says she does.' He was angry and hurt and I wasn't handling this very well.

'What do you think?'

'I think she loves me.' I could hear the uncertainty in his voice. He wanted this woman despite her having somebody else's baby. It was the uncertainty that was tearing him apart and the pain he was feeling, perhaps the disloyalty, maybe the affront to his manhood – all of that shit.

'Micky, look at me.' He raised his misery torn face. 'Why do you think that?'

He went quiet and was thinking. He wasn't quite crying but he was on the verge. He looked down again.

'Well, she writes and stuff. I think... I think she can, can't she? She... Well, you know.' That didn't make any sense to me; the emotion was creating confusion.

'Micky, look at me.' He looked up. 'Micky, I don't know. Please tell me.'

'She was screwing with this, this arsehole.' There was bitterness in his voice.

'You know him then?'

'Yes, I fucking know him.' There was contempt in Micky's voice now.

'And?'

'He is a real snidey creep.' The anger and hate was clear. 'The bastard's done this before when a guy gets banged up; you know, he goes round all sympathetic and helpful, and all that shit. Helps with the social security and stuff like the computer, you know, getting stuff online, and fixes things what are busted and then he shags them.'

'Micky, why are you telling me?'

'Cos I want to know what to do.'

'Do about what?'

'This shit bag, that's what.'

'What do you want to do?'

'I want to kill him.'

'And if you do, what then?'

He was thinking about it and his head dropped again. 'I end up back in here.'

'Is that a good idea then?'

'No, it ain't.'

'What about the baby?'

'She wants to keep it.'

'Why?'

His head came up and he glowered at me. 'I don't fucking know. I asked her to have an abortion and she said she couldn't kill a baby and now she doesn't want to have it adopted.'

'Okay, so let me see what we have here. Your wife wants you back because she loves you. You love her and you have two kids who need a dad and a mum. Your wife has another one, so you'll have three kids and nobody need know the baby isn't yours. Is that the situation?'

'Sort of, but I want to get the greasy shit.'

'What about your mates?'

'I would have to tell them.'

217

'And you don't want to?'

'No, well I can't, can I?' Logic was making a break-through. This was a proud man and he was feeling responsible for what his wife had done. I could relate to his pain.

'So when do you get out?'

'In a couple of years.'

'Let me see. You can sit in here and be miserable and depressed or you can make the best of it. The other options are to take action against this guy in a couple of years or get your mates to take action now. The problem with that is you could end up back in here or your mates can and you get extra time as an accessory.'

'What would you do?'

'I'm different from you so what I would do is irrelevant, but if I were you I would talk to my wife and work something out so that the pair of you can get on with your lives. You, your wife, your kids and your mum are the important ones here.'

'I s'pose.' He was nodding. He seemed to be more balanced. 'Can I come and talk to you again?'

'Only after you've talked to your wife and found out what she wants.'

'Okay, Captain, I'll do that.' He left. I wasn't sure I'd done any good but then again, I wasn't an agony aunt.

38

My second visit was approaching and I was having difficulty in suppressing my excitement. There'd been a leak somewhere along the chain of command and prisoners were trying to get their visiting day changed so they could see Sam. Crazy things happen in prison. The rumours of her beauty were rife if a bit over the top. I just wondered what the partners of the prisoners would think when they saw the reaction of their beloved ones. Then I got a message that turned everything upside-down; somebody was coming with her. The other odd thing that happened was that prisoners, most of whom I'd had no contact with, were sitting or standing close to me. It was most odd. It was almost as if I had some magic dust that would brush off onto them just because I had a beautiful girlfriend. I recognised they wanted to share in seeing Sam as if being close to me might result in that miracle. I supposed that sexual deprivation is a massive problem in prisons and undoubtedly, led to homosexual behaviours and that was destructive for all concerned. The thing that was clear to me was the extreme level of homophobia in this prison despite the high level of homosexual behaviour between heterosexuals. Clearly, what was happening because of Sam's suggested beauty was the creating of a psychosexual imbalance that I suppose was different for each prisoner.

The day came and both Bennie and I went down to the visitors' suite (the word 'suite' was a strange word to use for this bare, austere, over-videoed room). Bennie was at the table to the right of mine. I knew he'd fixed this but I didn't know why or how; I suppose Family men could just fix things. I sat watching the door. The tension was tangible. I was sure that if I closed my hands in this room I would catch a handful of tension and I knew it would be like being hit with an electrical charge. I could feel every nerve in my body stretching and tingling with that tension. Then the door opened and the tension shifted to expectation mixed with concern, a concern that the expectation wouldn't be realised. This to me was the real dehumanisation of prison, the ripping asunder of our innermost emotions. And they came in like a chain gang of people seeking that which they longed for: the person that had meaning in their lives.

I saw Micky with, I assumed, his wife. She was at least eight months pregnant and had a girl of about six or seven with her. She clearly adored him. You could see it in every look and every move. She flicked her hair and slowly stroked her neck while maintaining eye contact and she was quite oblivious to the fact she was doing it. He was talking to her and she placed her elbows on the table, then one hand on top of the other, her chin on her hands and her face directly to him. She was listening and admiring him. He was admiring her.

I looked back at the door. Sam hadn't come. I was so tense I thought my very blood would boil. Control, Jake, control; don't let the emotion explode. And then she was there and I wanted to cry. I could feel the tears and I fought them back. My throat contracted and my mouth went dry. Sam was there. She was a goddess of beauty; she moved like silk across a round polished beam: smooth, shimmering, undulating flawless perfection in motion. I saw nothing but Sam, tunnel vision; there was only Sam, my Sam, and she was looking at me and she was smiling and I was hit by a range of different emotions at once: relief, love, joy, exultancy, pride. I thought my chest would burst and my head was spinning.

I loathed my job and I hated those that had helped me to get into this hellhole. I despised myself for coming here and being damaged, for it was then that I knew I was damaged and I knew unless I controlled it I would drift into a place that I didn't want to be. And now the light of my life was walking towards me and I knew all eyes were on her and all those men wanted her and I knew she was mine and I would kill to keep her.

It was then that I saw the woman with Sam and I returned to the real world and really saw her for the first time. I'd never met the woman with her; she was smart and attractive. She had fine, dark-brown hair brushed straight back from her high forehead, falling almost to her shoulders with a slight inward curl at the ends. She had pale skin with an ivory sheen at her high cheekbones and a gentle, natural, pink blush on her cheeks. Her eyes were deepest green, a startling colour, wide apart and lightly made-up with a faint blue. Her nose was straight, perhaps slightly long for a fashion model, but she'd a mouth most girls would pine for and most men would want to kiss. It was broad with full lips, finely etched and using exactly the right colour lipstick for her skin tone. Her chin detracted slightly from the near perfection of the rest of her face, being a little sharp. She moved smoothly, following Sam. She knew how to walk; it was the sort of walk taught in ballet schools and clearly she was fit and looked it, with her high bust and tight backside that was firm and rounded. Yes, she had what might be called a faultless, athletic body.

How prison had screwed me up and screwed up all the other men in this room who watched these two models of beauty move smoothly, definitely and gracefully towards my position.

Sam sat first and smiled. We didn't speak, we just looked at each other and that was all we needed.

'Jake,' a voice said.

'Hi.' I didn't know her name.

'It's a bit like being in a goldfish bowl in here, isn't it?'

Both Sam and I laughed. Normality washed over us as our vision moved from each other to notice the eyes in the room focused on us (well, on Sam and this new woman) and as we looked around the embarrassed and furtive looked away and some just stared.

'I'm Petal,' said the new vision.

'Aha.' Well, what do you say when you want to be polite but wished the person wasn't there?

'I work at the CPS.'

'Wonderful. You going to serve me with something?'

She laughed, more of a giggle. 'No, you're off the hook for the killings you carried out.'

'Thank you, but is that an official notification?' It was then that her words registered – '...for the killings you carried out.' So they knew I did them and they were clearing me.

'No, not really. I've a delivery to make.' She turned to Bennie. 'Hello, Bennie. Who's your friend?'

Bennie was sitting with a beautiful West Indian woman.

'Ezola meet Petal,' said Bennie. So he knew her. 'And the one making cow's eyes at Jake is Sam.'

Petal turned back to me. 'I've got two messages to deliver. A simple message first. It's to tell Peter Jackson to get back into line or he'll end up very dead.'

'From whom?'

'He'll know.'

'Why not tell Bennie the message?'

'Because it's better coming from you. Oh, and Jake, when I leave here Bennie will have the tool.'

'The other message?'

'Yes, just to let you know that your potty friend, Joe Nokes, is in the process of review and an appeal is likely. The review has indicated that he only killed one person, Mable Nokes. The police should never have questioned him in the mental state he was in at the time so some wrists will get slapped.'

'Will he get out?'

'Most likely a transfer to a mental hospital and then we'll have to see.'

She stood, kissed me on the cheek and turned and kissed Bennie. By the time the prison officers reacted she was walking towards them. I knew Bennie had the weapon because I didn't and I'd no idea what it was or how it had been transferred. So she was CPS and Family. They were everywhere. She walked towards the exit and then Micky's wife was by us.

'You're Jake?'

'Yes.'

'Thank you.' She was crying. 'Micky's okay now.' She smiled through her tears and went back to Micky. I wanted to cry. I felt for both of them.

'What was that all about?' asked Sam.

'Well, Micky was having some problems and came and talked to me and it seems he's sorted them out with his wife.'

'Proper little counselling service, aren't you?' There was sympathy in her voice; she didn't know what it was about but she understood. No wonder I loved her.

'Well, I have to do something when I'm pining away in here for you.' Bravado, that was my solution, but I knew Sam would understand.

'Piss off,' she said and reached out for me and then sharply pulled her hand back. 'Oops, no touching.'

39

It was lunchtime in the exotic dining hall of the prison, with its plastic-topped tables, plastic stackable chairs, plastic cutlery and plastic trays with indentations for food, plastic mugs and plastic condiment containers. Not that I have anything against plastic, you understand, but perhaps it's not such an exotic dining room after all.

The queue was long and winding and I was slipping down it as prisoners made way for me in the mysterious way they did for those that they'd decided warranted some form of respect. I reached the serving area with my plastic tray thingy just as Dad arrived, so I helped him and we walked together to our normal seating area. It was odd really; the tables were supposed to be filled from the front right-hand side of the room and some people did that and they normally came in as groups. If there were not enough of them to fill a table of six the empty seats were not filled. The screws sometimes tried to make that happen (well, new screws did) only to end up with a mess of food down the backs of their uniforms, so they learned to let the prisoners sort out their own seating arrangements and in general, to stay out of the way of flying gravy-soaked mash or curry sauce or some other easy-to-flick and sticky missile. At least plastic cutlery was useful for something.

Minutes later, Arty joined us. Dad and Arty were very quiet. I knew Dad had been for an assessment for some pains a few weeks before and had been to see the specialist yesterday. Arty had been allowed to go with him so we knew it was serious. I wondered what the results had been. They were both picking at their food.

'Are you going to tell me?' I asked. Arty just got up and left. He was upset.

'We need your help, Jake,' said Dad.

'To do what?'

'Tell us what to do.'

'About what?'

'I have cancer and the doc says I have anything from six weeks to a year, depending on how it develops.'

'He told you about treatment?'

'Well, sort of, and no.'

'Go on.' Boy, Flash and Sergeant were trying to look as if they weren't listening. What Dad had said so far was hurting them; they loved the old man. That was not the sort of thing we, us hard men, us outcasts from society, could admit to.

'Well, I could have had this chemotherapy thing but I'm too old and the dicky ticker wouldn't take it and anyways, it's probably too late for that. If they'd found it earlier they might have been able to cut it out, but the scan thingy says it's now invasive, whatever that is, so it's up to drugs now, pain killers, and the doc said I will have to take more and more to kill the pain and well, that's it really.'

I could ask what sort of cancer but I couldn't see how me knowing that would help. 'You might request compassionate release.'

'How would I do that?'

'I don't know, but Mo could find out.'

'I don't know him.'

'I do. I'll ask him.'

'I'm not going if Arty can't come with me.'

'I'll ask Mo.'

I looked around and could see Mo with a group of people

225

racially similar to him. He was finishing up so I wandered towards the door and reached it as he did.

'Hi, Jake,' he said. 'My plan's working well.'

'That's good, Mo. Can I ask your advice?'

'Anything, Jake. Just anything.'

I explained Dad's problem but that he wouldn't go without Arty. He asked me some questions and said he would do some digging and then talk to Dad. That was that then.

40

I passed a message via Boy to see Peter Jackson. I got a message back to see him on the wing mid morning. I entered D-Wing, Level 3, which was a special place. The cells were larger than the cell Harry and I shared and level 3 were all singles. These were for lifers who had served a number of years. To pass along the walkway at this level was an experience. Peter Jackson's people guarded it. Bennie Copland met me at the top of the stairs.

'Welcome, Jake.' He turned before I answered and walked along the walkway. I followed. I passed cells that contained people I'd seen, such as Bookkeeper and Smarts. I knew what Bookkeeper did (it was in the name), but what Smarts was supposed to do I didn't believe. They said he could remember everything he read – a sort of living computer – but he had to spend most of his time in a quiet room as he could become overloaded and have fits. I wasn't sure I believed this, although I'd heard of people with an eidetic memory so I suppose he was an example. It was said that he murdered his wife with an axe because she forgot the milk at the supermarket but that may just have been a myth.

Peter Jackson's cell wasn't a cell at all; it was an apartment. The inside must have been designed by one of the guys who design caravans where everything kind of fits and the place contains everything. In this 'room' with Peter was Bennie. I had learned that Bennie had served as a corporal with Major Michael Carmichael when he was a captain and he knew Jase Phillips. I had also picked up that Bennie had been busted in the army on a drugs offence and had served in Parkhurst before ending up here.

'Welcome, Jake. You wanted to see me?'

'I had a visitor, Peter, and I was asked to give you a message.'

'From your girlfriend or her companion.'

'Via her companion.'

He turned to Bennie. 'Leave us please, Bennie.' Bennie left. 'I see. Deadlier than the male I'm told.'

'Perhaps, Peter. I know nothing about her.'

'You're very lucky, Jake, and the message?'

'I don't know who the sender is but I was told you would know.'

'I understand, Jake. The message.'

I was nervous so I just said it like I was given it. 'Tell him to get back into line or he'll end up very dead.'

Peter sat there, thinking. 'Do you know who it was from, Jake?'

'No.'

'Do you know what it means, Jake?'

'No, but I might guess.'

'Guess then, Jake.'

'That you've done something that isn't what somebody wanted done.'

'Will you be the one who kills me, Jake?'

'I shouldn't imagine so for one moment, Peter.'

'Can you send a reply for me?'

'I've no idea who sent it. I did ask and was told you would know.'

'Jake, you were a policeman. If you had a piece of information such as you've given me could you identify the potential killer?'

'The opportunities are too great, Peter. It could be a

228

member of The Family in here, it could be a contract killer in here who's a prisoner or even a member of staff. Why don't you do as you've been asked and get back into line?'

'It's not possible, Jake. The instructions I had were to have Jase Phillips killed so I did. Then you turn up and you kill the killer, Raymond Tidy, and want to kill me for telling Ratty to do it. I then receive instructions to have you killed. So I tried and it went wrong. Marty Clifford was supposed to kill you and he's still in hospital. He's gone blind you know; it was the brain damage to the back of his head that did that. Costello wants to kill you for what you did.'

'I didn't know about Marty.'

'No, he'll be in rehabilitation for a while.'

'And Costello?'

'He's a loose cannon; he may try to get you but I've told him no.'

'So if you tell him yes you'll be off the hook.'

'Not that easy. Costello kills you and now Sergeant and his black boys kill Costello and then me. This whole thing has got out of hand.'

'It can't be right, Peter. The Family aren't stupid they don't go around murdering lots of people. Something is wrong here. They work below the surface using brains rather than brawn.'

Peter's eyes were bloodshot, probably lack of sleep, and he stared fixedly across the table at me. There was something already on his mind worrying him. He slowly tilted his head backwards and gazed into nothingness. His voice was mild; it had an edge of surprise in it, 'I didn't really believe you didn't know, even when Bennie told me.' He was a quiet man but he demanded respect.

'Let's start again, Peter, and get this clear.' Peter looked at me; he wasn't a well man. 'Are you okay?'

'I don't think so, Jake. Talk me through what you see and perhaps we can reach some sort of solution.'

'Okay. You were told to kill Jase because of something he knew or believed about Carmichael. You told Ratty to kill Jase. Jase is dead. That stopped him passing on what he believed or knew and it stopped the legal action to get him freed. Now, he had visitors and perhaps one of them knows what Jase believed. I killed Ratty for killing Jase and I was going to kill you but found out you were just a link in the chain, so I still don't know who gave the order but I know it wasn't Mabry.

'You're then told to have me bumped off and Marty Clifford gets the job. He fails and ends up seriously injured, blind. You lied to me about that, suggesting others acted without your instruction. I don't know why you just didn't tell me. Perhaps you thought I was Family.

'Now you, Peter, are being threatened because you're out of line, but I'm not sure what line you're supposed to be in.'

'No you've missed a step, Jake. I ordered your rape and you killed Wharton and Wilson. I think *that* was me being out of line and I didn't tell them to kill you.'

'Okay, Peter. Your conclusion?'

'Two bosses: one wanted Jase killed and the other didn't care. The one who didn't care got you in here to sort this lot out. That has to be Mabry. Only he could pull the strings in the legal system. Why? I can't even start to understand. I think it's Mabry who has told me to get back into line because I ordered your rape, but I don't know what that means except protecting you because he knows that Costello is after you and he wants you alive and again I don't know why he wants you alive as you're not in The Family. Perhaps somebody else with clout is pressurising him.' He was looking at me to read any reaction to what he said. He saw none. 'Only one man could pressurise him.' He stopped; he wasn't going to say it, so I did.

'Rupert Carmichael.'

'You know one hell of a lot about The Family as a non-member, Jake.' I ignored the gentle thrust.

'How would Mabry know, for example, that Costello would want to kill me?'

'Good question, Jake.' He sat and thought about it then shook his head, almost as if he didn't believe something. 'Mabry has somebody else, somebody else close to me, somebody who can't operate as you can but is just feeding him information, somebody who may just be tracking you and me.' Again he was just looking at me. 'Are you a member of The Family, Jake?' He wanted to be certain.

'Good, Lord, no. You know I'm not.'

'Who do you work for then?'

'Me, I work for me. I wanted to avenge Jase. I know that may sound crazy. Mabry owed me a favour and another friend fixed me getting in here and I hope getting me out, and he fixed the liaison with Sergeant.'

'Right, ex-RMP, Captain. Who do you actually work for?'

He might as well know. 'Sir Nicolas Ross.'

'The barrister?'

'Yes.'

'No wonder you can get in and out of here.'

'Who ordered you to have Jase killed and why?'

'I daren't tell you, Jake, but you'll have to solve the Costello problem or you're dead meat. I can't stop him.'

'How do I do that?'

'Two choices: a hit – I don't recommend that because you've been lucky to escape the long arm of the law so far – or a yard fight, and I don't give you much chance of winning that but if you live, it will all be over.' Again he went into thinking mode. 'It must be Bennie.' He was thinking about the leak he had into The Family.

'Why?'

'Family man, came in about three weeks before you, and I

231

was asked to look after him. He transferred from Parkhurst.
Odd transfer that, but I knew he was Family'

'By?'

'You don't give up do you, Jake.' He laughed.

'Okay, Mabry needs to know there'll be a yard fight that
I've agreed to so that will keep you in the clear, Peter.'

'So Mabry wants you alive, Jake. You best go. It's been
good talking to you. I now know you're good but don't give
you a chance in the yard.'

41

I got back to our cell and Harry came in.

'Harry –' I began.

'Stop right there. You're going to fight Costello.'

'How did you know?'

'You started with "Harry" and I knew something was coming and the only thing at the moment is Costello wants to kill you, so I reckon your only option is a yard fight because he won't go for the ring; it has too many rules.'

'You can fix it for me, Harry?'

'Yes. Weapons, and when?'

'No weapons. Normal prison clothing and boots at next association with his wing.'

'Why no weapons?'

'Loose clothes and boots are all I need and neither of us spends life in here if the other one dies.'

'Area?'

'Twenty-five to thirty feet square, marked with seats to prevent encroachment.'

'That's big and will favour you. Will he agree?'

'Tell him it will let more people see and it will also look more acceptable to the screws.' Harry nodded. He accepted the logic. Anyway, it was only a bit bigger than a boxing ring.

'You only have four days.'

'I'm fit, Harry. Not sure Costello is.'

Harry sat and looked at me. He was thinking and I could

detect concern. He was working through the options and he clearly reached the same one as me.

'Okay, Jake, we start training tomorrow. Now I'm going to talk you through a load of stuff you already know but as you don't handle this stuff often I think you may need to be reminded. Remember, Costello has massive street-fighting experience. He does it for a living and he's killed doing it.'

'Thanks, Harry. I really needed cheering up.'

'Jake, he's pissed off with you but he won't want to kill you, just beat you to a pulp, cripple you a bit, maybe. You won't be pretty when he's finished with you.'

'Why won't he want to kill me?'

'He wants to get out of here one day, as you said. Let me give you an overview of what I think will happen.' He walked to the window, looked out and then came back and sat down on his bunk. I was sitting on the chair. 'It'll be fast and explosive. He'll just go for you. No feeling you out like in boxing. It'll be unpredictable, ugly and brutal, and there's likely to be a lot of blood. I know you like blood.' He smiled at his reversal of my dislike. 'He'll target your head and in particular your face. He's unlikely to use kicks; it isn't the way he fights. He's a fist man. Street fighters tend not to use kicks. Well, not the way you use them. They just swing a boot in an arc, and kicks are your main weapons. You've an advantage there with your ability to kick. If you go down he'll come down on you. He's more experienced than you at fighting on the ground and he outweighs you, so he has a double advantage there. How we doing?'

'Can I go home now, please?'

'No, you bloody can't.' Harry smiled. 'Remember there are no rules. You're used to using Eastern, unarmed combat techniques and boxing. Both these can be useful but remember there are no rules here.' He paused to let me understand his message. 'He goes down you kick him in any vulnerable place you can. Not once, but as many times as you can and hope, just hope, he can't get up.' He stopped to let what he'd said sink in.

'You know all about the centre-line theory: on which are some of the most vital targets that you must protect, like your eyes, nose, chin, throat, solar plexus and groin. They're also the areas you must attack. Use a stance that best protects your centre-line. Create an even balance that will enable you to move in any direction and will give you the stability to withstand and defend against strikes. Speed is another advantage you have. Carry your hands high. Okay, anything there you need more information on?'

'I don't think so, Harry. A good reminder so far.'

'Now: range. He'll not be used to fighting anybody who can use kicks. So keep your distance from him. This will do three things. One: it will keep his punches out of range. Two: it will cause him to come to you so increasing the power of your punches. Three: enable you to use kicks. If he closes into punching range move in close to again nullify his punches or skip back out of range. Up close, you must use elbow and knee strikes, head butts, gouging and biting; biting is a fantastically good weapon.

'You're fitter and faster than him so mobility is important. Move quickly and freely and stay balanced. This will require using your footwork skills and will set you up to be able to use the unarmed combat stuff. Evading his attacks will be much better than parrying them. He's big, strong and knows how to punch from a whole range of angles – hooks, crosses, straights, uppercuts used in a variety of patterns – but he's slow and when you're in doubt attack. You get no points for defending in this game.

Tomorrow we'll start training and I'll get some little helpers like Arthur and Big Fred. Okay?'

'As long as neither of those two little helpers hit me I'll be fine.'

42

I had been working my socks off training all day when I got a message from Mo to take Dad and Arty in the classroom that evening. So I did. When Mo arrived we were expectant but as usual we expected the worst; it was just the norm for prisoners. We sat in a circle. We waited. Mo started.

'The chances of getting both of you out are slim to non-existent, but you have a good chance, Dad, if your daughter will look after you.'

'Is that it?' asked Dad.

'Well, let me give you the background.' He waited and we nodded. 'Okay, the power to grant early release is up to the Secretary of State for Justice. But they don't do it very often; only about fifty people were granted permanent early release in the last five years.'

'How many requested release?' I asked.

'It's one of those things you can't find out. I've obtained Prison Service Order six thousand and that tells me how it can be done but the conditions are strict. It may be considered if a prisoner is suffering from a terminal illness and death is likely to occur soon. You may fit that, Dad.'

'May?' I intervened.

'Yes, the time limit is probably about three months. This is not an exact science, but they do expect the prisoner to be bedridden. The second kind of compassionate leave (note *leave* not *release*) is for family circumstances. I don't think you can swing that one but it may be that things will

236

change. Two issues are in the favour of compassionate release. The first is we're in a rapidly aging general population and that applies equally to the prison population and applies to you, Dad. The other thing is the pressure on prisons as space is now at a premium and at the same time, the general population want criminals locked up.'

'So what do we do?'

'No, what do *I* do? I'm going to make the applications. I will forward two cases: this one and Old Man Peter's. His is a dementia case.'

'What do you need, Mo?'

'Money.'

'For what and how much?'

'I need money for a barrister, and I have one in mind.'

'How much?'

'Not sure but it'll be bloody expensive.'

'How much?'

'I reckon about fifty K.'

'Okay, Mo, I'll find that.'

They just looked at me.

'Where from?' said Arty. There was surprise in his voice.

'I'll just rob a bank.'

Dad started to laugh then stopped. 'You *will* find the money, Jake?'

'I'll find the money, Dad.'

'Mo, I want Arty out of here to look after Dad. It may require some clause that when Dad dies Arty comes back in and some bureaucratic rubbish like reporting to the police each day or a curfew, a tag, but I want Arty with Dad. I want you to write me two brilliant cases. I want the first one, not for a legal brain, but for a powerful politician who is also a businessman. It should contain the political arguments that are difficult to argue against and will appeal to the voters of both sides. I want a different case written for a barrister, a legal argument you know: issue, rule, application and

237

conclusion. There's two men I may be able to get to help us behind the scenes but they'll be invisible so your guy won't know.'

Mo gave me an inquisitive look.

'Mo, I know some people who know some people, but I need the right tools for them and the tools are well-written briefs and these are not the briefs Officer Pretty Legs wears.'

They smiled; they had all watched Pretty Legs climb the stairs. Her skirts were shorter than they should be and her legs were longer than they had any right to be and the prisoners just watched her walk through the prison, hoping she would climb the stairs. She knew it so she teased us all.

43

The day of the fight came and it was dark, miserable and raining – no change there then. I walked out into the area and two groups of prisoners, one group from each wing, were moving seats into a square. They were soaking wet but didn't seem to care. There was some chi-iking between the two groups but it lacked edge, more fun than fury. The betting I'd heard was that I might last a maximum of five minutes. It wasn't a case of who would win but how long Pete would take to win and there was no doubt the winner would be Pete Costello. There were 300 bets, as there were 300 seconds in five minutes, and there were three books being run, so 900 bets could be placed. The bookies would take the money for any winning time a bet wasn't placed; there were ten blanked numbers for each of the bookies. The winner would take all the money laid on in those five minutes. There was a rumour that the bookies weren't taking any bets on Costello to win as only one person had bet on me. Wow, I had one supporter. Even Harry hadn't laid a bet. Now that did worry me. Perhaps he thought I wouldn't win. Me, I just wanted them all to be wrong. Well, not the one who had bet on me.

The rain ran down my neck and soaked my shirt and the rain cascaded off my jacket and soaked through my trousers. Squelches came from my boots as I walked; my socks were soaked. There was an hour to go. The prison staff knew what was happening but they weren't going to interfere. 'Too risky,' as one of them said. This seemed to be the latest catchphrase in the prison.

I went back into the prison building and was walking towards the gym.

'Best of luck, Jake,' said a female voice. It was Senior Prison Officer James. 'I've a fiver on you to win at two hundred to one. How they're going to find a thousand quid to pay me I've no idea.'

'Bit of a risk then, ay, ma'am?'

'For them, Jake. I've watched you for the short time you've been here. You're a winner. This one is a bit close but if you stay out of trouble for six or seven minutes you'll win.'

'I best get my running shoes on then.'

'That's what I'm guessing you'll do. You said to me when you came that if any of these bozos picked a fight with you you'd kill them. Don't kill him, Jake; you won't get away with it for a fourth time. Just win.' She smiled and strangely that gave me confidence. Her job here was to understand people.

I went to the gym, stripped, dried and lay on a bench. Harry was there with Doc. Doc had been a doctor and had been struck off for doing some naughties. He had then become a physio, which enabled him to do even more naughties.

Doc worked my arms and legs while Harry talked. Harry talked sense but I wasn't listening. I knew what I was going to do. Firstly, I would cripple Pete Costello so he was slow. Second, I would tire him so that I could move in and out and weaken him so that I could finish him. Frederick the Great in his instructions to his generals said, 'Those generals who have had but little experience attempt to protect every point, while those who are better acquainted with their profession, having only the capital object in view, guard against a decisive blow and acquiesce in small

240

misfortunes to avoid greater.' I've only the capital objective in view and I'll have to take some small misfortunes to get there. No, I wasn't really listening to Harry.

I watched the crowd gathering from an upstairs window. I watched Harry move through the crowd below. I looked across, ahead of his movement, through the crowd. He was heading for the Peter Jackson group. They were at the front. It's true that rank has its privileges but Peter Jackson never made a big thing of his power in here. Harry stopped near Peter Jackson's seat and an underling held up his hand, stopping him. Harry spoke to him, I could tell by the movement, and Peter Jackson just raised a finger, allowing Harry's approach. Harry had a brief conversation with Bennie that lasted about ten seconds, maybe a little longer, then Harry and Bennie went to Peter and Bennie gave him something. Peter nodded. I had the feeling that he had just received the black spot. Harry spoke. Peter shook his head and then nodded again. There was an acceptance. I knew that was Peter Jackson out of the picture. There was no argument. No point in arguing. When The Family has made a decision you just have to comply: less messy that way. It did concern me that Harry was involved but I knew he wasn't Family.

Dressed and ready for battle, I walked to the crowded, noisy yard. The crowd had parted to let us through. The rain had stopped and the ground was drying underfoot. The weak sun shone through the weakening blanket of clouds. Good omen, I thought. I had Arthur and big Fred in front, Harry by my side and the rest of my class behind me. We had a bunch of seats in a corner. As we approached the ring I saw another passageway through the crowd, through which Pete Costello and his entourage were walking. I entered the ring with Harry and my group, and sat where Malcolm Tunes, the head of the prisoners' entertainment committee, directed us. Malcolm had been a disc jockey on some minor TV channel, but had done some naughties with some very willing teenage girls who were, unfortunately for him, under sixteen: a bit like Doc really. Actually, not at all like Doc; his were the wives of patients and when the husbands found out he eliminated them. He fought the case as a straight murder so avoided Rampton or Broadmoor but that's where he should be; he was as nutty as a fruitcake but at the same time a great healer.

Malcolm called for silence on his megaphone and silence descended. He then called each contestant forward to check for weapons and that they met the requirements: standard prison gear with no protective clothing. Harry represented me. He challenged a belt Pete was wearing and that was removed. Trainer from the gym checked me and missed the cricket box I was wearing. I'm sure he knew it was there.

Malcolm then announced the rules. In short, there weren't any. If one person capitulates (capitulates was his word), he would declare the other one the winner. He announced the timekeepers; three of them, with stopwatches and the mid-time of Malcolm's declaration of the end was the recorded time for the betting. The end would come in two ways: a fighter being incapable of continuing or surrendering.

He called us to the centre. His instruction was simple. 'Go to your corners. When there, I'll start to run for that gap over there and you two can get on with it.'

We walked back to our corners and Malcolm ran for safety.

44

Pete came at me as if he were in a sprint, fists as high as his temples on either side of his head and eyes glaring at me. I felt the crowd behind me move back, such was his aspect. I ran towards him, two steps to give me momentum to launch myself into a flying kick. My left foot hit his chest and my right leg straightened to smash the sole of my boot into his face. We both went down and I rolled clear and onto my feet. Pete staggered to his feet as silence hit the crowd. This wasn't expected. Then my supporters exploded into a wall of sound. I could see the blood streaming from his smashed nose and split lips. There was a heel mark on his left cheek and that eye was closing. I was so keyed up I could have seen a pimple on his ear. Pete was made of stern stuff and was moving as I attacked with a stabbing kick to the side of his right knee. He was damaged and from his left side I threw a left hook that found his left eye as the target.

With terrific speed and the whole weight of his shoulder behind the blow, he whipped his right fist into my solar plexus. I was moving backwards so that reduced the impact but not enough. I felt my knees go and the pain racked through my body. More than pain – agony. I couldn't breathe and my body wanted to just stop and lie down, but my head wouldn't let it. I was fighting for my life here. I was on my feet and went to my right, desperately trying to breathe as instinct pushed me to avoid the right upper-cut that just touched the very tip of my nose. Contact would have finished me for good.

Frantically, I buried my left fist into his left eye and back-pedalled like mad to gain a picture of the situation and get my breath back. This was no fight; this was a battle. Blood streamed into his eye so he didn't have much sight to his left and he was limping like he was crippled. His right eye glared at me through the bloody mask of his smashed face.

I moved to his left and around him so that he was turning to see me. I delivered a sidekick so the sole of my right boot slammed into the side of his undamaged left knee. He went down on his knees and I delivered a roundhouse kick so the toe of my boot hit the base of his skull. I thought that would be it, but it just seemed to enrage him. He staggered to his feet, lowered his head and charged me. I got my avoidance wrong and his head slammed into the left side of my ribs as I tried to twist away. I was sure they were broken but Pete Costello was on his hands and knees. I was behind him and I took a penalty kick aimed at his crotch. It was a goal. He let out a yelp and clutched himself as he writhed on the ground. I kicked him twice more in the body before a pair of strong arms grabbed me from behind and a voice said, 'Enough, Jake.' It was Harry and I collapsed. I think I was crying with pain and exhaustion.

The announcement was made as fifty-two seconds and I was the winner. I didn't feel like a winner. I felt that I had been run over by a steamroller.

Doc was working on Pete and shouting for an ambulance. He was thumping Pete's chest to get his heart going. He stopped and gave artificial respiration by holding Pete's nose and blowing into his mouth. Somebody then arrived with a stretcher and I was put on it and taken at what seemed to be a trot to the sick bay. I can remember Nurse Carstairs passing me, heading for the ring with an oxygen cylinder and an assistant with the portable defibrillator. This was serious then.

I came to my senses in hospital. It was morning. Senior Prison Officer James was there and a uniformed policeman.

'Okay, Jake?' she said.

'How's Pete?'

'He's okay, Jake. He's resting at the moment, having been bandaged up, but they'll have to operate on his right knee and do some repairs to his face. He'll live though, but it's probably good we don't have conjugal visits because I don't think he could function.' It was only then I remembered scoring a goal.

A man in plain clothes came into view. 'I'm Detective Constable Carstairs,' he said waving a card at me that I couldn't read. 'Tell me what happened.'

'Oh, we were just sparring, trying out stuff and as you can see, it worked.'

He stopped making the notes. 'Sparring you say?'

'Yes, sparring.'

'A bit violent for sparring wasn't it?'

'Well, if you're going to learn anything you best do it for real, Detective Constable Carstairs. Are you related to Nurse Carstairs?'

'Yes, she's my –'

'Enough, DC Carstairs. Let's wait until tomorrow when we can talk to both of them.'

'Yes, Sergeant.'

I didn't see the speaker but he was a smart cop, saving time on something that he sussed was going nowhere. I was pleased that Pete was okay; well, as okay as could be expected. If he had had a coach like mine it would have been a very different story and probably I wouldn't have been able to write it.

I never did find out the relationship of the detective constable to Nurse Carstairs. That afternoon I was transferred back to prison and put in the sick bay.

After lockdown that night, there was a commotion. We knew immediately that somebody had died; it was that sort of commotion. Harry was looking out of the window and I knew he was the root cause of the commotion.

'Peter Jackson, Harry?' I asked.

'I think it might be, Captain. He made a phone call today.'

'Will you be in any trouble?'

'No, I shouldn't think so. I received a call to tell him to make a call to his brief.'

'Petal's weapon? Peter said she was deadlier than the male.'

'Oh, she is. I think she was some form of reptile in a previous life and brought all her venom with her.'

'Want to talk, Harry?'

'No, not really, Captain. When it is my time to go I'll ask Petal to fix it. Go to sleep and then it's all over.'

'It's after lockdown; how would the screws know if it's that quiet?'

'Simple. The phone call must have told him there was no reprieve. He took the stuff and set an alarm. The alarm would keep going until the screws opened his cell to turn it off and they would find him dead.'

'How you feeling, Harry?'

'Bloody awful, Jake. I had an obligation to meet and I met it but I really can't feel any upside to that.'

'So you are free and clear.'

'Yes, Captain. Free of all obligations now apart from keeping you alive.'

'Thank you in advance for that, Sergeant.' We had moved through the emotional support to the reality of our jobs.

'What will happen now?'

'Bennie Copland will take over as the top man. We will ensure a smooth transition. Well, I'll ask you to get Arty and Big Fred to nursemaid Bennie and you can be an advisor to him. That's what Peter Jackson wanted as you won't be around long enough to do the job. Peter was really surprised you were undercover; he wanted you as his successor, but he had doubts about you surviving the fight.'

'Wow, thanks for that, Harry.'

'I knew you would survive, Captain.' There was something in the way he said that but I wasn't going to ask. Was it in what he had just said? 'Free of all obligations now apart from keeping you alive.'

45

Four days later, I was sent for by the governor and escorted to his office. In his office were Sir Nicolas Ross and two men I didn't know. As I walked in Sir Nicolas stood and held out his hand.

'Great to see you again, Jake, and we've some more good news.' We shook hands. 'This is Mr Christopher Hughes of the Home Office, and this is Mr Mark Hoffman of the Foreign Office.'

Both were in dark suits, white shirts and club ties. Forty years ago they would also have had bowler hats. Times change, but only slowly in the civil service. They stood, I shook hands formally with them and they sat down again. It was a ritual that they probably just did and didn't recognise. Sir Nicolas turned to the governor.

'Governor.'

The governor now had the attention, and spoke. 'Please have a seat, Mr Robinson.' He didn't look a happy bunny. 'You'll be aware that Sir Nicolas has been attempting to secure your release and have the case against you quashed.' He didn't specify which case. 'That, it seems, has been achieved. Mr Hughes brought the documentation for your release from this prison. I'll release you into his charge and you'll go to the American Embassy and there the formalities will be completed.' So it was the case that got me in here undercover.

'Thank you, sir.'

'I trust you'll not be in trouble again, Robinson.'

Mr Hughes replied. 'I sincerely hope not, Governor. Captain Robinson will return to his post in the security service, assuming he wishes to do so, now that this unfortunate error has been satisfactorily resolved.'

'I think we should be going eh, Jake. Mr Hughes, Mr Hoffman, Governor,' said Sir Nicolas.

'There's the matter of Captain Robinson's belongings,' said the governor.

'Please give them to charity, Governor. You can have your natty blue suit back and I'd like to say goodbye to Harry Mount.'

'Certainly, I'll have him brought here.'

'I'd prefer to go and see him.'

I waited in the governor's office while my clothes were located. Sir Nicolas smiled and said, 'It seems you stirred up some more trouble then, Jake.'

'What have I done now?'

'The Home Secretary has been talking to his opposite number in justice. It seems they're considering, on a trial basis, the release of three prisoners from here. Not settled yet, just an experiment.'

How did Mabry even know? Of course, the thing I asked Mo to write. Why would he bother? The power of contacts thumped home to me. No wonder The Family was so powerful they could manipulate the law as a favour to someone. I knew where my £50k for this job would have gone.

I got changed into my own clothes and then went to see Harry. As I walked up towards our, now Harry's, cell Senior Officer James met me.

'Goodbye, Batman,' she said.

'Batman?'

'Yes, you fly in here and meet up with your mate Robin. You permanently get rid of three very bad guys while doing

249

good things with some others who needed help. You also get rid of two prison officers who were a disgrace, teetered on the brink of disaster that could have had you beaten to death, and you've magically resolved that and now you fly off. I expect Robin will be out of here in a few weeks.'

'Ma'am, you've a magnificent imagination but I'm glad you were my personal officer. I'd never had one of those before.'

She laughed. We shook hands and as we were about to part, she placed her hands on my shoulders and kissed my cheek.

In the next half hour I said goodbye to Harry. It was clear the whole prison knew I was out and I was surprised at the send-off. The landings were full and they looked down on me. My class weren't very happy about losing their teacher but they were pleased for me.

Arthur pushed his way to me and took my hand. 'I don't know how I can repay you, Captain, but I will if I can.' He wrapped his massive arms around me.

'Thank you, Arty.'

Dad shook my hand. There were tears in his eyes and he and Arthur walked away. I felt emotional. I was walking away and Mo came up to me.

'Thank you, Captain. I'm already at point one of my plan. Thank you.' He held out his hand and we shook.

'You won't have heard yet, Mo, but you might just get a little help with your release plan for three prisoners on a trial basis. Watch the political press.'

I was driven away in a chauffeur-driven, midnight-blue BMW series seven, very relieved and able to fully relax for the first time in weeks. I settled back in the deep leather seats and felt free and scared. I suppose freedom is scary. I'd not noticed that before my incarceration.

I was out, I was free, I was going home and I was sure I could really start to find out what this killing was all about, but staying alive had been the real success.

Memories are strange. I thought Peasmarsh was a 'good' prison. Yet, it had also been the scene of violence and I'd been in the middle of that. Despair couldn't be hidden. I felt it before I walked through the doors, so that was probably just me, and I saw it all around me when I was inside. Some people in there should have been in other forms of institution and some should have had hard labour as the old prison system had. I now knew that one size didn't fit all. I also felt that rehabilitation was under-estimated but how to achieve that I'd no idea. Being able to read and having a job when leaving school struck me as essential for the reduction of crime and some of my students, if they'd been able to read and write, might never have gone down the destructive paths they took.

I can still picture the tier-upon-tier of cells, and the only colour I remember is grey, although I doubt the walls were actually painted that colour. My strongest memories were of the noise and the smell, an overwhelming drone punctuated by shouts and the clank of metal on metal as doors opened and closed, and the pervasive boiled cabbage. I must admit to the occasional panic when I thought I might never get out.

Yes, I was out, I was free, I was going home to Sam and I was sure I could really start to find out why Jase was killed and why he killed Michael Carmichael, but staying alive had been the real success.

251

Postscript

Barrow and Sam had a conversation which resulted in the conclusion that I had to see a counsellor. My counsellor was Pauline Byford. She was a very bright and an extremely ugly, dwarf, female psychiatrist. She was with MI6. That did worry me as I'd worked with them on interrogations. They'd the ability to get inside people's heads and didn't seem concerned at the psychological damage they might do. She had a large head with protruding forehead, a large bulbous nose, thick lips, no chin, very short legs and a long body, short arms and stubby, thick, podgy fingers. She was about 4 foot 6 inches tall. However, despite looking so odd, she was extremely pleasant and totally non-judgemental – unlike me, with my stupid assumptions, that because she looked odd and was a psychiatrist she would be unpleasant and judgemental. I suppose that demonstrates how screwed-up I'd become. It didn't take long for her to get me to recognise the problems that I had.

Her office was like a mad psychiatrist film set. She had a bookcase that covered one wall and a desk that sat in front of a massive window overlooking a small, enclosed park that only residents could enter. Another area of her office wall had at least eight framed certificates. I was on a leather psychiatrist's couch and felt like a prat and she sat out of sight behind my head. This was like a scene from the horror movie, *Dr Umust Bumphimofski.*

She quickly identified that I was depressed, with some

other bits. Much of that was resolved by her taking me through the events of that day in the showers from my perspective and then from the perspective of the now-dead men and finally from the perspective of the other prisoners, particularly those who were later showing me respect. The biggest revelation was when she got me to celebrate killing them. If anybody had come in her office when we were doing that both of us would have been locked up. I ended up rolling on the floor, laughing so much that I thought I would wet myself. Laughter is always the best medicine or so I had been told.

I was amazed how quickly I recovered. Logic back, anxiety gone, sexual functioning restored, nightmares gone; all I wanted now was to get on with the job. I was again Jake Robinson, or was I? I now had the basics to go forward and find out why it was that Jase really killed Carmichael and to explore the question of whether Carmichael was a killer. If Carmichael was a killer, who had he killed and why? Why was that a problem for The Family? Anyway, Barrow wanted to know, because of the connection to The Family and finding answers may have helped in the battle against organised crime.

So, now I'd another project to drive: to hunt the killer.

Hunt the Killer

When Jake leaves prison there is a contract on him. Why? Others who had contact with Jase had been killed.

The leads from the prison reveal the real reason that Jase killed Major Michael Carmichael and Jake teams up with Inspector Kitty Halloway to hunt for a horrendous serial killer. Was it Michael Carmichael?

The story wheels and rolls in a helter-skelter of excitement and suspense as Jake and Kitty hunt for who the killer was and feel their way through the shadowy world controlled by The Family. But who in The Family is Jake's 'friend'? And who has taken out a contract on him?